M000191923

Cover by: Cate Ashwood Designs

Edited by: Jean Malherbe

Proof reading by: Alex J Adams

Ebook ISBN: 978-1-7776524-8-7

Print ISBN: 978-1-7776524-9-4

FINDING THE RIGHT FOREVER

R.M. NEILL

For J, you bring light to everyone you meet.
Shut up, and say thank you.

Contents

Prologue

OWEN

"I THINK YOU'RE GOING to fit in just fine here, Parker." I extend my hand to shake on the job offer.

"I got the job for real?" His smile lights up his face, ecstatic to be working for me at The Screaming Bean. He's just become a full-time baker. I'd wanted to expand my offerings to the area, and I thought a baker who would be creative in the kitchen, and who actually knew what he was doing, would be a good place to start.

I nod in affirmation. "Yep, if you still want it."

"OHMYGOD, yes! This is so exciting! I can't wait to start. When do you want me here?"

Parker is levitating off his chair. I don't think I've ever seen anyone this excited about getting a job. But he has his pastry chef papers and comes recommended by the teacher, so I'm giving him a chance. I hope he's not always this damn perky, though.

I push a form over to him for payroll. "I just need your info so you can get paid. Fill this in now if you want to, and when you're done, I'll show you around and we can discuss a schedule."

He takes the pen and starts scratching in all his info while I check my phone. Almost lunchtime, so this is perfect. I have an excuse to get him out the door. I shouldn't complain about having an enthusiastic employee, but I'm not in the mood for it today. I need lunch and I have a lot of work to do, including ordering new ovens to upgrade the kitchen now that I have someone to use them.

"This is so exciting." He bounces to his feet, wearing an eager smile waiting for the tour and I scowl at his enthusiasm. He's like a can of shaken soda pop, ready to explode as soon as the cap comes off.

"It's just a tour." Rolling my eyes, I motion for him to follow me. I don't deal well with this kind of happy.

His smile falters, but he needs to know I'm not exactly a cup of happiness and this is what he's working with. After showing him the office and staff area, we end up in the kitchen where he'll be spending all his time.

"Next month, I'll upgrade the ovens to something more industrial. That way, you can bake more at once and be far more productive. I expect more than a batch of chocolate chip cookies. I'm looking for unique creations that will draw people back here. Cupcakes, muffins, tarts, scones — whatever you can think of."

I watch as he wanders around, opening the fridge and looking over the equipment I already have. He's curious and eager as a beaver. I hope he can bring that enthusiasm to his creations.

"Can I make a request or would that be too forward of me?" He rubs at the back of his neck and I wave a hand for him to continue. I'm not put off by his boldness at all. I prefer people to be straight up with me. "Would you be able to get some cannoli horns and springform pans? Also, some extra cake pans. If you ever want to sell whole cakes, I'll need more than the four you currently have. I'm also getting good at cannoli. I'd love to offer those."

I blink my surprise away. The boy has plans. I like it. "Yes, that can be arranged. How about I give you the supply catalogue to look over and you can make a list of what you think you'll need or like? That way, I don't have to pretend to know what a springform pan is."

A moment of silence passes before he barks a laugh. "I wasn't sure if you were serious or not. You have a great poker face, but I bet if you smiled, it would really throw your opponents off."

Now it's my turn to laugh. It sounds foreign and unused to my ears. "I'll keep that in mind whenever I play poker again."

Parker trails me back to my office, and I dig out the supply catalogue for him. "Are you okay with starting Monday? 4 A.M?"

"I am! Four is my lucky number. See you Monday, boss!"

Parker's first full week as my baker has been a huge test on my nerves. On his first day, he returned with the catalogue and handed me a list. It was reasonable, and he'd included notes on what he wanted to use them for and make. He'd also included several smiley faces along the margins, making me try not to gag in front of him. On day two, he came prepared to start small and had insisted he needed to sing while he worked. It helped his creativity and he found comfort in singing, he'd said. Who am I to argue? I gave him the radio I had in my office, which I never used, and he cranked it as high as it could go. He sang at the top of his lungs in a voice that should send any animal running in the opposite direction... ALL. DAMN. DAY. If I entered the kitchen, he would smile and dance and go about his work as if I wasn't there.

Being ignored was great because I didn't have to be polite or make conversation with his cheery ass so early in the morning. I get up and do my stuff in the morning by nature. I don't sleep well, so many mornings, the coffee keeps me in a functioning human state until lunchtime. So, him ignoring me and continuing to sing like I'm not even there makes me even more cranky. Because, why must you bop along to Wham at 5 A.M without a care in the world?

By Friday, when I meet Dominic for our lunch date, I have to get some of it off my chest. Parker is a good worker, but Lord almighty, I don't know if I can handle him all the time throwing rainbows wherever he goes.

"How's your new baker working out so far?" He spoons soup into his mouth and closes his eyes. "God, I love your soup, O. You make the best tomato mac soup ever. I will never get sick of eating this."

I snort. "I know. You eat it three days a week already."

"Anyhow — baker. What's the update?"

With a sigh, I recount the week so far and Dominic laughs at my surly attitude. "Don't laugh at me, asshole. You know I'm not happy like that in the mornings. The whole smile and lollipops thing," I wave a hand in the air. "It's exhausting trying to keep up."

"Maybe he'll make you less grumpy one day, then. If you can't beat em' join em', right?"

"Not fucking likely." I shake my head. No damn way I'll *ever* be someone's little ray of sunshine. Not in a million years.

ONE

Parker

MOST MORNINGS, I PINCH myself on the way to The Screaming Bean. I still think it's all a dream. But with every day that passes proving it's a reality, I smile a little more at how my life is coming together. I'm a recent graduate with my Le Cordon Bleu Pastry Diploma and I'm now the head baker at The Bean. Well, I'm the only baker, but it doesn't matter. It's something I never thought I'd ever achieve, but here I am, creating yumminess every day *and* getting paid for it. Life is good.

The staff is great. The pay is great. I would even say my boss is great. It's not that he's mean or anything, he just never seems happy. Like every day somebody pissed in his cornflakes and his face can never crack a smile. If you can ignore all that, it's a fantastic place to work. I can't understand why Owen, my boss, never smiles. He has a successful business and does what he wants. He even has a great best friend. Why wouldn't you smile at all that?

I stretch out in my bed to wake up, and roll over to my side. My face lands in a pile of fur, tickling my nose and making me splutter. I wipe the hairs from my tongue and sit up, sending an evil eye to the source of the fur in my mouth. Cheddar, my giant, lovable orange tabby cat, is on my pillow again, crowding out my personal space. I shove him off and wipe my lips again. "Really Cheddar? How about you learn how to live with boundaries and not attempt to smother me while I sleep?"

It's my day off this week. The last Sunday I'll have off before the Christmas rush and all the custom baking for December starts. As soon as the calendar hits December first, people go insane and ramp up their Christmas orders. While I'm thrilled to get my start at custom orders and work my way up to a specialty baker for wedding cakes, Owen constantly second-guesses my decisions.

I've worked there for months now, and he still second-guesses my skills. I'm good at what I do. And the constant scowl on his face throws off my morning mojo. I don't like to not be happy. It attracts bad things.

Cheddar jumps off the bed with a thud and paws open my door to go wander the group home. I'm temporarily staying at Auslo's Loft, a shelter for the LGBTQ youth who keep getting the short stick in life. I landed here several years ago when I needed to escape a situation and it was the best thing that ever happened to me. Jacob and all the boys here became my found family, and I couldn't have been more grateful. After I graduated with my pastry papers, I needed a place to stay while I looked for work.

Jacob offered me a spare room here, so I took it. It's not much, but it's home until I find one of my own, and finding one has been harder than I thought. I was only supposed to be here for a month, tops, and it's now my fifth.

I poke my head out my bedroom door and sniff. Smelling the coffee brewing, I head downstairs to the communal kitchen and pour myself a cup before plopping into a chair at the kitchen table. Jacob wanders in, looking just as bothered to be out of bed as I do. In a house full of mainly teenagers, the quiet moments are few.

He pours a cup and joins me. "Hey Parker, day off today? You're usually out of here before the sun comes up."

I smile over the rim of my coffee. "Yep, day off, but I'm still up with the chickens. Need any help with anything today?"

"Actually, yes, if you're offering your only free time to me."

I would do anything for Jacob. The man is there for so many of us when we need a safe place. It's only right to give back everything I can to him. When I landed on his doorstep alone and afraid in the middle of the night, he saved my life. How can you repay someone that rescued you from the edge of a cliff?

"Of course I am. What do you need me to do?"

"It's December first tomorrow, and I've done no decorating. The two younger kids here need to feel welcome. I want them to look forward to a holiday for once instead of dreading it, you know?"

Oh, I know. A little too well. I know what it's like to dread a holiday. With the shitty foster family I landed with, and my own so-called family before that, holidays were not something I looked forward to. Since the first time I spent holidays here, my outlook has changed, and I know exactly what Jacob is saying.

"I would love to do that today, Jake. The kids might even help?"

He nods. "They might. Caleb doesn't talk much, and Katie is still adjusting. All you can do is ask."

"If they don't have homework to do first, I'll drag them into it then. If we have the ingredients, I'll make some cookies now too. Nothing to get you in the spirit like Christmas cookies, right?"

We continue to talk as I rummage through the cupboards and find what I need to throw together a batch of sugar cookies. Jacob manages this shelter and the animal shelter next door. His brother Austin, and Austin's husband Logan, built them when they envisioned a place they would have liked as younger boys. All three of them devote so much time and effort to the shelters. It gives me hope there are more wonderful, accepting people out there. I can't believe how much Jacob takes on with both facilities and it all comes from his pure heart.

My mom overdosed when I was only eight, placing me in a foster care merry-go-round. I had hoped it was a new beginning. One that would get me into a house with heat and food in the fridge and parents that hugged you instead of telling you how a kid ruined their life and was a waste of space. So yes, I get where these kids come from, and I respect the hell out of Jacob for giving his time to help people like me. He's like the big brother to every kid that comes here, and he loves playing the role. From what he's shared with me, he and his brother Austin didn't have great home lives either. While they'd had all the basic needs covered, there was no love, and they had even arrested his dad for some shady happenings while he was mayor of their town. Jacob hasn't talked about it much, but I know he's even closer to his brother because of whatever happened.

Jake snags a hot cookie from the tray, juggling it with a hiss. "You could have waited until they cooled." I laugh.

"I'm afraid there won't be any left!" He kisses me on the cheek as he leaves for his suite. "I need to do planning for the Christmas day dinner. I'll catch up with you later."

After placing the cookies on a rack to cool, I pull on a pair of shoes to lug in the Christmas decorations stored outside in the garage. Thank God Jake is a stickler for organization or it would take me twice as long to find everything. Everything is marked and colour coded in green and red. I don't even read what's in the boxes, I just start carrying them all inside to the common room where we'll put all the decorations up.

"Did you already bake cookies this morning?"

I poke my head up out of the box and whirl around to find Katie. She's holding Cheddar, my disloyal cat, and judging by the bags under her eyes, she had a rough night of sleep. "I did, yes. They're in the kitchen and you can even eat some for breakfast." I wiggle my eyebrows with a grin, hoping she'll crack a smile and I'm rewarded for my efforts.

"You're a bit weird, you know that, Parker?" She plops Cheddar on the sofa and heads to the kitchen, returning with a stack of cookies and watches me while I assemble the fake tree.

"Weird is okay. It's better than boring, right?"

"I guess there are worse things to be called." Her voice trembles. I stop what I'm doing and sit beside her, pulling the giant overfed cat onto my lap. "You want to talk about it?"

Her lower lip quivers, but she shakes her head no. I know how she feels. I don't know what happened, but she'll tell one of us eventually. Until then, I just need to do my best to let her know she's perfect the way she is. A fifteen-year-old bisexual girl, not accepted by her family because she didn't have the same tastes as them, is a fragile girl. Add in her coloured hair and piercings, and I'm damn sure they've picked on her at school. School attendance is the only hard rule here. You have to go to school, even if it's online learning; you can't stay here if you don't want an education. Katie is a vibrant, funny girl. She attends the local high school, but I have a sneaky feeling she reached the end of her rope yesterday.

"You know, I almost didn't become a baker because a kid called me fat when I wasn't much older than you." She reaches over to pet Cheddar while I talk. "I thought he was right. I was bigger than the other kids and it sort of made me hate myself for a while."

"What did you do?" She whispers, keeping her eyes focused on Cheddar and not on me.

"I lost a lot of my self-confidence that day. But to make a long story short, one day I decided enough is enough. I loved baking and one stupid kid's opinion shouldn't matter. So I kept on and became a baker." I'm leaving out the part where my self-confidence still hasn't recovered and I hide behind sunny smiles, but she's listening, anyway.

"You're a great baker. I love it when you bake for us."

"Thank you, love. It makes me happy to feed people things that make *them* happy. If it brought a smile to your face today, my day is complete."

Katie giggles and her gloom seems to have lifted. She chatters away and helps me unpack decorations before she disappears to her room to do homework. Jacob shows up not long after and together we finish decorating the tree and the common room. Micha and Dominic want to decorate the outside later this afternoon, so we carry the outside stuff back to the garage for them to deal with. Apparently, Dominic, Micha's new boyfriend, is insane with outside decorations.

"It's nice to see Micha back to himself, isn't it?" Jake collapses into a chair with a hot chocolate.

"It is. I really like Dom. He's at the Bean all the time. He makes no secret how he feels about Micha."

He stares into his mug, and I wonder if he has a future in marshmallow readings.

"We'll find that someday, Parker. We all have someone out there for us. It might not be as great a love story as those two, but we'll find it."

I nod in agreement. Sure we will. I won't hold my breath for it to happen, though. Families don't seem to want me. Why would a man want to share his life with me?

TWO

Owen

S NOW IS LIGHTLY FALLING in the early hours. The sky is still black as tar, but the flakes cross the soft light thrown by the streetlight in the parking lot and it reminds me of a snow globe I had as a child. The soft quiet of a snowy morning always makes me smile and takes me back to a simpler time. A time of snuggling into my warm, fuzzy Scooby-Doo blanket in my bed, hoping school buses wouldn't be running. The freedom of playing in the snow and drinking hot chocolate all day.

Those days were long ago. As I approach The Screaming Bean at 4 A.M, I know it's going to be an eternal day. A staff member called in sick and Parker, my pastry chef, will need help today with all the orders needed for Christmas parties coming up. Hard to believe it's already the first of December and they've booked us with orders since August. Since I expanded and started taking custom bakery orders, business has exploded. I reach the door of my coffee shop, my pride and joy, and I use my key to open the door. The alarm has already been disarmed and there are snowy prints leading to the back. Parker is already here.

Parker.

He's only worked here for a few months and he's tested my patience every step of the way. But he was the only applicant. Well, not completely true. Of the two applicants he was the only one with a certification and his creations didn't end up on one of those memes with the phrase *Nailed it.*

Banging pans signal Parker moving in the kitchen and I detour to my office to drop my coat and turn on my computer before going to check in with him. I pause outside the kitchen door when I hear him singing along to a popular song. If singing is the word you want to describe the off-key screeching and squawking I'm listening to. Just when I thought he couldn't get more annoying, there it is.

I open the door with a heavy cough and a stomp in my steps, hoping he stops singing once he sees me there. Ah, but see, that's not how Parker operates. He takes one look at me, ignoring the bags under my eyes and the scowl aimed at him, and sings louder. Asshole. Yes, I'm his boss. Yes, I could make him abide by some kind of rule of silence or threaten him with something, but I can't. As much as he irritates me like a nasty rash, he's a phenomenal baker and he does wonders for The Bean. I can't afford to lose him.

I just wish he wasn't so fucking cheerful. It's 4 A.M, act like it.

Crossing to the sink, I wash my hands while he continues to massacre the song lyrics. I'll cook the soup for my lunch with my best friend today and let Parker do his thing. Maybe tomorrow I'll bring earplugs. I assemble the ingredients for a small pot of tomato macaroni soup I make from scratch three days a week just for Dominic and me to eat at lunch. It's his favourite.

As the ground beef sizzles, the singing finally stops. Thank fucking god.

"Good morning Parker. Thanks for coming a little early today."

"Sure thing Boss. Are you my help?"

He pulls out the clipboard of bakery orders due for the next two days, and it's a massive stack. My eyes widen as my mind races over how we're going to get all this done. He notices my shock and laughs. "You don't think I can get all this done, do you?"

"I never said that. I was thinking I'm not going home soon with a list that long."

He snorts. "Oh, ye of little faith. I can do this with my eyes closed." He grabs a dry erase marker and writes on a white board what needs to be done. The list is long. Very long. My heart rate picks up with each new order he adds to the board. I should have monitored this better. He thinks he's invincible, but it's my business and reputation on the line if we can't deliver. Why can't he learn to say no to people when they try to weasel in an order for a day that is already over booked?

"Parker, I need you to handle all this without overdoing it. I have a reputation to uphold here. I'd rather have you turn away business than fail to deliver a booked order."

He raises an eyebrow. "I told you, I've got this. It may mean some extra work today, but it's manageable." He smacks the radio and flashes a smile. "Nothing a bit of tunes can't get me through." He continues writing on the board, humming under his breath as I grit my teeth. If getting these orders done means extra singing time, I'd rather eat off the floor.

"As much as I'd love to listen to your singing, if you want some help, you're going to have to stop singing and tell me what you need me to do." I wave my hand at the ever-growing list on the whiteboard. "This is your opportunity to order me around and use me as best you can."

He taps at his lips with a finger. "Well, sometimes it sucks when I sing and I have no backup vocals. Can you do that? You know I bake better when I sing." He cocks his head, struggling to keep a smile from forming.

"I'm not fucking singing."

I return to the soup and drain the noodles, Parker cackling at me all the while. I clean up the mess I made and ready a workspace for whatever Parker will need me to do — which will *not* include singing.

He's so used to working on his own, he hasn't got back to acknowledging me. I watch him as he mutters under his breath and double checks the whiteboard several times. He reminds me of a rabbit running from a dog, his eyes darting everywhere and his body going off in multiple directions at once. I sigh and walk over to him. Placing a hand on his shoulder, I force him to stop for a moment.

"Would you like me to do the dishes for the next batch of batter, or would you like me to make some icing?"

"Oh ah, icing, I think. Yes, the icing. I'm going to get the dough going for the gingerbread cookies next and then we can separate the icing into batches while the cupcakes cool. When you're finished with the cream cheese icing, can you start a batch of regular stuff for cookies?"

I smile. "See? Not so hard to ask for help. I can do that."

He hums under his breath, and I narrow my eyes. "What?"

"You can only do the icing if you sing with me. I have to get into the groove. These are gingerbread, Owen! Santa's other minions. I need to be happy to make them happy." He turns up the radio. "Surely you understand that about me by now?"

What god have I angered in my life to deserve this?

I run a hand over my weary and caffeine deprived face. "Parker, just tell me how much you need or what recipe you follow, and I'll do it. In case you haven't noticed the last few months, I'm not exactly chipper in the morning." I grab a bowl from the nearby shelf. "Surely you understand that about *me* by now?" I slam the bowl down harder than needed and narrow my eyes. I don't feel like doing his sunshine bullshit today. Or any day, really.

He flips open a binder to the icing recipe he wants me to use. "You know, early mornings are better when you smile. One day you're going to try it and love it."

I mumble under my breath as he breaks into song. Thank god it doesn't take long to make the icing, because once it's done I cover it and place it in the fridge before fleeing to my office.

I need quiet. And Tylenol. Lots of Tylenol.

"Excuse me, boss? Do you have a minute?"

I lift my head to find Parker at my office door, an effervescent grin still glued in place. Running a hand over my face, I sigh. "Sure, come in."

He bounces over to my desk with a small paper bag. He must eat pixie sticks every morning, I swear. How is he still this perky and alive after the day he's had in the kitchen? "Paige is on her break. Did you know it's her birthday tomorrow?"

Shit. Yes, I knew, and I forgot.

"I did, but it slipped my mind."

"I ran out once the gift shop opened and got her a card. You can sign it." I nod, reaching for the pen, grateful Parker has caught this and Paige didn't think I totally fucked up on her. She's worked for me since I opened and I never forget her birthday. I get her a card and have flowers sent to the front while she works. I guess I'll have them sent to her house instead.

"Thanks for doing this, Parker. I'm usually on top of it and I appreciate you asking me to sign the card."

"Of course, I only knew because she mentioned the flowers you send her every birthday are her favorite, so we got to talking and... here we are." He smiles at me again and he's happy as a proverbial pig in shit. I'm certain it's not because he's saved my ass with Paige, it's just him. Him and his stupid ball of happiness.

Parker tucks the card back into the bag, and he shuffles his sneaker-clad feet. "Uh, so now that December is here, could we maybe decorate a little?" This is the most I've ever seen Parker not smile, or be bouncy or just generally a hyper toddler type. "I know you don't like Christmas but — "

"Why do you think I don't like Christmas?" I cut him off, barking the words rather than speaking, and his eyes widen.

"I... uh... you're not very excited about it and it's like the happiest time of year. I just assumed... I'm sorry." He clutches the bag to his chest and I feel like the biggest asshole for being so rude.

I sigh again. "I'm sorry for snapping. I like Christmas just fine, it's just not something I get into like other people. Of course you can decorate."

His face lights up like a damn Christmas tree. "Thank god because I already found the boxes and dragged them out. It would've been hella awkward if you had said no." He's back to lighting up the room with his smile and speaking so fast, it's like a record playing at double speed and I can't even keep up.

"Please stop." I raise a hand to get his attention. "Go decorate. I'm sure Paige will help." He squeals, an honest to god squeal, before he spins on his vibrating feet and bounces his way out and down the hall.

It's going to be an extremely long month if I have to put up with cheeriness turned up to the maximum level. I should restock the bottle of Bailey's in my desk soon. Something tells me I might need it.

His visit to my office has at least jogged my memory concerning my usual Christmas charitable activities. Each year, the town has a children's Christmas party for families that struggle, and each year I receive a request, just like all the other town businesses, to contribute to it. I find the papers in my stack and sign off on their request, sealing it in an envelope to have Paige drop off on her way home. I don't even question what they ask of me anymore, I just agree to it. Of course, I can provide cookies and juice for fifty odd kids and purchase the wish list items for the three kids attached.

I keep the list of asks for the kids aside for Paige. She loves doing it and I give her full power to buy what she deems appropriate. I don't love the commercialization around Christmas, but I love the aspect of giving, especially to kids that may have nothing through no fault of their own. I'm not that big of a Scrooge. Everyone deserves to be happy and if buying an enormous stuffed unicorn or a giant box of makeup for a kid makes their life better in some way, I'm going to do it. I just don't like to tell people about it.

I swipe the stack of mail from my desk and head out front. Paige and Parker have the artificial tree set up already and their easy camaraderie makes me pause. They jostle and joke with each other like siblings and have obviously grown close since Parker started here.

Paige notices me first. "Hey Owen! We're gonna need you to put the star up for us. Can you help?"

"Isn't the star supposed to be the last thing on a tree?"

"True. So how about this? Help us decorate it now and put the star on when it's done." Paige smiles in the way I know she's going to get her way without even asking.

"What if I don't want to help?"

"Owen, if you don't help, I'm telling my gram and she's going to have words with you. Just help us and spare us all that misery, please."

I groan. "I knew you would play the grandma card." Placing the mail on the counter for Paige, I take one of the coffee bean ornaments out of the box.

"What's the grandma card? I feel like this is a need to know story." Parker rubs his hands together, bumping shoulders with Paige.

"My gram was Owen's grade four teacher. She was also his art teacher." Her eyes sparkle at me as she continues the tale I will never, ever hear the end of. "One year for a project she asked the kids to decorate a Christmas tree in a unique way, something that represented what Christmas was about to them."

"Are you going to tell me this guy who never cracks a smile once loved Christmas? Is that where this is going? If so, I may need a chair."

Now they both throw impish grins at me, as I shake my head and silently place ornaments. Paige is going to tell the story whether I like it or not and I know damn well, she will tell her gram if I don't go along with all this.

"Go ahead, tell him what happened."

Paige giggles. "So my gram figured all the kids would do silly things with their trees, or make it about food or whatever... predictable stuff. Owen here was not predictable, but he sure was memorable." Her teasing eyes find mine as my lips turn up. Paige is not only an employee, but she's also like the little sister I never had. She knows I get embarrassed over this story and she's making sure I'm still okay before she continues, but I surprise myself and pick up the story where she left off. Maybe to prove to Parker I'm not a total Christmas hater, as he seems to think I am. Just because I'm not always smiling and happy doesn't mean I'm not a nice guy.

"Paige's gram was my favourite teacher. I may have had a crush on her a little bit and I wanted to impress her." I place my ornament and turn to face both of them. "I should also tell you I'm an overachiever."

Parker scoffs. "No kidding. Just tell me what you did. I'm dying." He probably is. He's wiggling around like he has ants in his pants.

I allow my lips to tilt in a small grin. "Mrs. Barker gave us a tiny fake tree to take home. It was maybe twelve inches tall, and she gave us instructions to make a tree that represents Christmas to us, like Paige said." Now I'm smiling for real when I remember Mrs. Barker's reaction to it. "I sewed a dress by hand with some scraps of material I found in my dad's shop and I put it on the tree; dressed the tree like a person with it. I poked some holes to have branches stick through and made paper angels to hang on it. For the top, I made a big smiling face to look like Mrs. Barker."

Parker gasps, eyes bugging out as he stares at me. "You made your tree into your teacher?"

I chuckle. "To me, Christmas meant being kind and good and Mrs. Barker was those things. She was an angel to a struggling ten-year-old kid and I'll never forget that. I wanted her to know I thought about her that way." I swallow the lump growing in my throat. "She cried and told me she thought I was the sweetest, kindest boy she'd ever known and asked if she could keep it."

"She still has it." Paige chimes in. "She doesn't go out much anymore, but when she does, she stops in to see Owen. Whenever I want to get my way, I just have to threaten I'm telling gram on him." She laughs as she hugs me.

I brush her off. "I know your game, Paige, believe me. Now give me the star and you two can finish tomorrow." I still love Mrs. Barker and I don't want to give her any reason to come down and chew me out. Ever since she broke her hip, she's become so frail. I'd feel terrible if I made anything happen to her.

I place the star on the tree and allow them both to ooh and ahh over it before telling them to leave for the day. Paige takes the mail for me and Parker pauses, shining as always. "Nice to see you smile, boss."

He pulls his toque on with its ridiculous wobbling pompom, beaming at me expectantly. Is he wanting me to respond to something?

I stare at him, hoping he gets the hint to leave, but he fumbles with his phone and Christmas music blasts out. "Oh, I love this one!" Again with the fucking singing, or the sound of wounded cats. Either would be right.

"You can leave now, Parker."

"Right, I'm on it, boss." He keeps singing as he walks out the door, phone in hand, music blaring, a smile splitting his face as he sings his way down the sidewalk.

I pinch the bridge of my nose as I head back to my office. It's going to be a long fucking December.

THREE

Parker

THE LIFE OF A baker can be very tiring. Early mornings wear you out and when Sundays roll around, it's a day to lounge and do your best impression of a lizard on a rock. Even if my rock is still at Auslo's Loft, the youth shelter in town. I'm a twenty-four year old man calling a youth shelter home due to the kindness of friends. Finding an apartment wasn't supposed to be this hard. Until I can finally find a place of my own, me and my feline sidekick, Cheddar will laze about here for the day.

I usually help Jacob with any chores he needs doing, but today I want to lie here and snuggle with my cat. Nothing crazy. Just stay under my blankets with my purring cat, lazy and in jammies; maybe I'll even eat junk food today, too.

Knock, Knock

"Hey Parker, are you up?" A whispered voice comes through my door and as much as I want to ignore it, it's Jacob. I can't ignore Jake.

"Sure, Jake. Come on in."

Cheddar meows in protest as I move him off my chest to the side so I can sit up. He velcros himself to my side instead and I scratch his ears.

"Sorry I'm in here so early. You probably wanted to sleep in, right?" He sits on the bed next to me, rubbing his hands on his thighs.

"What is it Jake? Obviously, there's something bothering you." I scooch over, shoving my dead weight of a cat even farther away. He stiffens in protest, but I win, moving his fuzzy ass further so I can draw Jake closer. "You always tell me to let things out and not keep them pent up. You're at my door for a reason, so out with it."

His voice quivers. "I think I fucked up. Austin's going to be pissed. What if he gets mad at me and we don't get along anymore?"

Jacob wrings his hands, and I wrap both arms around him in an awkward hug. Austin is Jacob's brother, and they've been through some nasty shit. I don't see how Austin would ever leave Jake behind. It would have to be something extremely terrible, and Jake's just not that kind of person.

"Lie down with me and talk." We both lie on my bed, facing each other with our hands pressed under our cheeks. My heart breaks to see the distress on Jake's face. Whatever it is, must be serious. "Can you tell me what it's about?"

"He won't be happy about something I've done. I don't want to tell you too much, in case he asks you about it. I don't want to get you involved, but I needed to talk to someone." He chuckles. "Even if I'm not saying much."

"I'm always here for you, Jake. Tell me as much or as little as you want. If I can help, I will, but whatever it is won't cause Austin to cut you out of his life. I'm sure of it."

He chews his lip. "Do you think so? Cuz you know how people can be. What if he turns out to be like my dad and disowns me?"

"Jake, that's not going to happen. Unless you murdered a puppy or robbed a helpless old lady, he's going to forgive you for whatever it is you think is so bad. Even then, he'd still probably forgive you." I stroke his arm. "You're his only brother. He loves you."

"You're right. He's supported me in everything and almost gave up his husband for me. He might be angry, but he'll get over it." Jacob nods with resolution. "That's what I'll keep telling myself, anyway."

Jake calms down some, but obviously whatever he thinks is a big deal is weighing on him.

"You know, when I first came here, Austin was the first person I really connected with. You were great, but Austin understood me a little bit more than I thought for a stranger." Cheddar walks on top of me and settles between us with a flop, tired of being ignored behind me, and we both reach to pet him. "Maybe it's because we both have orange cats. Whatever it was, he helped me over a tough time and I'm forever grateful."

Jake nods thoughtfully while Cheddar soaks it all up. I can't do any more than provide an ear and company for him. If I know Jake, he's worked up over something that isn't that big of a deal. He's just such a kind person, he takes it all to heart.

"Have you heard anything back from your apprenticeship application yet?"

I sigh. "No. It's killing me though." Jake's brother actually started a scholarship fund for the kids who stayed here. If I hadn't landed here when I did, not only may I not even be alive, I would never have gone to college. When I say I'd do anything for Jacob and this place, it's not said without weight. I mean it. "If I get in, your brother will freak out."

Finally, a smile graces his face as Jacob laughs. "He'll be asking you to send him cakes and showing you off like a new baby."

Jake rolls onto his back and we continue chatting until my stomach growls its disapproval of still being in bed. Jake needs to get back to check on the residents, and I decide to hit the diner for lunch.

A home cooked meal and then back to snuggling in bed with Cheddar sounds like my new plan for the day.

I'm at work, dancing away and singing to ABBA on the oldies station when Owen finds me in the kitchen with his usual scowl. I really wish the guy would smile more. He's already proven he's a decent guy underneath all that gruffness and it's easy to notice he's hot as hell. But would it kill him to be happy with his life and crack a smile?

"Parker."

I don't stop wiggling and turn to face him. "Owen." I mouth the words to Dancing Queen, not stopping as I wait for him to speak and I see it. He's trying hard not to smile. Am I maybe rubbing off on the guy?

"Did you already make the cupcakes for Dom?"

I turn the radio down and return my spoon microphone to the counter. Kitchen karaoke needs to pause. "I did. I was just about to ice them. He said he wanted me to make something special to celebrate his new dog." Well, that's not the entire story. I know he wants to impress Micha, so I'm going to do my best.

"It's been a long time since he's been this happy. If you knew his wife, you might understand why it's important to me you make this your best work."

"I try to make everything my best work. What was she like?"

Owen gazes into the distance, lost in a memory only he can see before he answers. "She was what genuine beauty is about. She was so kind, and she loved with her whole being, you know?" I don't. I've never been able to experience the love of anyone as he describes, but I let Owen go on. "Dom was devastated when he lost her and I was, too. They had the kind of relationship you looked up to and hoped you could find for yourself one day."

Wow. I know what that's like, though. Pining for something you wonder if you'll ever get. Maybe too much for my liking. "Sounds like she was the best. Do you ever think you'll have what they had one day?" I lean back on the counter as Owen does the same thing opposite me. He's relaxed and I like it. He's not happy, but it beats the scowl he always has.

He shrugs. "I don't know. I used to want it with my entire being. Then I opened this place, and it's become my priority. The last relationship I was in ended badly and I guess I just gave up."

This is the most Owen has ever opened up to me. It's like a look inside his soul. Behind the hot scowly face, he has a tenderness about him he rarely shows. The more layers of him I see, the more I realize he's a puzzle I'm obsessing over figuring out.

"What about you? Ever think you'll find the person for you?" He half smiles again. If he'd just give in and smile, he could change the world. Or at least my world.

I go back to filling my icing bag. "I've never had a good relationship. I never see a person for what they are until I'm already too far into it." I sigh. "Maybe I'm not supposed to find my soulmate and I'll live in a bakery forever, like a Keebler elf, but I won't stick to boxed cookies."

Owen laughs and smiles, and for a moment I'm so struck by the ease of his laughter and the beauty of his face... smiling, I don't realize I'm staring. Holy crap. He's gorgeous. Does he even know how he looks?

When he notices me staring, he closes himself off again, turning off the smile and going back to his usual scowl. "Um, that's all I came for. Just wanted to make sure the cupcakes would make Dom happy. Thanks Parker." He clears his throat and exits quickly, like he's embarrassed he'd said too much, or revealed more than he'd wanted.

I return to my cupcake task, but the image of a laughing, smiling Owen is burned into my retinas. His laughter is deep and right from his belly, filled with joy. His smile is something I know I'm going to dream about. He's a very handsome man — I've noticed, believe me. But the smiling face is out of this world and it's not something I'll easily forget.

I need to see him like that again and it can't be soon enough.

FOUR

Owen

I HANG UP THE phone in my office after a lengthy morning of calls with suppliers. It seems my usual coffee supplier has had a massive shipment delay, and I had to scramble to find an alternate source before I ran out. Nothing worse than a coffee shop running out of coffee. Of course, with Christmas coming soon, everyone is working past their capacity and running low on their own stock. Thankfully, I secured a shipment before the day ended, but there's no avoiding the fact that I'm exhausted.

I need to let Paige know there will be an order coming in at an unusual time tomorrow, so she doesn't ignore the buzzer if she's busy.

A glance at the time means I should catch her now before she gets into her end of day procedures. Paige is nothing but a creature of habit and don't try to screw with her routine. Parker has fit in well with her, but I won't be getting on her bad side if I can help it. With sure strides, my sneakered feet approach the front and I brace myself for what I'll find or hear today. Will it be more ear bleeding singing, or will it be dancing with a mop? Will he be planning tomorrow's baking, or will he be writing obscene poems to make Paige laugh? Any of those situations don't make me thrilled, but his work never suffers. So I say nothing and let him be himself — including tolerating all his happiness.

As I enter the main area and the front counter is in view, a man in a leather jacket is being rude to Paige. I linger to see where this is going before I step in. Paige likes handling things on her own.

"I asked for extra whipped cream. Did Parker tell you to treat me like shit? I'm a paying customer, you know. Where's your boss? I want to complain!" The man is leaning across the counter into her personal space, and I don't like his threatening tone.

I step forward. "I'm the boss. Is there a problem here?" Paige's tight-lipped face is my cue this clown has a story. I don't even have to hear her side. He has the slimy feel of over-cooked spinach oozing off him in waves.

"Your chick here fucked up my order on purpose and won't give me a refund."

Paige clenches her fists. "You ordered the mochaccino and specifically said extra whip. That's what I made you."

"Well, you heard wrong. I said no whip."

"Then why did you wait until it was half empty to tell me that?"

I silently observe Paige stand her ground to this asshole trying to... get a free coffee? What other motivation would he have? I'm about to tell him to leave, but a voice behind me speaks first. It's Parker.

"She's been serving you for weeks, Marcus and you always ask for extra whip on everything. Even if you asked for none, it's an honest mistake."

He knows this guy?

"I'm so happy you see it that way, baby. I've made a mistake. I was hoping to see you. I made a mistake with you, too. Can we talk?"

Baby?

What the fuck is going on here? I feel like I'm in a soap opera episode. Paige is still furious. Parker seems wary and slimy guy is putting on an academy award worthy performance with his about-face, admitting to a mistake with Parker and the coffee? I'm seriously confused.

"Anything you want to say, you can say it in front of my friends." Parker stands tall, not breaking eye contact with the guy.

Slimy turns his lip up in disgust. "You have no friends. Drop the act, Parker. You can't do better than me, so I'm here to take you back. You've been too proud to ask me yourself, so I'm doing you a favour."

He was dating this guy? Am I in another dimension? How does my cute sunshine baker end up with this ball of shit? Holy crap, I think he's cute?

"I'm not going anywhere with you, Marcus. You made it pretty clear what you think of me. I'm not as stupid as you think."

I've been ping ponging back and forth with their exchange, and I don't know what shocks me more; that Parker actually found this guy attractive, or me wanting to stand up for my employee that I just admitted to myself I find cute.

Slimeball removes the lid of his coffee and pours the rest on the floor in front of us. Parker lunges forward, but I put out an arm to stop him and step in between them. "You have thirty seconds to get out the door before things get worse for you. You heard him. He's not going with you, so I suggest you leave immediately."

He laughs before breaking into a disgusting coughing fit and hacking up a giant chunk of phlegm as he spits on my floor. This is when I break from my usual laid-back demeanor and get pissed off. Like a tiny twig under the weight of a giant beast, I snap. In one quick stride, I have the slimeball's arm behind his back and drop him to his knees.

With a muffled grunt, his knees hit the floor, and he knows better than to struggle. I've got at least 100 pounds on the guy. He's not going to win.

"Paige, give us a roll of paper towel please."

She thrusts it into my hand, which I hold in front of the slimeball, named Marcus. He hasn't said it hurts yet, but I'm sure that's coming. Guys like him get off on bullying, and it's not happening in my place of business. Not now and not ever. "You will clean up the mess you just made in my shop and then you will leave. You will never come back, and you will never bother my staff again. Do I make myself clear?"

He only nods while snatching the paper towel out of my hand and cleaning the mess before he struggles to his feet. Without another word, he leaves, throwing the door as hard into the wall as he can on his exit. I turn to find Paige and Parker with wide eyes trained on me.

"What?"

"You totally went superhero there, boss man. I didn't know you had that in you. Wow." Paige shakes her head, returning to her closing duties after locking the door behind the poor excuse of a man.

Parker, I can't read, and a weight settles in my gut. I would have behaved that way no matter who slimeball had been trying to intimidate, but for some reason I'm hoping Parker doesn't see it as a negative thing.

"Are you okay, Parker? Who was that guy?"

"Uh, my ex. Not sure why he decided to come and beg for forgiveness weeks after he kicked me to the curb. Must have been missing the coffee, I guess."

Jesus. This guy did a number on Parker if he thinks he liked coffee more than his boyfriend.

He's still staring at me like I have three heads and I have a feeling that I may have scared him. I wouldn't want him to be afraid of me. It's not like I use force with people all the time. This was a one-time thing, and for whatever reason, the fact he was in Parker's face really bothered me.

He shakes his head. "Thank you for standing up for me, Owen. That means a lot." His warm brown eyes never waver from mine and a fizzy feeling spreads over me. It's been a while since I've felt the gaze of admiration bestowed on me and it feels... good. I let my eyes roam his face and it's the first time I've seen him without a blinding smile.

He breaks the trance first, clearing his throat and stammering an awkward sentence. "Um, ya, so I'll leave now. It's time to ah, leave." He spins on his heel toward the kitchen, and I'm left staring after him, wondering what just happened.

The following morning, Parker arrives at his usual time, earbuds in and screeching along to some song, as usual.

He waves in my direction. "Hey boss!"

Parker continues to the kitchen as I prepare yet another coffee for myself. I didn't sleep very well last night because of yesterday's incident. I have to clear the air and make sure I hadn't made him uncomfortable. It would kill me if he felt that way around me and I get the impression he's had no one stand up for him before. That doesn't sit well with me either. He has to know he's worth more than a cup of coffee to people.

I feel like it's my duty to let him know he doesn't deserve to be treated like that. From the bits and pieces I know about Parker so far, I don't think he's had a good hand dealt in the game of life and I want to make things better.

I brace myself, entering the kitchen to the most terrible rendition of Genie in a Bottle I've ever had the displeasure of hearing. "Parker!" I have to raise my voice and he spins around, dropping a hunk of cream cheese on the floor with a splat.

He reaches over to turn down the radio. "Shit, you scared me. I'm sorry Owen. That's a wasted block of cheese now."

He finds some paper towels and cleans up the cheese, wringing his hands when he's done and looking at me with... fear?

"It's just cheese, Parker. It's fine. I'm not mad or anything. That's actually what I wanted to talk to you about."

His eyes widen. I use a softer voice and reach for the right words. "Listen, about yesterday. I wanted to say I'm sorry if it scared you when I went off on that guy. I don't, as a rule, get physical in anger." He remains still, eyes cast to the floor. "I... ah... I also wanted to say that people shouldn't talk to you like that. It was rude and uncalled for."

He fiddles with the hem of his apron. "I wasn't scared. I've just had no one defend me like that before. I didn't know what to do."

I'm glad he's not scared of me, but why would he have no one stick up for him? Even if you don't like his happy, smiley persona, he's still a nice guy. "Well, I don't let that shit slide, no matter what. I'll do it again if I have to."

Parker still fidgets, not looking at me, and I can't handle that. I step closer and with my fingers, I raise his chin to look at me. "Hey. It's just me. Everything is fine, okay? Don't let people walk all over you, Parker. You're worth more than that."

His shining brown eyes stare back at me, and I spend a beat too long reading the sadness in them. What could have happened to him for that sadness to cling to him like a wet blanket? I drop his chin and turn to leave the kitchen. His whisper has me pausing. "Thank you for thinking I'm worth something. I'll try harder to not let it happen."

He turns up the radio and launches into singing, leaving no room for conversation.

As I return to my office, I can't shake the look in Parker's eyes. Nobody should ever feel like that.

FIVE

Parker

G OD DAMN IT. I needed that cream cheese earlier. Now I have to wait for another brick to soften before moving on. I clean up what I was working on and pause for a breath. I'm still reeling over Owen standing up for me yesterday. He brought Marcus to his knees, for crying out loud. I'll be lying if I say it didn't make him more attractive. Not even Marcus had stood up for me — and he was my *boyfriend* at one time.

With a sigh, I remove the gingerbread from the oven. I've made both men and women and my plan is to decorate them with cute Christmas t-shirts in rainbow colours. The lettering will be difficult to make so small but I'm up for the challenge.

After placing the cookies on a cooling rack, my mind wanders back to Owen and the past few days. The fact is, he hasn't left my mind since I saw him smile. Piled on top of all the other stuff I've learned about him, I'm crushing hard. Not sure it's wise to want my boss, but I can't really help it. I place more trays of cookies in the oven, then lean against the counter and grab my newly filled coffee for a quick break.

"Parker, I need to know when you need me to deliver the cupcakes over to the city hall party."

Owen startles me, barging into the kitchen and I slosh coffee on my shirt. "Shit." I hiss, as I pull the fabric away from my body. "They should be ready by 11 A.M at the latest."

I reach for a cloth to dab at my wet shirt as Owen hovers. "I didn't mean to scare you, sorry. You're usually singing out loud and never hear me come in." He's got a point. I am usually loud.

"It's fine. You're right. You just happened to catch me at an odd moment of quiet."

"I'm sorry."

Owen's voice cracks and I whip my head up, abandoning my dabbing to find his eyes trained on me. "I'd never hurt you on purpose, Parker. I'll be more careful next time."

I swallow the lump in my throat. His concern is unnerving. Should he be that concerned? I only spilled coffee on my shirt, I didn't cut off a finger. "It's coffee, Owen. No hospital trip needed."

The timer goes off for the batch of cookies and I quickly tug an oven mitt on. I don't know how I feel, being the center of his attention right now. It's making me feel things I can't put words to, and I'm overwhelmed by it. He never does anything more than grunt or snap at me. Why is he concerned now? When I sneak a glance his way, my focus moves from the oven for too long and my arm connects with the hot oven rack. "Fuck!" I manage to not drop the pan on the floor and throw the pan onto the table to save the cookies. But before I can tear my oven mitt off and get to the sink, large strong hands are already pulling me there.

Owen turns on the cold water before shoving my arm under the faucet and practically spilling me into the sink in the process.

"Jeez Owen, let me go. I can handle it."

"Stop squirming around and let me look at it, Parker."

"It's not serious, just let me take care of it." It's not the first and it won't be the last time I burn myself in the kitchen. I'm always careful, but sometimes I make mistakes. Like when I glance at my boss and see an emotion on his face I can't understand.

He turns the water off and drags me to a chair, forcing me to sit as he reaches for the first aid kit on the wall. I have a look at the burn — the best I can anyway, since it's near my elbow and under my arm. It's already starting to blister. Great. Just what I need to deal with today. He places the case on the table, pulling out gauze and burn ointment.

"Oh, Parker." He breathes as he gently dabs the water away. I hold my breath at the gentle way he handles me. It's a complete paradox to his intimidating nature. Large hands like his should not be so gentle. I've already seen him use them to protect me, now they are caring for me.

It's no longer the burn on my skin distracting me, but the touch of his hands as he gently takes care of my wound. Nobody has ever taken care of me like this. If I skinned my knee or cut myself, it was only me washing out my wounds in a rusted sink with a bar of soap and sacrificing a piece of towel to serve as a bandaid. No motherly, fatherly, or any other type of figure was there to assist me. I was always on my own.

Owen applies ointment and trims a non-stick bandage pad to cover it, then wraps it with gauze and secures it with medical tape and waterproof wrap. It's overkill for a small burn, but I am working in a kitchen, so I should protect it properly.

"Are you okay? Can you still work?" Owen's genuinely asking because he cares. His eyes scan my body, cataloguing the rest of me to ensure I'm not hurt anywhere else.

I bend my arm and move it around to show him I can function with the bandage. It doesn't hurt; it's awkward and it stings, but I can live with it. "Of course I can work. It's a little burn on my arm is all."

He quietly packs away the first aid kit and places it back on the wall while I survey the cookies I threw with haste onto the table. Only a few broke, but they were spares. I should be okay with what remains. The oven timer goes off again, this time for cupcakes and I make sure I take them out without losing focus, even though I can feel Owen's eyes burning into my back. Dropping the pans on the table, I turn to face him.

"Thank you for your help. I'll let you know when the cupcakes are ready for delivery."

He nods and leaves without another word, and I release a whoosh of breath. Jesus, the man is starting to get under my skin and I'm not sure how I feel about that. I don't know if I'll ever wrap my mind around what makes him tick.

I return to my tasks, auto pilot kicking in and my hands work of their own accord. That's a good thing, because I can't concentrate. I'm too busy thinking of Owen's hands and how they felt on me.

Six

Owen

"**H**E WORE A REINDEER onesie to work today."

Dom chokes on his coffee, sending a fine spray across the table. I pass him a napkin to wipe his face and use another to soak up his mess as he gets himself under control. "You're kidding. How does he work in the kitchen with that on?"

I shrug a shoulder and sip my coffee. "Fucked if I know, but he's getting on my nerves with all this Christmas crap." Parker knows I'm not a huge fan of anything cute. Christmas is just another day. I don't hate Christmas. I just hate how perfectly sane people seem to lose their ever loving minds over it.

Ever since I hired him, it's been non-stop cute and cheerful and it's not my thing. The turkey suit at Thanksgiving should have been my clue he was that kind of guy. Who dresses up for Thanksgiving?

"Are you still coming to our Christmas party? Parker's invited. Is that going to be a problem?"

Ah yes, the first party Dom is going to host with his new boyfriend. The party will be fun. Hard not to like a party, even if I haven't been to one in ages. Dom and I still enjoy each other's company and Micha is cool, but Micha is a lot like Parker. It's going to be full of cuteness and rainbows and whatever other kind of shit people have at parties for... fun.

"It's not a problem. He's my employee. Of course I'll still come." My employee that I find cute, but I'm not about to admit it. Not out loud, anyway.

Dom scratches his ear with his left hand and I narrow my eyes, bracing myself for whatever he's left out. It's his tell. If he scratches with his right, it's just an itch, but if he uses his left, that's different. There's something he's not telling me. When you've been friends as long as we have, you pick up on these things.

"What is it?" I sigh.

"Ah, Micha asked if it could be a theme." He cringes, waiting for my reply. It's a fair response. I'm not big on themes. I just want simple: Food, drinks and company. That's fun enough.

"And what has he suggested as a theme?"

"It's nothing outrageous. He wants an Ugly Christmas Sweater party."

I groan.

Dom laughs at me. Just as I knew the fucker would. "I'll lend you one. You just need to show up."

I raise an eyebrow. "You have more than one ugly Christmas sweater? Since when?"

He throws his head back in more laughter. "You have met Micha, right? He takes impulsive shopping to a whole new level." He shakes his head in what he thinks is a sign of annoyance, but the slight tip of his lips tells me otherwise. A fool in love, and I couldn't be happier for him.

My own chuckle slips out. Micha can be over the top. If I had to guess, he has matching sweaters for the pets too. But he makes my best friend happy. So I'll suck it up and follow along.

Dom snorts and covers his mouth, his whole body shaking with laughter as he looks beyond my shoulder. I know immediately it's Parker.

"When you said reindeer onesie, I wasn't expecting him to be all furry and have a hood. Good Lord, he must be dying in the kitchen with that." Dom is still snickering and snorting, so I turn in my chair to see what the reindeer baker is up to.

Parker is sliding a tray of, you guessed it, Rudolph cookies into the display case. He's flipped the hand coverings over on his outfit and now it looks like he has hooves, which I suppose is cute. If you like cute, that is. But the part I think that has Dominic in stitches is the giant light up red nose he's now wearing. It's blinking like a stoplight and perched right on the end of his nose.

I shake my head — sending a prayer for the rest of December to pass at warp speed — and turn back to Dominic. "He's nuttier than his own fruitcake."

"I like it. It's fun. *He's* fun." He peers over his cup at me. "When's the last time you had fun? Just let go of all the adult stuff and have fun for the sake of it?"

"I don't have time for that stuff." I slant my eyes away from his because I know what's coming next, and Dominic doesn't disappoint.

He sighs. "You know, even business owners can have fun. It's called balance. You should try it."

I fiddle with my coffee cup as I let his words settle. I know he's right. He always is for this stuff. I used to be fun. I partied far too much. I was always that guy who met new people on a night out and randomly went off with them to do stupid shit, only to come back with unexplained bruises and a garden gnome. It was nothing for me to function on 3 hours of sleep, and I never turned down a good time.

Then something happened. I used the life insurance from my parents to start up The Screaming Bean and put my business degree to use. I poured all my free time into making it successful. It was my joy and still is, but somewhere along the line, I lost the part of me that was separate from the business. It's been years since I had the random fun Dominic is suggesting, but I also don't miss it.

"I'm not even sure if I know how to do it anymore, really. It's been a long time."

"Owen, nobody forgets how to have fun. You forget the combination of a lock or how to play a card game. You don't forget how to have fun."

A hollow laugh escapes me. "Apparently I did." I drain my cup and spin around to see Parker again behind the service counter. The proverbial pain in the ass with his sunshine smiles and can-do attitude. Sure, I've got a few years on him in the department of life, but he lives at the youth shelter while he's trying to find his own place. Don't even get me started on the poor excuse for a boyfriend he had. Yet he's prancing — actually prancing — around my coffee shop, acting like a reindeer as a few children giggle and look on. Like it's the best part of his day, he plays along with them.

Dominic stands, clapping me on the shoulder. "You should think about fun, O. You could use some. Talk to Parker."

I snort. "About what?"

"Oh, I don't know, maybe fun things? If anyone could show you fun, my bet would be on him."

Dominic leaves to go back to his butcher shop next door, and I clear our table. When I enter the kitchen, Parker is humming Christmas songs as I dump our dishes at the dish wash station.

"Hey boss! Have a good lunch?"

Parker continues humming under his breath while he decorates more cookies. This time it's Santa cookies. He's taken his hoof mitts off and pushed up the sleeves of his reindeer suit. As he pipes black icing edging on the Santa's, his antlers bounce on his head. He has to be so hot in that damn suit back here near the ovens, but if he's uncomfortable, he's not complaining. His cheeks are flushed rosy pink and his sweat soaked hair sticks to his forehead; the only signs that give away he's hot.

"Yes, it was good. It's always good to talk with Dom."

He nods his head, bobbing his antlers, and I feel my lips threatening to tip into a smile. "Friends are always good, boss-man."

I reach over to take a cookie, because they look so damn good, and he smacks my hand.

"You can't eat these."

"Uh, I own the place. I can eat what I want." I reach again, and this time he smacks my hand with a spoon. "Ow! What the hell, Parker? Give me a cookie."

"They're for the kids. If you eat one now, I won't have enough for everyone."

"What kids?"

He faces me, passing a fuzzy arm over his forehead. "The kids' party at the town hall tomorrow afternoon? Remember? You're supposed to be Santa?"

Like hell I agreed to be a Santa. "What're you talking about?"

He marches over to a corkboard, reindeer tail bouncing on his butt, and plucks a sheet of paper from the board and hands it to me. It's a letter of donation from the town for their annual kids' party. I donate every year. I know this. Not sure why he's staring at me. He sighs. "Owen, right here." He jabs a finger at the bottom where Janice, the clerk at the town hall, wrote a note asking if I could be Santa. In my handwriting is a scribbled *Yes*.

"When did I agree to this? I'd never be a Santa. I'm going to be a horrible Santa." Make this a reminder to *read* the shit she sends over from now on. There's no way I can back out of it without looking like a massive asshole.

His laugh is light, with none of the stress and frustration in it I'm feeling right now. "It'll be fun. You'll be great."

There's that word again. Fun. Plunking me in a Santa suit with kids on a sugar high, potentially crying on my lap when they get scared, is fun?

"Since you seem to know all about this, what are the details?"

He claps his hands together and barely holds his happiness in check. "We're coming to work at our normal times. The Santa suit is already at the hall. We'll go over just after lunch with the cookies. Paige also has the gifts done. We can take those over too."

"You and Paige did all this without me?" I know I give her free rein, but she usually gives me a running commentary. I'd also let the days go by and didn't even notice we were close to the day of the party.

He shrugs a shoulder and returns to his icing. "We know you don't really like Christmas, so we just took care of it. Paige has the expenses for you, though."

I silently watch him make perfectly iced pom-poms on each Santa hat cookie and wonder if maybe Dominic is right, and I have lost the fun in life. I'm not keen on trying to find it at Christmas, but what must my staff think of me to not even approach me and remind me this was going on?

"Um, do you need me to do anything now?"

Parker's smile is carefree and blinding. "Want to sing Christmas songs with me?"

"That would be a hard no. I meant anything productive to help with for tomorrow."

He shrugs again. Only this time, his smile falls. Shit, why does that make me feel bad about making him unhappy? "Nothing constructive, as you like to say, Owen. It's all good."

When he turns his back to me, humming again and bopping to the song only he can hear in his head, I find myself envious of how he finds joy in the smallest things. How he's always... happy. How can someone always be happy like that?

With a sigh, I leave Parker in the kitchen and return to my office. Paige's expenses are on my desk, and also, a sack of wrapped gifts marked for each child. Clearly, I need to do something more for my staff if they're willing to do all this on their own time. I write a cheque for Paige right away. It's only seven days before Christmas and she spent her own money for this.

I power through some admin work needing to be done and when the clock says it's almost closing time, I wander out front to hand Paige her cheque before she leaves.

"Oh, thanks for being so fast with that, Owen. I didn't go over your budget, did I?"

"No, it's all fine. It's reasonable, actually." She stuffs the cheque in her pocket and I rock on my heels. "Uh, are you okay with it, though? That was a lot to cover on your own so close to Christmas. I should've been more aware."

"It's okay boss." She pats my arm. "I saved and dipped into my own Christmas fund. I knew you were good for it."

"Paige..." She waits while I try to gather the words. "Um, I'm not the type of person to make big gestures of thanks. You know that." She chuckles. "But I just want you to know I appreciate what you did. If you need me to give you cash instead, I can do that. I just don't want you to be in a tight place over something you did for me."

"It's all good, Owen, but thank you. I'm just happy to see you going for the Santa role. I still can't believe you agreed to it."

"That makes two of us."

Paige gathers her things and flits out the door. I poke my head into the kitchen and see everyone else has left as well. The cookies Parker was working on sit on a tray with a note: *Do not eat or you're on the naughty list.*

I return to my office to collect my things for an early night. If I'm going to be dealing with spoiled, crying children to find fun, I'm going to need all the rest I can get.

Seven

Parker

I BOUNCE UP THE stairs to my room, as any reindeer would, and immediately strip out of my reindeer suit. I was sweating like a beast in that thing today, but it was so worth it. Seeing all the customers smile when I had my light-up nose on, was the icing on the cake. No pun intended.

I step into the shower and wash away today's grime, and wonder how it will all go down at tomorrow's town Christmas party. I'm not sure why I've made it my personal mission to get Mr. Grumpy pants, my boss, to crack a smile and have some fun, but I have. After he revealed it to me the first time, his smile has been the only thing I can think about. Well, that and how his hands had felt when he treated my burn wound. That was amazing and I have wondered more than once what it would feel like to have his hands touch me in other places. Instead of coasting through my workdays with his quiet and frowny good looks, I have to make it harder on myself by trying to coax out devastating smiles. I'm nothing but a sucker for making myself suffer, it seems.

I dry myself off as Cheddar barges into the bathroom and sits down to stare at me. Judging my nakedness in a way that's both accepting and critical. We both carry extra weight, and he knows he can't shame the hand that feeds him.

"Do you mind? You've left the bedroom door, and now my bathroom door, open. Privacy is a thing you know." I quickly wrap a towel around my waist and close my bedroom door. I'm still staying at the LGBTQ shelter, which was only supposed to be temporary. Five months later and I'm still here. My over-stuffed orange tabby cat has full roam of the house. He visits whoever he wants, when he wants, but always comes back to sleep with me. That's why my door is always open, but man, learn some manners.

I continue to dry off — now that I'm no longer in danger of another resident seeing my dick hanging out — while Cheddar meows away. So I meow back, hoping I say the right thing. But I don't speak cat, so who the hell knows. He seems to enjoy conversation at least.

I pull on a clean t-shirt and lounge pants and head to the common area. I'll unwind and see if Jacob needs help with anything before the early bedtime I need to function tomorrow. Jacob is on the couch with a cup of tea and his feet up, while he types madly on his phone.

"Hey Jake." I plop beside him and prop my feet up as he shoves his phone in the pouch of his hoodie.

"Hey Parker. How was your day?"

"I had a fantastic day. Thank you for asking. Who ya texting?"

His ears turn red, and he shakes his head. "Just a friend. Are you staying here for Christmas, by chance?"

Ah, the master of deflection, my friend Jacob is. I can take a hint. "Well, unless I find a place to rent in the next few days, yes. No home, remember?"

He winces at the reminder of my situation, and I feel bad for saying it. "I'm going to visit my brother and Logan for a few days over Christmas. I arranged for Janice and Brandi to come and stay while I'm gone, but if you're around, do you think you could help them out too? There's only the two younger kids right now. I believe Joseph has an aunt he's going to visit. Martin has a boyfriend he'll be with, Katie of course, and then you."

I nod at the reminder I have nobody of importance left in my life. My dad was never in my life. My mom died of a drug overdose when I was only eight. After I bounced around the foster care system, I had hoped the last family I was with would adopt me, but that never panned out. I toughed it out there until I could afford a bus ticket, and ran away when I was sixteen, landing on the doorstep of, first a homeless shelter in a large city, then finally finding myself here. I was literally on Jake's doorstep in the middle of the night and praying to God this place would be different. Thankfully, my prayer was answered because I was at the end of my rope.

"I don't mind helping at all, you know that, Jake. Unless Santa brings me a boyfriend that actually likes me, I'll be here."

"Great, thanks for that, P." He holds out a hand for a fist bump. "Are you excited about tomorrow?"

"Oh, my god I am! I think I'm most excited to see Owen as Santa though." I know he's going to be adorable, even with his perma-scowl in place. Maybe not adorable, more like Sexy Santa. A Santa with a lap I'd race to sit on. Apparently I have a Santa fantasy. Who knew?

Jacob regards me with furrowed eyebrows as he chooses his next words. "This crush on your boss isn't going away then?"

Okay, so I'm not as covert as I thought I was. I may have over shared far too much with Jake one night after my ex humiliated me for the last time, and I drowned my relationship sorrows with shots of peach schnapps. I've had a crush on my boss since I met him almost five months ago. He's gorgeous, with his dimpled chin and messy brown hair and eyes so blue you'd swear they were from the ocean and you'd drown if you stared too long. Which I have a few times, but he hasn't mentioned it. The man can rock a tight t-shirt and ripped jeans like nobody's business. Don't even get me started on how he helps friends. He's been a regular visitor in my fantasies for a while now. So yes, that crush has grown, and it's weighing on me like store-bought fruit cake.

I shake my head. "No, it's not. I was a goner when he twisted Marcus's arm in The Bean and stood up for me. I know he's not interested, but I can't help it." Which is true. He may have a hard time being happy, but he's given me so many peeks into what he's really like. I know he's a puzzle I'd love to figure out.

Should I be interested in my boss? Definitely not, but I'm not good at what you'd call making good choices.

Jake pushes to his feet. "I need to do the house rounds and check in. Parker?"

"Ya?"

He chews on his lip. "Be careful, okay?"

With a nod, he walks off and I'm left considering his words. I have nothing to be careful about. My crush is one sided. I'll try to get him to smile more and that's my mission simply because it makes me happy. Maybe a Christmas miracle happens, maybe not. If he was actually into me, things would be different. Fact is, people like Owen don't get involved with hot messes like me. I can hope all I want, but it will never happen.

Choking on that dose of reality, I head to the kitchen to eat my loneliness away.

My alarm comes far too early and I smash my hand on it blindly, searching for the off button until it halts its piercing wake up call.

With a groan, I stumble to the bathroom and go through my morning ritual of waking up. I perk up once I remember what's happening today. Hello sexy boss man Santa. If he doesn't smile when he sees my elf suit, I don't know if I'll ever make him crack a smile over Christmas. I thought for sure I had him with the reindeer suit yesterday, but no deal. Bloody guy didn't even poke fun at me. Who can't smile at a grown man prancing around in a reindeer suit?

I pack my elf costume in a duffel bag. I can't wear it to work and show up at the party covered in flour and icing. For work, I'll wear something else festive. Good thing I have no shortage of holiday attire to choose from.

With a grin, I pull on my favourite Christmas t-shirt that says *Jingle My Balls*, with a pair of jeans. I can easily cover it up with my chef coat if needed and I'll be in an elf suit at the kids' party, so it's perfectly acceptable. I'm festive, fun and ready for the day.

I leave a dish of kibble out for Cheddar before I begin the cold but short walk to work. It's only two blocks away, so I can't really complain, but the air always feels colder at 4 A.M. When I get to work, Owen has already arrived, which means he's early by at least thirty minutes. I let myself in, careful to lock the door behind me again since we don't open for another three hours. As I walk towards his office to wish him good morning and let him know I'm here, I freeze in my tracks.

"Ho, Ho, Ho. Have you been a good boy this year?"

I bite my lip to stop the bubble of laughter threatening to spill out. Owen is practicing to be Santa. This has to be the cutest thing ever. I wish I could see. Instead, I stand rooted in the hallway eavesdropping and feeling a smidge guilty about it. But it's his self-talk — out loud — that pulls me closer to the door.

"Why did I say I'd be Santa? I'm hardly jolly. God, I hope I don't make their Christmas worse. Okay, Owen, you can do this. It's one day to make a difference for a kid."

He practices his Ho, Ho, Ho a few more times and now I've crept close enough to peek into his office. Owen is sitting on his chair to the side of his desk, practicing what Santa would do. He pretends to rummage in a gift sack and pulls an imaginary present out.

"Ho, Ho, Ho. This one says Lucas. Where's young Lucas?" He's too stinking cute, practicing every slight gesture and trying on different Santa voices. If he wants to practice with someone on his lap, I'll be the first to volunteer. I would push the kids out of line to get that opportunity. Take it for the team, if you will. A test drive on sexy Santa's lap would be a fantastic gift for me. A small moan passes over my lips at the thought of sitting on his lap, but with far fewer clothes on. Owen's eyes snap to the doorway, locking on mine, and I can't breathe.

"How long have you been listening?" He stands and pushes his chair back behind his desk, shoving his hands in his pockets. I thought he would be angry to get caught, but now I think he's embarrassed. Oh, my heart. I didn't think it was possible for a stupid crush to grow, but it just did.

I clear my throat. "I'm sorry. I didn't mean to eavesdrop like that. You've got a great Santa voice. That ho, ho, ho is on point." I nod my head with the enthusiasm of a bobblehead doll, hoping he believes me and doesn't back out of it. "You're going to be great. You got this."

"You think so? I'm not really a kid person. I don't know what to say to them. Sometimes I think they're scared of me because I'm just a big guy, you know?"

Oh crap. He really is nervous. His beautiful blue eyes are asking for reassurance and, of course, I'm going to give it. I'd give him anything he wants, he just has to ask. Owen doesn't give me much apart from snarky comments and scowls, but the few times I've had more than that, I'll never forget. Like now.

"It's not that you're big, really. I mean, you're a mountain, in a good way don't worry, but I think it's because you don't smile. Little people look at faces for reassurance and if you're scowly, that scares them."

He's silent for so long I think I've made a giant mess of things and I should turn and leave, but he surprises me with what comes next.

"Dom says I don't know how to have fun anymore. I guess it makes sense. I don't smile because I'm not having fun. This is going to be fun, isn't it?" His eyes search mine and I hope he doesn't see what I'm hiding.

"Well, I think it's fun. But I'm a giant kid at heart. I find anything to do with Christmas fun." I step into his office, shoving my hands in my pockets to keep myself from pulling him into a giant hug. His insecurity, coupled with his handsome features, is making my body ache to comfort him. I would never have expected that under such a confident and powerful façade, lived a man who lacked the skills to play a simple charade with children. "I'll be right there with you; your right-hand elf." I chuckle at my own joke, and there it is. His lips pull up at one side in an almost smile. Even that slight change sends my heart racing.

"Okay, I trust you, Parker."

Shit. He trusts me. No pressure, I can do this.

I grin back. "In that case, if you feel you want to practice with someone on your lap, let me know." His eyes balloon to the size of dinner plates, but the other side of his lips tick up and a genuine smile is aimed my way, making my knees shake.

"I'll keep that in mind."

Before I can let my mouth say anymore of my inside words out loud, I shoot a finger gun and spin out of his office.

I practically run back to the kitchen with a pounding heart. I just made Owen smile.

EIGHT

Owen

WHEN I ARRIVED AT work earlier than normal this morning, I thought I'd be alone. I didn't think Parker would walk in on my Santa role-play practice.

I spent a lot of time last night tossing and turning. It's true, I'm nervous about doing this and I really can't put my finger on why. I understand why some people are nervous about this kind of thing, but I'm a big guy. I'm 6 ft 4 and 250 pounds. I have one forearm covered in tattoos and sometimes that freaks people out, even with my baby face that doesn't betray my age of thirty-two. I'm not a wall of muscle, but I'm fit enough; if you want a bowl full of jelly squishy kind of Santa, I'm going to need a pillow.

While I spent my night working up anxiety over whether small children would piss themselves in fear while sitting on my lap, I also couldn't stop thinking about what Dominic said about having fun. How he said I should ask Parker for help. Since then, I've been playing the last five months of interactions with Parker over and over in my mind, like those shitty films in grade school that always seemed to get stuck in the projector at the most interesting parts.

While I've always written off Parker's antics as annoying, I'm seeing his efforts in a new light. He's an outstanding employee and I know he had a crappy childhood. He has no blood family, and instead, has the other people from the shelter as chosen family, one of which is Micha, Dominic's boyfriend. Even knowing Parker's history on the most basic of levels, I wonder how he can be the happy-go-lucky guy he always is. Maybe all his craziness, reindeer suits included, is a way for him to be happy and forget the bad stuff?

I'm no psychologist, but I know singing is therapeutic for many. Parker is always singing off key and dancing around in the kitchen. Instead of laughing and singing along, I've scowled and huffed away. He creates new words for his creations that are borderline certifiable, and instead of laughing, I scowl and tell him to label it a cream puff and I walk away. He wears fun outfits on holidays and again, I frown and walk away.

I run a hand down my face and stare at the space where he stood a few moments ago. He didn't even laugh at me practicing Santa. He encouraged me and told me I was *on point,* whatever the hell that means. But why did he offer to sit on my lap for practice? I have to admit, I'm glad he walked off after that comment, because my brain has decided now is the time to unpack what he meant by it. The image of him on my lap — and not just sitting there well behaved — is taking hold of me. Why now?

With a groan, I move back to my laptop and try to get my mind focused on the work I need to do before leaving for the party. With Christmas being so close, and The Bean being closed for a few days so the staff can have time with their families, I don't have nearly as much work as I normally do, and I find myself at loose ends. I push away from my desk with a huff and stalk to the kitchen.

What I find in the kitchen stops me in my tracks. Parker is dancing as he mixes something by hand and is belting out the lyrics to *All I Want for Christmas is You* like he's a contestant on American idol. While I'd normally ignore him and go about my business with my usual scowl on my face, I see a different Parker today.

I see a beautiful young man with a dazzling personality. A man who has been underappreciated by people who say they care about him. A man who tried —and failed — to hide how much it meant to him for me to bandage a simple burn for him. He's someone who has every reason to be bitter about life, but isn't. Parker has been trying to teach me to enjoy life while it's here, but I've been ignoring his message. As he changes songs and gets his body into a full-on shimmy, my eyes roam over his body, noticing everything physical about him I've tuned out before. He's wearing jeans today, which he normally doesn't, preferring baggy chef pants, and I'm stunned at the body he's hidden for so long. His jeans mold to his ass in a perfect denim hug, and cling to his thighs like a second skin. He hasn't even turned around, so I wonder what the front looks like.

As if I sent him a subliminal message to turn, he spins around with his eyes closed, screeching into his mixing spoon and belting out *Run Run Rudolph* like nobody is listening. His t-shirt is fitted, accentuating his smaller stature and of course, it's Christmas themed. But my eyes continue to skim the front of him quickly and I find my skin prickling with heat at the thought of what's behind his bulging zipper. I clear my throat to get his attention over the music and his eyes fly open. Instead of being embarrassed to be seen like this, he maintains eye contact while dancing. A bright smile graces his beautiful face and I again wonder why I never took the time to appreciate him like this before. Why have I been going through life with my eyes closed?

His brow is damp with sweat and he's panting from the exertion of mixing and dancing. He turns the music down. "Everything okay, boss man? You look worried."

He stares at me with his giant, brown doe-eyes. Fuck me, how have I not noticed him after all this time? I clear my throat and find something else to look at instead of him. Anything but him. My brain is scrambled, and I need to get it back online before I do or say something stupid.

"Everything is fine." My voice breaks like a prepubescent teen and I spin around to enter the walk-in cooler to collect myself. I grab the first thing I find, inhale a deep, settling breath and exit to find Parker still watching me.

"I just needed to get some..." I look at what's in my hand and silently curse when it's not something more practical. "Whip cream. For ah, the pie I'm making tonight."

"Oh, you're making a pie? Can I help? Are you taking it somewhere?"

Jesus, why is he asking me all this? Can't he notice I'm not my normal self here? "Um... a kind to use whip cream on."

Smooth Owen, your brain has officially vacated.

Thankfully, Parker must pick up on my discomfort. He turns his back to me again and I bite my lip when he dances, shaking his ass without a care in the world and leaving me, once again, mentally kicking myself for being so oblivious.

I rush back to my office with a can of whip cream I don't need and stash it in my bag. I need to get myself under control and back to focusing on being Santa in a few hours. Right now, I don't know if my heart is racing because I'm about to step out of my comfort zone to play Santa, or because I just noticed Parker as another man for the first time. Both scenarios are equally terrifying and making me dizzy.

This whole *learning to have fun* thing is rapidly getting out of control...and taking the fun with it.

I pull my coat off its hook and head out front. Our morning rush is in full swing. Paige gives me a quick nod as I signal I'm stepping out for a few minutes. Filling my lungs with the cold December air grounds me and I walk the short distance next door to Wild Baloney, Dom's butcher shop. If anyone can help me focus, it will be him.

The bellowing moose call goes off as I enter the storefront and Jade smiles a greeting. "Hey Owen! Long time no see. Dom's in the back."

"Thanks Jade. He's not busy? I didn't call him."

"Gosh no, nothing he can't do with you talking to him, anyway." She shoos me towards the back and I enter Dom's domain of meat cutting.

"Why is it that every time I come in here you have a sausage in your hand?"

Dominic startles at my voice and looks at his hands holding a giant hunk of meat and laughs. "This is a bologna chubb, my friend. There's only one sausage I handle and..."

"Stop! I don't need to hear any more of your lovey dovey stuff. I know you're in love and all that, but I'm selfishly here for me."

He drops the giant hunk of bologna with a thud near the slicer and focuses on me. "You know I'm always here. What's going on?"

I inhale deeply. "So, you know yesterday you said I need to learn to have fun again?" He nods. "And you said maybe I should talk to Parker because he's fun?" He nods again, so I continue. "I'm going to be Santa this afternoon at the kids' party the town is hosting."

His eyebrows shoot up. "Say what now? You're going to be *Santa*?"

I laugh and stuff my hands in my pockets. "Yep. Big Ole Owen was practicing how to Ho, Ho, Ho this morning in the office."

FINDING THE RIGHT FOREVER

Dom snorts and laughs. "Go big or go home. I tell you to learn to have fun and you pick playing Santa to start with. The happiest thing on earth next to a kid cranked up at Disneyland is what you're going to start with."

I chuckle. "You didn't let me finish." I chew my lip. If I say it out loud, it makes it more real. "Parker caught me practicing the whole fat and jolly bit. He was very supportive, and he made a comment that I can't get out of my head."

"What could he have possibly said to have you this rattled about it?"

Okay, here goes. "He said if I wanted to practice with someone sitting on my lap, he would volunteer. Then he shot me with a finger gun and left a fire behind him as he all but ran to the kitchen. So, me being me, I can't stop thinking about him on my lap now. Weird, right? I go to the kitchen when I think I'm under control, but he's dancing all over the place and singing stupid Christmas songs which usually pisses me off, but... Jesus Dom." My voice cracks. I swallow hard and continue. "I'm staring at him, shaking his little ass and I'm lost in his puppy dog eyes and I'm so flustered I had to step into the cooler." Dom chuckles softly, but I point a finger at him. "Don't laugh at me! Dom, how did I never look at him like this before? Why is it right before I'm about to try on the fun thing with Santa? Now I'm worried about popping a boner when some kid comes over to my lap because Parker is going to be there too." I plop into a chair, dropping my head in my hands.

I'm a wreck. One small comment has taken root in my brain like an annoying worm, and I can't stop fixating on it. Dominic's hand is on my shoulder and another chair scrapes along the floor as he settles next to me.

"O, you can handle this. What is it you're really bothered about in all that?"

I don't answer right away, instead I take a breath and screw my eyes closed. My usual calmness returns. The rational train of thought is back on track. I take a moment to gather the morning's events and replay them, watching them again for the first time, but with a different perspective. I know I can play Santa, it's not hard. You wear a suit and say a few things and give a kid a gift or two. That's not what's bothering me.

I lift my head and look into my best friend's eyes. "What's bothering me, is that I just noticed Parker as a man for the first time, not an annoying employee."

Dom nods and rises to walk back to his slicer. "What part of that is causing you to freak out so much?" I watch as he assembles his slicer and goes through the safety procedure.

I puff out my cheeks and find Dominic watching me. "The part where I want to find out what it's like to have him on my lap."

NINE

Parker

AS THE CLOCK CREEPS closer to the time Owen and I have to leave for the Christmas party, my usual happy exterior is being nudged aside and replaced with anxiety. Over what exactly, I don't know.

Something shifted with Owen's behaviour towards me, and I'm not one hundred percent sure what caused it. Although my gut is saying it's the lap comment and it leaves me wondering if I maybe went too far. That would be the way my life always goes. Everything is going great and I open my big mouth and say something stupid to ruin it all.

With a sigh, I finish bagging the Santa cookies, tying the cellophane tops with pretty ribbon and attaching name tags I made with each child's name in calligraphy. I also tie a giant candy cane to the top of each bag. It's a beautiful presentation and when I was a child, it would have thrilled me to receive a gift like this. Anything handmade always carries that extra bit of love. An item you crafted with your own two hands, especially for me, bears extra special meaning. It could be a jar of jam, a loaf of bread, or a pair of knitted mittens. It all carries that extra bit of love with it you can't find in toys or gifts from a store. I've been accused of being old-fashioned, but one of the very best gifts I ever received as a child was a pair of mittens made by one of my foster sisters. She had just learned to knit and given me her first pair. They weren't perfect. She missed a few stitches, and one thumb was shorter than the other, but they were perfectly imperfect to me. I didn't know it then, but those mittens would become a symbol of what genuine love looks like to me. It takes thought to create, patience to build, and even if it turns out a little wonky, they still do the job.

I shake my head to clear away my melancholy mitten thoughts and finish curling the ribbon on the packages before placing them with care in a padded flat box to make the brief journey to town hall. Humming another Christmas song under my breath, I head to the bathroom to freshen up before I wrangle Owen.

Staring at my reflection in the bathroom mirror, I see my flushed cheeks with a dusting of freckles across my nose and my large brown eyes. I always thought my eyes with their long thick lashes were my best feature. I wonder if Owen sees something different from what I see. He was acting so weird. Like I was a foreign object in the middle of the kitchen, and he couldn't figure out what I was. And grabbing a can of whip cream randomly? That was just bizarre. Maybe I should ask him if there's something wrong. What if I ask and he tells me it's me?

Shit, I can't ask. I'd rather not know if I've displeased him somehow.

A loud knock on the door has me jumping and slamming into the wall.

"You okay in there, Parker? We have to leave in five."

"Uh, yep, be out in a minute."

I listen to his footsteps fade away and I give myself a final pep talk. "You're awesome Parker. You've got this. Even if something's changed, it won't be bad. You've got this."

I give my reflection two thumbs up and exit the bathroom to find Owen waiting out front and chatting with Paige.

"Do you have the bag of gifts?"

"Already loaded in the car. Are the cookies ready?" Owen shrugs into his coat and I go to the kitchen to gather my duffel with elf suit, box of cookies, and somewhere along the way, the rest of my sunny disposition so my sudden nervousness can take a hike. When I exit, I hand the cookies to Paige as I put my jacket on.

"Wow Parker, these are great! The kids will love these." She looks at the special tags and runs a finger over them. "You really went all out. Your calligraphy is amazing."

"Thanks. It was fun. I just hope they take the time to notice it before jamming the cookies in their mouths."

Owen stares blankly at the cookies, giving none of his thoughts away on the cookies or the tags. "Ok, let's get this over with."

I wave to Paige and gingerly follow him across the parking lot to his Bronco. Sliding in, I place my bag at my feet and hold the cookies on my lap like the precious cargo they are.

Owen has said nothing to me since this morning with the awkward exchange in the kitchen. His knuckles are white, gripping the steering wheel with far more force than needed and his jaw muscles bulge with the strain of clenching. He keeps his eyes straight ahead on our short drive.

I clear my throat and attempt to break the tension that's drowning my good mood faster than a cookie sinking into a glass of milk. "Your suit will be ready in the hall. Janice said she rented one for you, so it won't be anything nasty or gross."

He cuts his eyes briefly to me, but remains quiet. I squirm in my seat and, for the first time since I've met Owen, I feel uncomfortable with him.

"What about you? Where's your suit? You said you'd be an elf, right?" His fingers flex on the steering wheel and I watch them, lost in a daydream of them flexing on my hips instead. Wishing we were together someplace less stress filled, more fun filled.

"It's in my bag. I'll change there."

"Of course you have your own elf suit." His lips threaten to smile and I'm buoyed by the awkward tension between us breaking.

"Well, you know me. Spreading Christmas cheer requires full effort, nothing half assed from me. Dress the part is not just empty words. I take it seriously. Very seriously."

We pull into a parking spot at the town hall and Janice rushes out to meet us. She carefully takes my tray of cookies and ushers us inside. "Okay boys, you're going to need to follow me around the halls the back way. Some kids are already here and you need to change and make a grand entrance. You know, make it seem like Santa magically arrived and all that."

We follow along as her no-nonsense rubber-soled shoes squeak on the tiles and she stops at a door to a small office. "This is where I set you up to change. The Santa suit is hanging on the back of the door. I'll take the cookies down now, but you keep the gifts." She walks over to an old intercom box on the wall. "This still works, so I'll buzz you when you can start your way down. Just press the button to respond if you need to." She closes the door behind us and it's only then that I realize we're changing in here... together.

I place my bag on the desk and sling my coat over the back of a chair as Owen removes his coat and comes to the same conclusion I have.

"Um, if you want to get dressed first, I can step out if you want and then we can switch." I rock on my heels. "If it's uncomfortable for you, that is. I don't want you to be uncomfortable."

"It's fine. We can get changed together. It's no different from a locker room at the gym, right?"

I bob my head like one of those dolls on an old person's car dash. "Oh pfft. Totally like a gym. I'm cool with it if you are." This is early Christmas for me and quite possibly spank bank material if I get a glimpse of Owen with his shirt off. God, if I see more than that, I might faint. Okay, Parker, practice some restraint and do this.

I unzip my duffel and slyly watch out of the corner of my eye as Owen removes the Santa suit from the bag. When he reaches down to pull his shirt over his head so he can replace it with the crisp new white one supplied, I hold my breath in anticipation. When the material clears his head, I press my lips together hard enough to hurt as I keep the gasp from escaping. He's not all ripped muscle, but he's lean and powerful. His back is broad and as he tenses to pull the new t-shirt on, I memorize the way his shoulders flex. What a sight, and I only watched it from the side. I swallow my tongue as he turns around to face me, flashing me an all too quick glimpse of his equally broad chest with a tattoo over his heart I'd love to have a closer look at.

As the t-shirt clears his face, I tear my eyes away to concentrate on my dressing. When I tug the top half of my elf suit on, I know I made a mistake and I should have tried it on first. If the top is snug, I can only imagine how the rest will fit. Oh dear lord I hope I don't traumatize any children.

"You doing okay over there, Parker?" I glance over to catch Owen pulling his Santa pants on over his very fine ass and I silently wish for a problem, so he'd need to take them off again.

"Uh, ya I'm okay. Just a little more snug than I remembered." Understatement of the year. As I pull up the footless leotard and it clings to my body in all the wrong places like a drunken octopus, I pray to the gods I have a pair of shorts in my bag or the children might get an unplanned anatomy lesson.

Owen turns towards me and freezes with his hand half in his pants as he tucks his shirt in. If the floor could open up and I could disappear right now, it would be great. My sunshine bravado has taken a vacation because I might as well be standing naked in front of my hot boss right now with the way these clothes are clinging to me. As a person already self-conscious about their body, his penetrating stare causes my cheeks to heat and I tug on my shirt, hoping to find extra length to cover me.

His gravelly voice has me snapping my eyes to his. "You look great. Don't be shy." His throat bobs with a swallow as he continues to gawk at me, and I don't know what to do. Scratch that, I know what I have to do and that's reciting the periodic table or I'm going to have an epic hard on punching a hole in these tights. I normally like my ideas, in fact I'm proud of them. Not today. Worse idea ever was stuffing my junk into spandex around my hot boss. Fuck me.

I turn my back to him and mutter the names of chemical compounds, relieved it's working as I rearrange myself as much as I can.

"Do you think you could help me with this belly thing?"

Owen needs help to attach his fake belly. I pull on my bell shoes, at least those fit, and jingle my way over to him.

"Okay, it looks like we need to attach this strap around your back and these two attach to the suspenders." Owen slides up the suspenders and clips the top belly straps in place and I fumble my arms around him, trying to attach the buckle blindly while smashed up against the front of him. Not my smartest moment, because while I'm pressed into him with my arms around his back, I realize how I just invaded his personal space worse than a house cat in heat. His breath hitches and I jump away from him.

"You know what would be easier?"

Anything Parker. Any fucking thing would be easier.

I motion for him to turn around, and he does. "I should do you from behind."

It's at this point in my life, I wonder how I'm still alive, because phrases like that spew from my mouth far too often, and never at the right time. This is already one awkwardly filled moment. I just poured more gasoline into the awkward fire and lit a match. So much for getting Owen into the fun. If he even wants me working for him after this, it'll be a miracle.

"Uh, that came out wrong. I don't need to do you like rail you or whatever. Like sex or anything."

Oh my god make my mouth stop!

I find the buckles and fasten them to his pants. "So, having fun yet, boss?"

Owen turns back around, adjusting his fake belly into place and surprises me with... a smile.

TEN

Owen

I MUST ADMIT, WHEN we drove to the party, I had some apprehension about how it was all going to go down. The realization that I found Parker attractive still hadn't really sunk in. While I had acknowledged that I thought he was cute, I had never given the complete package of Parker consideration. I was supposed to be trying on how to have fun again, not fixate on my employee's cute little ass and brown eyes.

But now I have an even bigger problem. He's plastered himself against me, trying to attach my fake Santa belly in the most ridiculous, yet innocent of ways, and I'm not afraid to admit that I like the way he feels pressed up against me. His hands are fumbling around, trying to buckle the straps, but every time his hand brushes my back, shivers scatter across my skin. Parker slithering all over the front of me and pressing his spandex covered junk into mine is something I'm enjoying... perhaps too much.

How could I not notice his own outfit? He said his elf suit was tight, and he's right, but I can honestly say it suits him and I find myself wondering how I might be able to see him in tight clothes more often. I have to think of the least sexual thing I can to banish the naked images of him from my brain, otherwise Santa is going to have an epic woody — and not the toy kind.

As I am mentally running through the team roster of the 2011 Boston Bruins Cup winning team, he makes the innocent remark of doing me from behind. I don't miss how his voice cracks and I can't contain the smile when I turn around to face him. His eyes are wide, and he sucks his bottom lip in, like he's regretting what he said, but I'm laughing. Instead of scowling at his antics, I throw my head back and laugh.

"Just to be clear, you don't want to do me from behind? Is that right?" His flushed face and red ears, coupled with a lack of eye contact, are unexpected and I stop laughing. I fear I've overstepped, maybe even misjudged his behaviour.

He tugs at his shirt, trying to hide behind it, while his eyes drop to the ground again, taking my stomach with it. "Sorry, sometimes stuff just comes out of my mouth, and I don't know how to make it stop." He reaches out and pulls my Santa coat together, buttoning it up the front and smoothing it over my fake belly. "You really make a sexy Santa, though." He snorts and steps back. "See? I need to stop talking. This is supposed to be you having fun, not being hit on by your elf."

I continue with the buttons where he left off. "Maybe I like elves." I shrug and find the fake beard, as Parker, for the first time in his life, remains silent. The air is thick with a nervous energy as we quietly finish dressing and wait for the intercom to signal our departure for the party. This is supposed to be something for fun; me trying to get out there and enjoy things instead of being married to my job. We're not even thirty minutes into this and I've drained the fun from Parker faster than I can shotgun a beer. I don't like seeing this shy and quiet Parker.

Am I reading too much into his comments and actions? Maybe he's only been pulling my chain and I'm not supposed to respond like I'm interested. Apparently, I've not only lost the ability to have fun, I've also lost the ability to read social cues. Maybe this is why I stopped trying to have fun. Too many awkward social situations can happen.

I heave a sigh and run a hand over my face. "Parker, I didn't..." He cuts me off. "It's fine, boss. You're going to be awesome. The kids will be awesome. It's all awesome. Everything is awesome, you know, like the song?" I shake my head, but he waves it off. "Doesn't matter if you don't know the song. It's Christmas and you're going to be a fun Santa." He spins around, leaving me gaping at his ass again and wondering how long this afternoon party is going to last.

The intercom buzzes, causing us both to jump, and Janice's voice comes through. "Okay boys, it's showtime. Get those cute little butts down here before I drain my secret whiskey flask. If anyone asks, it's just tea. Why I volunteer to do these parties sober every year, is beyond me."

A bark of laughter escapes me. "You heard her. Get that cute little butt moving."

Finally, Parker returns to his happy-go-lucky self. His sass back in full force, he puts on a show, bending over to pick up the bag of gifts. "If you insist Santa, but let me carry your sack. It looks full and heavy. I'd hate for you to spill it everywhere." My mouth drops open.

He winks and again I'm voluntarily smiling. Who knew Mr. Sunshine and Lollipop, the royal pain in my ass, was this cute and snappy? Everyone but me is the likely answer.

I follow him down the hall with a smile so wide my face hurts. When we get closer to the party room, I pull up. "Parker!" I hiss-whisper. "How should I enter? Do I do the Ho, Ho, Ho thing or just wave or what?"

"Have you ever been to a parade or seen a single Christmas movie?"

"Of course, but THAT was like, at least ten years ago."

He snorts. "Santa is timeless. Just do your laugh and wave and hug any kid that asks."

"They want hugs!?" I'm not prepared for hugging little people. That was not on the list of Santa duties.

He places his hand on my arm. "Owen, it's fine. Just follow my lead. You're doing great."

Parker enters and commands the room filled with children like a pro, announcing that Santa's arrival is near.

He's making jokes and getting the kids so excited I almost miss my cue because he's such a natural at this. I'm captivated watching him be entirely comfortable as himself, in a too small elf suit with bells on his shoes. His relaxed and smiling face tells me he's loving every minute of it.

I enter the room to ear-splitting screams and so many kids, I'm momentarily frozen. But Parker is there, gently guiding kids back to their seats and promising that everyone will have time to visit Santa once they let me in. I ho, ho, ho my way to the chair set up in the front for me, as Parker takes my hand and squeezes it in support before shooting me a brilliant smile and darting off to wrangle another child back to their group. There are so many smiling and excited faces. All of them are bursting to come see me and still believe in the magic of Christmas.

Janice is at my ear with a booze laced whisper when I take my place. "I'm on my last nerve with these sugar filled sweethearts. I wasn't made for this many children at once, you know." With her jaw set and a curt nod, she pats my shoulder like we're about to take on a band of pirates, not innocent children. "Don't you worry, though. Your cute little baker and I have got you covered. We'll come through this fourth circle of hell and we'll do it together."

"He is cute, isn't he? Got anymore of that whiskey?" I whisper into her ear.

"Sadly, I'm all out, love. Next time, you should have a nip before you come." She bustles away and I don't have time to regret my choice of sobriety, because Parker is already leading the first kid up and plunking them on my lap.

"This pretty girl is Mandy. She's shy, but she wanted to give you a hug." Parker nods to Mandy in her special Christmas dress and she can't be older than four. Her blonde hair is styled in ringlets and bows and she's adorable. "Hi Mandy. Your hair is so pretty. Who did it for you?" I brush a finger through her curls and she beams a toothy grin, pointing to an older gentleman nearby. "My Grampy did it. He loves doing my hair because he doesn't have any."

I stifle a laugh at her honesty and Parker hands me a gift with her name on it. "Here you go Mandy. I hope this starts your Christmas off nice." Her chubby little hands grip the package tightly and before she slides off my knee, Parker prompts her to tell Santa what she wants for Christmas. I listen patiently, making noises where appropriate until I make eye contact with Parker. He nods and swoops in with her personalized Santa cookie, sending her back to her grandpa and pulling the next child forward.

The rest of our afternoon is a blur. Parker reads every cue I silently send, like we've done this dance a thousand times and we've memorized every step. Even though I'm growing tired of listening to kids asking for things I know damn well they won't receive, I have to admit, I'm having fun. The kids have made me laugh, Janice has been entertaining behind the scenes and Parker has been... amazing. He flits between adults and kids seamlessly, laughing and managing child-meltdowns as if it's just another day on the job.

When the last gift and cookie has been handed out, Santa and his helper-elf leave with a flurry of Merry Christmas wishes and waves and I'm following Parker back down the halls to our changeroom with him gripping my hand so tight it's going numb.

"So boss, did you have fun?"

"You know what? I really did. I didn't expect to, but it was different." I look down at our still clasped hands and Parker lets go. I wish he didn't and that our walk had been longer.

"Well, you did great for a grumpy dude, really."

I snort as I remove the jacket. "Uh, thanks I guess. Not sure how to take that, really."

"Take it as a compliment. It's nice to see you smile, is all." He drops his eyes as I turn around so he can unhook the buckle at the back for me.

I don't think anyone has ever told me they like to see me smile.

Parker telling me, though? I can't wipe the big, stupid grin off my face.

ELEVEN

Parker

A S OWEN AND I make the quiet walk back to his car, the only thing stuck in my mind is how often he smiled today. God, the man is devastating when he smiles. I melt faster than Frosty in a heat wave when it's aimed at me, too. But what really turns me into a giant melty puddle is how it felt when I smashed myself to the front of Owen like a bug on a windshield. Thankfully, he didn't make a big deal out of me being all up in his space, or rubbing my spandex covered junk all over him. In fact, his reaction was completely unexpected, and I'd be lying if I didn't admit it made me hopeful. Hopeful that perhaps he doesn't find me so bad after all.

I shiver, imagining how it might feel if he'd put a hand on me or touch me in a way that wasn't accidental. Or accidentally on purpose. I'm not too picky. As long as the purpose was to do good when he touched me, I'd take it.

"You okay Parker? Cold?"

Owen opens the door to the town hall and I'm grateful for the cold air to calm my heated skin. All day dreaming about touching Owen is making me a tad warm. "I'm okay, thanks. Do you mind dropping me off before you go home?"

"Sure, that's not a problem. How's the apartment hunt going anyway?" He backs out and points his Bronco toward my temporary home, a mere two blocks away. The downside of living in a small town. Yes, I could have walked there, but it's a dang cold night and I hate it. Plus, it's extra time in his car with him. I don't want the day to be over yet.

"Not well, actually. Turns out there's not a lot of apartments available and if they are, it's either too expensive or too far out for me to get to work." He pulls into the parking lot at the shelter far too soon and I feel a cloak of disappointment settle that there was not a longer route to travel here. "So, I have a room here until they need to give it to someone else. Until that happens Jake said I could stay with him. I'll just keep looking until then."

I reach for the door handle, but his deep voice, the one that warms me from the inside, no matter what tone he uses, has me pausing. "Parker, thanks for making today go so well. I mean it. I couldn't have done this without you." He clears his throat and shifts in his seat. His eyes drop before returning to mine, and I'm reeling with the heat in his gaze. He's not even hiding it. "If you ever need help with anything, you know, as a friend, not your boss, you can call me. I just wanted to tell you that."

His blue eyes are glued to mine, like a curious kid's tongue on a flagpole in winter, and I'm breathless. All oxygen has just left the vehicle and my head is spinning. Owen is a great friend to the few he calls friends. I've seen it firsthand. To be extended that honour is an enormous gesture. One I'm not sure how to accept. So I do what I do best, make it awkward.

"Thanks Owen. I appreciate that. If the friendship includes helping play Santa again, the offer to sit on your lap still stands. Can never have too much practice."

By the grace of god he smiles at me again and laughs, effectively turning my already oxygen deprived brain to mush.

"Thanks Parker. I'll keep it in mind."

I grin back, glad I could make him laugh, and that it comes easier for him now. "I'll see you tomorrow bright and early with my bells on." Before he can finish asking what I mean, I exit the car and bolt up the stairs to the shelter and enter my door code. I wave when I'm inside and he pulls away, turning back towards the main street to continue his own way home.

It's still early evening, and some of the kids are in the common room watching TV. I keep going down the short hall off the kitchen and poke my head into the office to find Jacob at his laptop with paperwork and a half eaten, dried up sandwich.

"Hey Jake. Are you busy?"

He removes his glasses, the ones he only wears for computer work, and motions for me to sit. "Nothing I shouldn't stop working on for the night. What's up?" He takes a bite of the dried-out sandwich and my stomach turns.

"Have you had anything decent to eat today?" I cock my head, looking closer and noticing the dark circles under his eyes. "What's going on with you?"

Jacob grinds his palms into his eyes, leaning back in his chair. "It's been a day, Park. I had to change my flights to my brother's for Christmas because he told me the wrong days he would be home. None of our volunteers for the animal shelter are available over the holidays. Not a single one!" He sighs and leans forward to eat his sandwich again, but I snatch it away.

"Hey." He whines. "I'm hungry. I was gonna eat that."

"Come to the kitchen. I'm going to make you something. This is nasty, Jacob. It looks like it's been sitting in a gas station display case, uncovered, since last Christmas." He laughs, but follows me along at least, and plunks himself into a chair while I rummage in the fridge and settle on making us bacon and eggs.

"How did things go at the Christmas party? Did Owen do well playing Santa?"

Did it go okay?

Did I see my boss half naked? Check.

Did I rub myself all over him unintentionally, like a cat in heat and he just stood there? Double check.

I shake my head to erase the images. Owen had fun. He even put up with my over the top-ness and smiled — multiple times. Every time he did, my heart stopped. I heave a lovesick sigh that would rival any teenage girl at a

Jonas brothers concert, and plate the food before joining Jake at the table.

"It was more than okay. He really enjoyed himself." I chew a piece of bacon and watch with horror as Jacob pours ketchup on his scrambled eggs. I swear he was raised by a pack of wolves with his eating preferences. "How do you eat that?"

"With a fork and a smile, Parker." He makes a show of eating a forkful of eggs as I shake my head. The boy ain't right.

"So Owen had fun. What's next?"

"What's next?" I snort. "I go to work and keep wearing stupid stuff to make him smile and one day he'll notice how truly awesome I am. We'll kiss and fall in love and live happily ever after." Oh, if only it was that easy to have your crush notice you and have a fairytale ending.

"Well, I love you and I notice how awesome you are. You've got my vote." He raises his water glass in a toast to me before taking a drink. Hopefully, it helps wash out the ketchup flavour.

"As much as I appreciate that, I don't think there's a voting system to get people to love you. Although, there's that show that gives roses so there could be."

He points his fork at me. "Change of topic. You said you would be around over Christmas, right?"

I nod. "Yep. The Bean closes for the week too, so I'm just hanging out. Do you need something?"

"I do. Remember, I said the volunteers for the animal shelter can't make it?" I nod. "Well, do you think you could take care of the animal shelter residents while I'm gone? I know it's a lot of work but you won't need to open for adoptions, just do all the cat care."

I raise my eyebrows. "Just do the cat care? How many do we have?"

"I think we had thirty-five at last count, but we just had a momma have kittens, and one of them isn't nursing well and would need to get checked on." He drags a scrap of toast along his plate, picking up the remaining ketchup, and I want to hurl. I might need to stop eating with Jake. "I won't be doing anything except looking for an apartment and most likely overeating while I read all day. I don't mind being on cat duty."

Maybe it will be fun. Or... maybe it's another fun thing Owen might help me with. "Can I ask someone to help?"

Jacob brings his plate to the sink, laughing the whole time. "You're about as transparent as a piece of saran wrap. You want to ask Owen to come and help?"

"Hell ya. Can you imagine him with kittens?" I know I can. Talk about catnip.

"It's fine to bring him over. You'll be doing me a favour. It's all good."

I help Jake clean up the kitchen and we chatter as we always do when we're together. Talking about his quick visit to New York for Christmas to visit his brother and Logan, and how he has to go to some jock party while he's there — his words, not mine. Not sure why he thinks that will be a bad thing, but this is Jake, and sometimes I don't understand his logic.

Cheddar follows me to my room, meowing along the way as if someone hasn't already fed him treats eighteen separate times today. I'm going to have to research treadmills for cats, or he's going to develop some serious health issues soon. He races ahead of me to sit in front of the treat drawer. "You know Cheesy, stop guilting me to feed you all the time because I'm not home. It's not healthy for either of us." I unzip the pouch and shake a few out before collapsing on my bed in an exhausted heap.

It's been a long day. The dump of adrenaline after I slithered all over Owen's body didn't wear off until I walked into the shelter and firmly closed the door behind me. Maybe it was just my overactive imagination and hyperactive libido, but the fact he didn't say or do anything about it has me clinging to the hope that maybe he might actually like me and not be as grumpy as he appears.

I turn off the light and switch on my rotating night light of snowflakes, burrowing under my blankets and replaying Owen's words from the car about being friends. I want to continue the banter and connection we had all day. If he said friends, I can text him as a friend, can't I? I open my contacts and stare at his name on my phone, which simply says *Boss*, because that's what he is. He gave me his cell number when I was hired in case I needed to call in, or be late, or anything else work related.

I want to talk to him so badly. My fingers itch as I type out and erase several messages before I finally settle on one and press send before I chicken out.

Cheddar head butts my shoulder and wiggles under the blankets with me for snuggles and ear scratches. "Cheddar, is it so bad to go after what you want? I mean, the worst he can do is say no, right?" He purrs and digs his claws in as he kneads the extra insulation I carry on my hips. "It's not like I don't have practice being rejected, right, buddy?"

If being tried on and returned was a sport, I'd have an Olympic medal by now.

No one ever wants to keep me forever..

TWELVE

Owen

I 'VE MADE MY WAY home after the party and no one is
more shocked than me that I enjoyed myself. By
playing Santa with kids, even. I shake my head again. The
disbelief that I even *did* such a thing still hasn't worn off.
With a soft chuckle, I flop onto the couch to relax with a
hockey game and a glass of Canadian whiskey on the
rocks. Searching through the channels, I settle on a
hockey game, Bruins and Leafs. If my grandfather was still
alive, he'd be cussing the defensive line for the Leafs right
now. It looks like someone filled their skates with cement.

The game isn't holding my attention simply because of
a few terrible plays. It's a bigger matter that's pulling my
attention away. My mind goes back to the sight of Parker
in his tight green elf pants, unintentionally showing off his
rather large package. I nearly swallowed my tongue when
he turned around with those pants on. He was self-
conscious about gaining a little weight, but there was
nothing for him to be worried about. At all. My annoying

little baker has been hiding under his kitchen clothes. Now that I know what he's hiding, I'm trying to figure out more ways to see it and I'm unsure of how that really makes me feel.

The ice clinks in my glass as I swirl it around and think of my attraction to Parker. People miss things that are right in front of them all the time, don't they? This can't be the first time in the history of romance that a person failed to notice someone in the beginning.

The TV blares as the Bruins score another shorty and I pump my fist in the air. I wonder if Parker likes hockey, or knows how to skate? Why do I even care? Because it would be fun to have someone to watch with, a Dominic-sounding voice shouts in my head.

It's been a long time since I've even considered having fun with another person, let alone the quirky baking twink who's also my employee. I drain my glass with a sigh and turn off the TV to head to bed.

After my bedtime routine, I lie in bed staring at my dark ceiling, listening to the ceiling fan spin. I turn my head to the side and sweep an arm over the space where another person could sleep next to me. My heart squeezes with a pang of loneliness, but I push it aside. Fun thoughts are what I need. To be specific, naked fun is what I need to think about. I'd be lying if I didn't acknowledge how amazing it had felt with Parker pressed up against me — all wiggly and squirming like an adorable puppy — to help me with something that only required me to turn around. It took all my strength to keep myself from wrapping my arms around him, to keep him there for longer. Did he mean to tempt me like that, or was it an innocent mistake?

It's hard to tell with Parker sometimes. Although twice now, he has told me he'd sit on my lap if I wanted, and there was no innocence attached to those invitations. But do I dare take him up on the offer?

A soft moan slips from my lips as I reach between my legs to stroke my dick. I close my eyes, imagining him on my lap right now, wiggling all over like he did today and holy shit, I'm hard as granite. A few pumps and my hand is already slick with precum as my cock weeps with anticipation. I quicken my pace to match my heaving breaths as my imagination works overtime. Squeezing my eyes tighter, I picture Parker naked and grinding on my lap, spilling filthy words in my ear. He bats my hand away, jerking me with an expert grip to milk me for every drop. My skin is on fire and my breath comes in brief gasps as my orgasm rapidly closes in.

"Come for me Owen. I want to taste it. I want to lick it off you and paint you with my own."

The image of Parker lapping cum off my body tips me over the edge and I explode over my stomach. I shudder through the most intense solo orgasm I've had in a very long time. As I lie there panting, covered in my spunk, it's only then that I realize I just jerked off to my employee. The one who is so much the opposite of me, I've never looked at him twice. The one that gets under my skin just by being there and who seems to make it his mission to make me smile.

I roll out of bed and grab an old shirt to wipe myself off with before washing up in the bathroom. Crawling back under the covers, closer to sleep now than I was before, and I'm about to drift off when my phone rattles with a text message. I reach out to see if it's important and my heart jumps to my throat.

It's Parker.

Parker: *Can a friend ask a friend to have dinner with them tomorrow?*

My easy slumber has vanished and I'm back to being wide awake. Clutching the phone, I stare at it, reading the message over and over until it all blurs in front of my eyes. Is he asking me on a date? Does he only want to be friends and I've just misread his humour this entire time? Fuck, I just jerked off to him.

I haven't been this twisted up about someone since college graduation. That one fizzled pretty fast when we both realized we had different ideas on how to transition from being a student to an adult. I thought we should focus on jobs and build a life. He thought we should continue to day drink and fuck other people. Ever since then, I've just drifted along, not wanting to be attached to any single person for the sole reason of *why bother*. It's not a solid reason, but it made sense to me. But that was ten years ago and if I've learned anything from the past twenty-four hours, it's that sometimes things change. People change. I've changed.

I'm still looking at Parker's text, and with a giant leap of faith, I decide I'm going to embrace change. I text him back and finally drift off into a sleep filled with dreams of an adorable man in an elf suit.

When I arrive at work the next morning, Parker is there before me, as usual. I can hear him rattling around in the kitchen and singing at the top of his lungs; a horrendous rendition of Jingle Bell Rock. At least nothing is changing in that department, still annoying as fuck with his singing. Although, I am curious to know if he has a new outfit today, and that's new for me. I shake my head and continue to my office.

When I woke up this morning, he had responded to my text, and it appears we have a date of sorts tonight. I'm not sure what he's got planned, but I told him to decide where he wanted to go, and we'd take it from there. Until I walked in here today, I wasn't nervous about it, but now I'm jittery over saying good morning to my baker and doing my usual routine.

As I enter the kitchen and his screeching tones hit my ears, I stop and once again reevaluate this version of Parker before he notices me. Today he's a snowman. Not just any snowman, but Olaf, the snowman from Frozen. The music is blaring as loud as it can go on the little radio back here and he's swinging his giant snowman butt around as he measures and mixes cake batter into the giant mixing bowl.

On normal mornings, I grit my teeth and make soup for my lunch with Dominic until he notices me and turns it down. We go through a series of questions with me grunting answers and barking orders and we continue on with our day. But today, I feel out of sorts. Like I should try to smile at him, maybe? Should we discuss this new friendship thing at work or should I only be friends outside of work? Are there rules for this kind of thing? Do we even call it a date?

Of course, as I'm standing there struggling with something that shouldn't be so hard, he spins around to find me watching him, like a creeper with a snowman fetish. Instead of saying something intelligent or boss-like, I stand there while flashes of what I did last night play through my mind. I feel my cheeks heat and my cock jumps as I drink in the man before me in an entirely different light. Even wearing a snowman suit, he's attractive.

Parker still sings and sways, not even caring that I'm staring at him. Or maybe he knows why I'm staring? Why the hell can't I find any words right now? He spins around again, and I silently watch as he pours batter into the pans, opens the oven and places them in. After setting a timer, he marches over and stops a few paces in front of me, tilting his head back to look up.

"You okay, boss? You're just standing here staring at me. While I'd normally be okay with that, I'm getting concerned."

I blink out everything, fuzzing with my head and focus on him. His hair is damp with sweat, cheeks pink and rosy again from all his dancing. My fingers itch to push a curl off his forehead, but I shove my hands into my pockets. It's too soon to touch him like that and if I do, what will happen next?

"I'm fine. Thanks. Aren't you fine?" I should have just stayed quiet, that's some real intelligent words.

A giant smile graces his face and my heart pounds. "I'm as fine as baking sugar. Do you have time to talk about tonight?"

"Right tonight, yes. Tell me what you came up with." I finally come to my senses and begin my soup while Parker fills me in.

"It's the last night of the outdoor Christmas town market. I really need to finish shopping. And they have the food trucks there too. It's nothing fancy, but I thought it might be a fun thing to do. We could get to know each other while we support more local businesses. Win-win."

"I think that would be nice. I've never been to the Christmas market."

He gasps. "How could you not go? The food alone is worth it. Until I learned how to bake them myself, there's this amazing calzone place; best dessert ever. Oh! Ever have a peach bum?"

My spoon clatters on the stove top as an image — which I'm sure he doesn't mean — burns my eyes. "Uh... no? I'm not sure what you mean." I'm definitely sure we're not thinking the same thing.

"Oh, you're missing out. It's delicious. My treat. I'll get you a peach bum."

His eyes twinkle with a mischief I'm slowly learning is the real Parker. He's up for whatever and he's loving playing this game. At least I think it's a game. If I'm the only one playing, I might be disappointed and isn't that a further revelation for me?

"As long as it's from you, it's a deal." I wink and turn back to my task, not missing how his eyes widen at my comment.

"There's no way I'm letting a friend sample a bad peach. I got you." He bounces back to his baking, resuming the current song of Frosty the Snowman and acting his usual ridiculous self.

With my back to him, I finally allow myself to smile, and it feels great.

THIRTEEN

Parker

I KNOW SOMETHING IS up with Owen. He does nothing but grunt replies and issue orders like a military master in the morning. Yet today, he was staring and awkward. I want to say he was flirty, but I'm not sure. It's out of character for him to wink and chatter. I didn't quite know how to respond.

When I asked him to have dinner as friends, I totally expected to be told no. Or at least put off. I was not expecting to wake up to a text from him this morning saying he'd love to do something with me tonight. Not just something pleasant and passing, but he'd *love* to. Just seeing that in a text from him has had me on edge all morning. I knew what I wanted to do. The Christmas market is fun and casual. There would be people around, so it wouldn't feel too intimate and there would be many things to talk about as we wander, not to mention food choices. I don't want him to think anything romantic about the outing. As much as I want it to be a romantic outing, there's no way he's interested in me that way. Being friends is all I'm hoping for. More than that is a pipe dream.

He's going about his normal morning as he always does, making soup for him and Dominic. He makes soup from scratch for his best friend because it's Dom's favourite. What kind of man does that? A damn good one is the only answer I can come up with. But today, instead of barging out of the kitchen when he's done, he surprises me and takes my coffee mug out to the front for a refill. He wordlessly takes my favourite travel mug with Santa Baby on it and returns with an adorable smile, causing my heart to beat faster than the beaters on my mixer.

"Two cream and a shot of hazelnut syrup, right?" He places my cup back on the counter.

Stunned, I can only say one word, and it's very eloquent. "Yep."

"Have a good day. I'll see you tonight."

With a nod of his head, he leaves me, and I'm left wondering, for the second time this morning, if my mind is playing tricks on me. Was this just a friendly gesture, or did it mean more? He paid attention and knew how I liked my coffee. I take a sip and hum with pleasure. And he made it perfect, too.

The day couldn't have dragged any slower. After a quick run home to change and shower, I exit the shelter to find

Owen already waiting.

"I hope you haven't been out here waiting for long."

We start the short walk to the market behind the shelter as I pull on my toque. "No, just a few minutes. I didn't want you waiting for me."

The snow crunches under our feet as we travel the path, and nervousness takes over. I don't understand why, though. It's not a proper date. "Would you like to eat first or look around?"

"Let's look. Is that okay with you?"

His blue eyes seek agreement with mine, and I nod. When we finally reach the stalls of the vendors, the Christmas feeling I love washes over me and I'm like a puppy jumping with excitement. "I know you're not a big Christmas fan, but can't you smell it?" I breathe deeply as he laughs. "It's apple cider and peppermint. Evergreens and snow. It's the best smell next to fresh baked sugar cookies."

Owen takes in the stalls before us, inhaling his own deep breath before unleashing his smile on me. "It is a good smell. I'll give you that. It's not that I'm not a fan of Christmas, it's just that I don't see why people have to do all this spending and gifting for it. Can't we just have an enjoyable meal, get drunk and call it a day? Why is there always pressure to find the perfect gift and go into debt for it?"

Well, at least I have some insight to him now. "Yes, many are like that. I just love the magic. How kids believe in Santa and get excited. How people come together and friends get closer. The food. All the food." We both laugh as I lead him to the first stall. It's a lady that makes soaps in her home and she makes an amazing one that smells like coffee.

"Hi Arlene! Merry Christmas!" I lean in for a hug. She gives great mom hugs.

"Parker! How are you? Doing some shopping for you, or friends?"

"Both, of course. Do you still have my favourite?" She turns around and hands me a bag, and I clap my mittened hands together. "You're such a doll. Is this all the coffee ones you have?" I turn to show Owen and hold a bar to his nose for a sniff. "Oh, that's real nice. I'd try that."

I snatch it back as he reaches for it. "Depends if she has any left. Right, Arlene?" Owen raises an eyebrow my way, drawing a snicker from me.

"That's not nice, Parker. You shouldn't tease your friend." She waits expectantly for me to say more. Arlene and I have a banter and while we know each other's names and situations, it's not like she knows my secrets. "My friend here is Owen. He owns The Screaming Bean. Owen, this is Arlene. She keeps me smelling irresistible and makes the best soap I've ever tried."

Owen shakes her hand. "Pleasure Arlene. Have you ever considered selling in a storefront?" She shakes her head. "No, overheads are far too much for what I do. Markets are the best place for me."

I pay for my purchase, and Owen buys a bar of his own. "Here's my card. Why don't you contact me in the new year? Maybe The Bean could carry the coffee soap for you. If it's as popular as Parker says, it could be a good fit for you."

She pockets the card and reaches for his hand. "Thank you so much for the offer, Owen. I'd love that. You have a Merry Christmas too, and I'll be in touch."

We shuffle out of the way for the other patrons and leave her booth behind. When I glance at Owen, he's smiling like a kid in a candy store. "That was really cool of you to do."

We stop at the booth for apple cider, and he gestures if I want one. With ciders in hand, we move along to more vendors and Owen talks. "She obviously means something to you. If she has an excellent product, I can help. She also reminds me a bit of my mom."

He's never mentioned his family to me. I actually know nothing about his life. "Can I ask you about your mom?"

We stop at the bonfire roaring in a small clearing, finding an empty bench to sit at while we drink our ciders. "My mom had me very late in life. She was almost fifty when she got pregnant unexpectedly. She was told she'd never have kids. So I was what she called a miracle." He smiles in memory as he stares into the fire. "She was my best friend and Arlene reminded me of her, hugging you and knowing what your favourites were." He shrugs. "My mom loved Christmas; seemed like the right thing to do."

We sip in silence, watching the fire dance. "What about you? I don't know about you at all. If you want to share, that is."

I said friends get to know each other. But I'm touched nonetheless, that he's wanting to know about me at all. "My mom died when I was eight. Drug overdose. I don't miss her."

His eyes snap to my face. "I'm sorry Parker. That had to be hard to deal with. What about your dad?"

I shake my head. "Never knew who he was. My mom was a junkie. *She* didn't even know." I've never cared about other people's opinions of my life before, but I bite my lip wondering if Owen will now think less of me, knowing my less than savoury past. That's not even mentioning my foster home nightmares.

A gloved hand settles on mine with a gentle squeeze and I turn my gaze from the fire to him. "My dad died of a heart attack shoveling snow, when I was seven. It was early December. It's part of the reason I don't like to do much at Christmas. Sometimes I just miss him too much."

I squeeze his hand back before removing mine. I'm learning way more than I thought on this outing, and it's doing nothing to squash any of the feelings I have for Owen. It's making me want to hug him hard and I don't think whatever this is between us is ready for hugging.

"Ready to keep moving? If you like Arlene, there's a nice man with alpaca wool products next on my list."

Owen drains his cup and stands. "Lead the way. Sounds interesting."

When I introduce Owen to Arnie, they instantly hit it off. So much so that I back out of the stall and wait outside for him. I grin like a loon, watching as he gestures with his hands and both of them laugh uncontrollably. Owen pays for his purchase, and I notice he hands Arnie his business card as well. He searches for me and when he finds me in the crowd, instantly lights up and moves towards me. The happiness on his face takes my breath away.

"Arnie is so awesome. Did you know he has an alpaca that refuses to drink out of the trough and insists on a bucket that only he holds?" He snorts with laughter and my heart explodes as he grabs my hand, leading me to the food trucks. "I'm starving. Can we eat now?"

I'm left speechless because I've never seen my boss like this. He's been a close cousin to Oscar the Grouch the entire time I've known him. He smiles for his customers and for Dominic, but not much else. Yet, in the hour we've been here, he's been laughing like he just learned how, making new friends and smiling so much his face has to hurt. And when he's smiling at me with a nose all pink from the frosty December air and his blue eyes are bright and shiny, I'm fucking dead. It's killing me not to grab him and cover him with kisses and ask him to be mine.

"Yes absolutely! What do you feel like having?"

When he steers me through the crowd, he doesn't drop my hand right away and I'm so caught up in my imagination of what it would be like to hold his hand for real, I almost fall on my face when he yanks me to a stop in front of Nacho Taco.

"Do you like tacos? Dominic told me about these guys. Have you tried them?"

"I haven't, but I asked you to dinner, so you can choose. If this is what you want, let's do it."

We wait our turn, and when we order, Owen pays as I protest. "You buy dessert. You said you wanted me to try a peach, didn't you?"

"Okay, fine, but you better still be hungry for it after."

He chuckles and licks his lips. "I'd never turn down a good peach."

Okay, what the hell? He's definitely flirting. I did not misread that one. However, I suddenly find myself at a loss for words and wondering what I should do. When our order is ready, Owen takes it, and we find an empty table to eat at.

I remove my mittens and unwrap the biggest taco I've ever laid eyes on. Owen's is a soft taco, and he eats it with ease, peeling back the wrapper as he goes and watching me with great humour as I struggle to eat my hard shell taco without losing it all on the ground. Two bites in and most of it is crumbling into my wrapper as I fail to get it in my mouth.

"This is the most awkward taco I've ever had. What the hell was I thinking, having a hard shell taco to go at a winter market?"

Owen reaches into his pocket and hands me a plastic fork. "Don't worry, I got your back."

Why is the fact he grabbed me a fork for a taco he knew I'd have trouble eating, the most thoughtful thing ever?

"Thanks, I might have had to fill up on dessert instead if you hadn't had a fork."

"I can take it back. Feed you full of sweets until you're sick of them instead of your..." He gestures at my mess of taco. "Whatever you've created there."

I fold up the paper with the remains of my taco. "You know what? I like your idea better. Dessert for supper is something I'm down for." I stand up and throw my mess in the trash before I pull my mittens back on.

"Let's go get that peach bum for you. It's the best thing you'll ever have in your mouth."

I press my lips together, holding in my laugh, but the laugh dies a fast death when I see Owen looking at me with hooded eyes and licking his own lips.

"We'll see about that."

FOURTEEN

Owen

COMING TO THIS MARKET with Parker has been one of the best things I've ever done. Watching how friendly he is with people he only sees a few times a year and how they react to him, further endears him to me. He seems to be everyone's little darling. Now that I know a bit more about what his life was like as a child, I'm even more taken by his sunshine ways.

Sure, my dad died around the holidays, and it's bound to make people sad, but Parker has a whole different outlook on life and it's taking my breath away. I feel so alive and all I had to do was talk to a lady about coffee soap and an alpaca farmer about his herd. When I watch Parker, the feelings swirling in my gut are more persistent and I've never wanted to touch someone as bad as I do him. His rosy cheeks and pink nose, the giant, fuzzy pom pom on the top of his head and his innuendo-filled jokes are adding logs to the fire. I can't deny I'm attracted to him anymore. But what am I going to do about it?

This time he takes my hand and leads me over to his dessert place, Cream Queens. "Okay Owen, prepare yourself for the best thing to ever cross your taste buds."

I still think nothing can taste better than him, but I won't say no to dessert. "That's a mighty big claim."

"You'll see." He winks and takes the step up to the order window where a hulking bear of a man with the biggest beard and mustache I've ever seen greets Parker with a bellow.

"Parker! Hello baby doll, where have you been?"

The giant of a man opens the door of his trailer and in two strides is out front, scooping Parker into his massive arms for a hug. Jealousy courses through me. Who is this guy to Parker?

He releases him and cuts his eyes to me. "Roger, this is Owen. My friend." I don't miss the look that passes between them, and I suddenly feel like I'm under a spotlight. Roger extends his hand and grips mine in a squeeze so hard I almost wince. Almost.

"Nice to meet you, Roger. Parker tells me you have the best peach in town."

Roger roars with laughter and tousles Parker's pompom. "Is that right? You brought him here to have a peach bum, did you?"

"You know it. Give us two please and say hi to Trevor."

Roger passes a box to Parker. "I'll do that doll. Come and say hello soon. We miss you."

Parker carries the box over to me and we settle down at a small table. He hands me a fork and opens the box. Two very large peach looking orbs are inside. "Owen, these are peach bums. The middle is the most delicious custard you'll ever taste. The peach part is something no words do justice. It's a melt in your mouth cake with a subtle peach flavour and covered in peach sugar. That's what makes it look fuzzy."

"It looks delicious."

Parker watches as I load up my first forkful of what I can only assume is one of his most favourite things in life. I close my lips over the fork, sliding it out slowly and savouring my first taste of this thing called a peach bum. I can't contain my moan of agreement that it's one of the best things I've ever tasted. "Ohmygod, that's fantastic."

Parker cocks his head while he takes his own bite, closing his eyes with a sigh of food contentment. "I could live off these forever and not miss a thing."

"So how do you know Roger? He said to come visit soon."

Parker hesitates but reveals more of himself. "He's my mentor. He's a pastry chef and when I was trying to figure out what to do with my life, he showed me how much I liked to bake and create with food." His eyes take on that faraway look of remembering something both happy and sad, but I wait for him to come back to me and finish his story. "Trevor is his fiancé and business partner. Trevor was teaching me how to make fondant decorations for wedding cakes until he couldn't anymore. He has rheumatoid arthritis and his hands aren't able to handle all the small tools anymore. I used to go over and practice once a week with him, but..."

He chews on his lip, and I can tell he's holding back. "If you don't feel comfortable telling me, you don't have to. Some things are private. I understand."

"It's okay. It's hard to see him like that. I know he wants me to keep coming over, but I feel guilty because I'm still capable. I don't want to make him sad." He sighs. "He's a good friend. I should go visit."

"Good friends will understand, Parker. Don't pull away from him. I bet he finds happiness in seeing you succeed; become even better than he was."

I've polished off my peach bum and I could eat about six more. Parker makes some amazing pastries, but these things are a killer. He's off in his head again and I patiently wait for him to return. While I do, I realize our so-called date is about to end and I don't want it to.

"You might be right. Can I tell you something? You said you're here for me as a friend, right?"

Initially I was, now I'm not so sure. I think I want to be more than friends, but how do I say that? "Of course. Nothing you say will make me not want to be your friend."

"I want to be just as successful as Roger and Trevor. I want to have a wedding cake business. Be the most sought after baker and be selective of who I take on."

"That's great. It's good to have goals, and I'd be happy to help you any way I can. That's what friends do." Even as I say it, the words don't quite feel right, like I'm putting myself in a box before I even have a chance to be something else. But I need him to know I appreciate how much he's done for me in such a short time.

His infectious smile, the one I ignored for months, returns and he punches me playfully on the shoulder. "Thanks boss. If you're not careful, I might think you care." He sticks out his tongue and takes our box to the garbage while I stare after him, wondering what the fuck I'm doing. I can feel someone watching me and I turn my head back to Cream Queens. Roger is standing at the door to his truck, and there's no mistake. He's wary of me and that makes me wonder what the hell Parker has told him about me.

"Okay, Owen, are you ready? I don't have any other stops. Unless there's something you want to do?"

He gathers the bags he left on the bench, and I notice every little thing about him. The way his mittens have Santas on them and hold the handles of his bags like a chubby toddler. His green and red sparkling pom pom on his head that flops around when it moves and is so oversized it borders on the ridiculous. How the front of his jeans is faded at the thighs and one of his pocket liners needs to get tucked back in. The happiness in his sparkling eyes, even after telling me something so personal, is still there. A playful smile, always on his face.

A face with deep chocolate eyes I can get lost in. Full lips I imagine on mine and the cutest little nose, red from the nip in the air. A nose that I notice has a dusting of freckles across it, making him appear younger than his 24 years. I wonder if he gets a sunburn easily on his fair skin?

How did I become so in tune with Parker in such a short time, after tuning him out for so long?

I clear my throat, reaching for my bag before standing. "Yes, I'm okay. Do you want to take the board walk home? It looks like it's lit up nice for Christmas."

"Aww, you'd do that for me? I'd love to, if you don't mind."

We exit the Christmas town displays to the boardwalk that surrounds Dogwood Pond. A short section will hook us back up to the trail behind the shelter before our evening ends. Our boots crunch through the thin layer of snow and the chatter of the shoppers fades away as we approach the boardwalk. It's much quieter here, with Christmas lights hung through the trees and couples walking hand in hand, some stopping to steal kisses under the lights.

Parker has grown quiet as he stares at all the lights with the wonder of a child, that all too cheerful smile never leaving his face.

"Why are you staring at me like that?" He laughs as he catches me ogling him.

"Like what?" Did he see what I was thinking on my face?

He laughs again. "Like I've grown another head or something. You're being weird."

"I guess I'm just in awe that you can still find so much happiness in the little things. Something I need to do again, and you make it so effortless. I admire your courage."

We've reached the small path leading to the shelter and veer off, away from all the Christmas magic and lights. Parker has said nothing since my declaration, and I'm concerned I may have made him uncomfortable.

When we reach the parking lot, he faces me. "I'm not courageous. I'm just surviving. But it means a lot to me that you would think that."

He shifts around some before blurting out, "Would you like to come inside? Warm up before you go, maybe?"

He says he's not courageous. He just said what I've been thinking about for the last thirty minutes, but was afraid to ask.

"I'd love to."

Fifteen

Parker

M Y SHAKING HAND PUNCHES in the code to the building, and I let Owen pass before me. My heart is about to smash through my ribcage. I can't believe I actually asked him in, and he said yes. What the fuck do I do now? I've never allowed myself to imagine him here in my space. Sure, I'm cocky as hell and brave enough to first ask him to dinner and now ask him inside, but now I'm as nervous as a cat in a room full of rocking chairs.

I hang my coat in the mudroom and take Owen's from him and lead him inside. Owen is curious, looking all over and taking it all in.

"Is this the first time you've been here?"

He nods. "Ya, I've been in the animal shelter, but not this one. It's not what I expected."

"What did you expect?"

He peers around the kitchen and through the entrance to the great room, his eyes widening at the ten foot Christmas tree. "I guess I expected it to be more industrial and less... homey. It's very welcoming."

Good grief, he can't even understand how that affects me to hear that. "That's what we aim for here. We want all the youth, or anyone really, to feel at home here. I'm glad you do. Would you like something to drink? Has to be alcohol free, I'm afraid. Hot chocolate, tea, coke, you pick."

"Hot chocolate, but only if you're having one with me."

"Of course." I fill the kettle and plug it in before gesturing for him to follow me. "I'll drop my bags in my room and give you a tour while we wait."

Owen follows me up the short flight of stairs that has a line of doors for separate suites. We don't have to go far, as I'm the first one at the top of the stairs. My door is always open for Cheddar and my lazy cat is sleeping in my spot already. I deposit my bags on my dresser and sweep a hand out in my best Vanna White impersonation.

"This is my room. All the rooms here are the same. We have our own three-piece baths, which is nice, but I'd love a good tub to soak in one day. Not much to see, but this is home for now."

Owen glances around, then sits on the bed and says hi to Cheddar. My breath catches in my throat because not only is he in my room, but he's on my bed. My hot as hell boss, the one that only days ago decided it wouldn't kill him to smile, is on my bed.

"Hey there, big guy. What's your name?" He scratches Cheddar under the chin and the cat eats the extra attention up.

"That would be Cheddar. Or Cheesy, as I call him for short."

Owen smiles at my cat and it's all I can take watching him give the cat attention. At least he likes cats, which reminds me. "Do you have any pets?" I ask him while leaning in the doorway. If I sit near him on the bed, I can't be responsible for what happens.

"I don't. Never seemed to have the time, but I love animals."

Well, that's good to know. "Uh, well, can I ask you something?"

He flashes that sexy smile again and the dimple on his chin pops, rendering me stupid. "Jacob needs people to help care for the shelter cats over the holidays. All the volunteers have plans. Since I'm here, I told him I would." I assess his listening and those baby blues are watching my lips, listening to everything with a focus I wish I'd had in grade school. "It might be another fun thing for you if you have no plans and would like to help me?"

I rub my neck. Did I ask too much too soon? He's not saying anything right away. Just as I'm about to rush and take it back, I have to strain to hear his reply.

"I'd love to help you. It'd be my pleasure."

The air crackles as we stare at each other and there's a definite change between us. I know we have filled tonight with little jokes and innuendos and subtle touches, but something just happened. The grumpy boss I've been crushing on for months isn't looking at me the way he always does. This is different, and it's hard for me to swallow.

"Awesome possum." I try to lighten the mood with my characteristic goofiness, and it works. Owen laughs and stands, much to Cheddar's disappointment. Can't blame the cat, bet those hands feel good when they caress a body. Sort of wouldn't mind a body switch if I could. Before he gets too close to me, I turn so he can follow me downstairs, where I'm certain the kettle must have reached boiling long ago.

Owen excuses himself to the washroom, and I mix hot chocolates for us, using my homemade marshmallows, because why not? As I'm finishing up, Jacob bounces in and opens the fridge.

"Hey Parker! How was the market? Did Owen have fun?" He grabs a can of coke from the fridge and leans against it, watching me cut pieces of marshmallow.

"We had a great time. Learned a lot about each other. Had some food. Shopped. It was really nice."

"I'm so glad. So he's liking fun, is he?"

I chuckle. "He is. He's a different person."

"Does he know about your crush on him?" I suck in a breath and turn around to glare at Jacob, but it's too late.

Poor clueless Jake didn't even pick up that I was making a second cup of hot chocolate, and blurted out my secret with Owen standing right behind him. He'd just come out of the washroom around the corner, since I heard the door open as Jacob asked his question. Talk about fucking awkward.

"He does now."

Jacob whirls around. "Heyyy... Owen. I didn't know you were here. I'm just going to leave you guys alone while I get this giant foot out of my mouth." He turns back to me, mouthing a silent sorry, and leaves us alone.

Once again, I'm standing, staring at Owen, trying to read anything on his face. But he's giving me nothing to go on. I've come this far. I'm not about to let him run or hide. I'm going to do what I do best, make a joke and move forward and hope it works out for the best.

"Talk about awkward, right?" I laugh, but it's a nervous laugh. "Can we pretend that didn't just happen and go back to being the friends we are? You know, the ones that let friends eat tacos from take out trucks and drink apple cider at bonfires." He still says nothing, but I'm not letting this go and losing all the ground we've made for the last two days. If it's weird for him to know that I had — have — a crush on him, well, that's his issue, but we've had too much fun to just let it be an issue.

Finally he speaks. "I still can't believe you ordered a hard shell. It's like you've never had a taco before." He pulls out a chair at the kitchen table and I set a mug in front of him, relief rolling off me. He's also choosing to pretend that just didn't happen. Might make it harder on him to know, but it's out there now. I can't call on the universe gods to take it back.

I shrug a shoulder, happy to hear his teasing tone. "Well, I've never had a soft taco. Seems kind of wrong to not have it crunchy. Maybe that's me."

He sips his hot chocolate, slurping in a marshmallow piece. "Mmm... that's a good marshmallow. What kind is it?"

I sit up a little straighter at his praise. "It's a Parker special. I made them. They are pretty good, if I do say so."

"I didn't know you could make marshmallows. You should make some at the shop. Kids would love these."

"Um, yes, of course, I can do that. Maybe for Valentine's Day I'll create something — if I'm still around."

His shoulders tense at my unintentional slip. From the perspective of a boss, I probably shouldn't have said that. "Are you planning to not be there? Is there something I should know?"

"Uh, well, remember I told you earlier about the wedding cake thing? Trevor was teaching me all the shaping and decorating things because I applied to be an apprentice at the biggest bakery in Cloverton. You never know when you could get a call, because they only take on so many at a time." Normally this topic is one of my favourites and I could go on about it for hours, but now, seeing how Owen is deflating before my eyes, I don't know what to think anymore. Is he really that saddened to hear this?

"It's unlikely I'll be picked, don't worry. You can't get rid of me that easy. And I'd never leave you in the lurch." His blue eyes aren't as bright, and I feel like the biggest asshole now for letting this out. I'm ruining everything without even trying.

He drains his cup and stands. "I should get going. Tomorrow is a long day at the shop. You should get your rest, too."

I follow him to the mudroom and watch as he shrugs into his coat. I can't just let him leave like this. We had a great time before all the proverbial shit hit the fan. I want fun, smiling Owen back. I want the Owen that was my friend tonight.

"Owen... this isn't how it should be. We had fun. I want you to keep having fun, you know."

His lips tilt in a half smile. "I had fun. This was good. But... there's something I should say." He shuffles around on his feet and bites his lip as I wait patiently for whatever it is he needs to get out. The longer he takes to say something, the more knots form in my stomach.

"Don't leave me hanging, Owen. Just say it and we can move on."

His eyes meet mine and all the air leaves the room as he rocks my world with what he says.

"I like you too."

Crap on a cracker. This isn't possible. I did *not* just hear him say he likes me, did I? His hands are in his pockets as he bites his lip. "Um, do you mean like me as a friend or something else?" *Nothing better than being direct, Parker.*

His tongue darts out, licking his lips, and I squirm. "Something else." His gravel filled voice shakes as the admission crosses his lips and I'm left stunned by this piece of information.

His incredible blue eyes burn into me as he swallows with a gulp. Sounds of kids shouting and playing video games in the common room drift into the silence as we both stay frozen in our spots. But this string between us, drawing us closer and closer, is about to snap. I step closer to him, searching his face for any sign that he's not on board with this. He's not backing away, so I do what I've been thinking about for months.

I grab a handful of his jacket and reach on my tiptoes. Nose to nose, I offer a final out. "Last chance to change your mind before I kiss you. Unless I read this all wrong, that's what I'm doing, Owen. Can I kiss you?"

"Are you going to stop talking and do it?" He tugs me closer to him, dipping his head so I don't need to be on my tiptoes. "I've been thinking about it all night."

I press my lips to his and I don't ask; I demand he open his lips for me with my tongue. He does so with a groan and I'm so hungry for more, I push him back until he hits the wall with a thump and his hands clutch my shirt, pulling me tighter to him. Plastered against him, I can't get enough of his taste. He tastes like the marshmallows I made and a sweetness that's all Owen. I could do this all night. Be lost in his lips and feeling his hands on me.

"Glad to see someone is having a good night." Katie, one of the residents, is standing at the doorway. I drop my head to Owen's chest with a chuckle and Owen buries his head into my neck, body shaking with gentle laughter. "I'll be back in ten if you don't want me to interrupt a second time." She giggles and lets herself out with a blast of cold winter air.

"I guess that's the warning for us to stop making out in your mudroom."

I sigh over his lips as I press another kiss to his mouth. "I could do this forever."

Owen cradles my face in his hands. "How about we start with doing it every day and getting to know each other more?" He kisses my forehead before resting his own against mine. "I loved tonight, Parker. It was incredible and the past few days have been... eye opening. Can we do that?"

"I've waited this long. I'm not going anywhere."

He kisses me this time. Long and deep and my legs are turning to jelly as I sag against him and feel his semi in his pants. When we finally come up for air, it's with great reluctance, but Katie will be back and Owen really should get going.

With a last kiss on the cheek, he gathers his things and leaves. I watch him through the window and when he turns back and waves, I feel my heart fly out of my chest.

Owen Dukarski, my boss, my crush, just kissed me and told me likes me.

I couldn't get any closer to heaven if I tried.

Sixteen

Owen

I WAS NOT EXPECTING to learn tonight that Parker has been into me for a while. Nor was I expecting to learn so much about his future plans all at once. His hands waving around as he kept babbling away, trying to ease my mind; that he wouldn't leave The Bean in the lurch, did nothing to ease my mind.

That wasn't the part that was bothering me. Thinking of him no longer being here for me was unexpectedly throwing me for a loop. The business was not the priority. I'd only just noticed him and was still figuring it all out. I didn't want him to leave, that much I knew. With Parker, my days already seemed brighter, and I wanted to continue what we seem to have started. The only thing I could think of was to just tell him I was into him. Because tonight, I realized I was.

His raised eyebrows and gaping jaw as my words registered, were adorable. So damn adorable.

But that kiss? It's burned into my memory and I can't stop thinking about it. How he tasted like the hot chocolate he made me and something so sweet it called to my soul. How he was pressed up against me, this time separated by more than a cheap spandex elf suit. Holding him felt so right and after an evening of light and fun flirting, followed by more discoveries about him, I hadn't wanted to leave.

Something was happening with us. An incredible something, and I didn't want to miss out. I knew that much. Parker seemed to be the puzzle piece that's been missing; the part that I never got around to shaking the box for to see if it was still there. Then you sleep on it, only to come back the next morning and find it's been on the floor near your chair the whole time. He's been in plain sight for months, but I've done nothing except allow his antics to irritate me.

When I arrived home, I lay awake in bed staring at the space next to me, wondering if maybe he's the one who is supposed to be there.

Fuck. This sunshine boy sure didn't take long to get to me once I let him. What do I do now?

I should have slept like the dead after everything that happened yesterday, but I couldn't. I spent all night tossing and turning and wondering what the hell was going to happen today. Specifically with Parker. It's the last day we're open before I close my shop for the holidays, followed by a small get together with the staff before they go home.

Every year, the number of people who complained about me closing dropped and the number who thought it was a great idea grew. Not that public opinion was my goal. I do it for all my staff to spend quality time with family. They get paid any regular shifts they would have worked too. It's much easier than trying to juggle and find people to fill in for staffing, and then having to deal with the annoyance of unreliable part timers. It works for me, so I do it.

Now, if only personal life matters were as easy to deal with as business matters. I'm dragging my ass into work late and I look like hell. I'm also nervous because I gave the green light to Parker, and it's been so long since I've been with someone that wasn't a one night party fuck, that I'm feeling lost about it. Not just the feelings, but the whole... *everything*. Like, what's the etiquette for having someone stay over? Or asking without feeling like some sort of pervert. I'm going to have to trust Parker to lead me in where we take this next.

I know Parker has arrived at The Bean before me and after I shed my outside gear, I speed walk to the kitchen to see him. As I approach, I can already hear the Christmas carols and his loud singing through the door, and I don't even try to hide my smile. Once I'm in the kitchen and Parker is in my sights, all my guts jostle and flip. There's no puffy costume today; no chef whites. He's dressed in snug fitting faded jeans and a t-shirt. A t-shirt I'm sure has something Christmassy on the front, but the way it hugs his shoulders has me noticing his broad shoulders and the way his arms flex as he works, his ass wiggling even though it's I'm Dreaming of a White Christmas and nothing upbeat.

I silently debate if I should touch him from behind or wait until he spins around to notice me. I don't even need to be in the kitchen today. There's no soup to make, no real reason to be here except to say hello and see him. He turns around, still singing, and greets me with that damn smile again, and I feel it all the way to my toes.

"Hi boss. Fancy seeing you here. Do you need anything?"

I smile back. It's infectious now that I've *let* it be. "Nope. Just coming to see my favourite baker before the day starts." A blush spreads on his neck and I smile bigger knowing my words did that.

"Thank you. If you need anything else from your favourite baker, just ask." He winks and returns to work, leaving me as he would on any other day. But today isn't any other day. I will ask the baker what I want... just not right now.

I snag his coffee mug and refill it for him, placing it back on his counter with a smile before I return to my office. I don't have a lot to do today, it's all being done for me. A delivery service brought the liquor bottles over yesterday, a call to my banker had the cash ready for me to drop in for pickup, and the candy store made their delivery yesterday, too. Before I went home last night, I stopped at the dollar store and picked up gift bags to package everything and at the Christmas market last night I found some gorgeous handmade cards. Now I get to sit and make everything look pretty before Dominic delivers the charcuterie for our Christmas social.

Writing heartfelt thank yous and Merry Christmas wishes into cards and making packages look pretty takes me a half hour. When you only have 8 staff, it's not a large project. With time to kill, my mind wanders to what I want to say and do with Parker. I want to know him inside out. I want to know his favourite food, his best childhood memory and if he sleeps in jammies or nude. I want to know how it feels to have breakfast with him and hold him in my arms every night. I even want to hear him singing in my kitchen.

Maybe I should ask Dom what the hell I'm supposed to do now.

I fire a text to Dom asking him to stop by once he gets to work, and he replies that he will. While I wait for my best friend to help me talk this out, I replay the last few days in my mind for what feels like the millionth time. I kick myself for being so closed off these last four months. How might it all be different if I wasn't a grump with my head up my ass?

This is so damn frustrating. I sigh, dropping my head in my hands, but I have no time to wallow as there's a knock and I lift my head to find Parker.

"Is this a good time? I can come back if you don't want me here."

Quite the opposite, I'm afraid. "Come in and close the door."

He swallows hard, but does as I ask, moving closer to my desk. "What can I do for you?"

His laugh is soft and breathy. "Anything you want really." The air hums between us and my knee is bouncing so fast I fear it might detach and take off without me. Whatever this is that's happening, needs to be addressed... and soon. I was going to wait until after we closed, but I can't. He's close enough to touch, and that's what I want. I slide my chair to the side of my desk, spreading my thighs apart while keeping my eyes trained on his face.

His chest is rising and falling with little huffs, but his eyes are locked on mine. "Is the offer to sit on my lap still open?"

He bites his lip, stepping closer. "It never closed." I don't need to say anything else, there's no need to. Parker slides his hands up my chest and onto my shoulders before his hot breath ghosts across my ear.

"I'd give you anything without a second thought, Owen." He places a soft kiss on my ear, and lips trail down my neck, drawing a whispered curse from my lips. My whole body is on fire. "I'd sit on your lap... your face... your cock." He punctuates each option with a bite on my neck and my hands clutch at his waist, pulling him closer. "Your choice."

My choice? My brain is so fried I want it all. Right now. I can't decide, like a kid in a candy store with an unlimited wallet, I want to have it all. But I'm having an issue forming words because Parker's mouth on my neck and ear is pushing me to the edge of insanity. My want for him is overriding rational thought. He knows this; he already knows and makes the choice for me. Pressing the lever to lower my chair with a thud, he straddles my lap before finally putting his lips on mine. It's the sweetest thing in the world and sensory overload. My hands roam his body with greed, to cover every square inch all at once and my mouth wants to do the same thing. But I don't want his lips off mine. I'm so fucking overwhelmed I don't even know where to start.

Hands are on my face and Parker tears his lips away. "I got you. Don't worry, we've got time to do it all. I know what you're thinking." He presses his hips into mine, pulling a whimper from my lips. He touches his forehead to mine, both of us panting. "I've wanted nothing more than I want you. I know what you're thinking because I'm thinking the same thing."

And we sit like that, my hands on his neck, his on my cheeks. I could get lost in his eyes if I had the time.

"You're so beautiful. I don't know how I never noticed you until now." I run my fingers across his jaw, loving how his stubble feels under my fingers. "Is this crazy?"

"Isn't life crazy, though? Why do we have to second guess ourselves every time something feels right?" He places a tender kiss on my lips. "I'm okay being crazy if it means I'm with you."

I don't know how long we make out like teenagers with him on my lap in my office, but it's long enough I forget all about Dominic coming by. And I also forget it's my office and I should be more professional. A quick knock, which I recognize, and the door opening confirms I was right about being so lost in Parker, I spaced out.

"Hey O I only have... whoa! Ah, I'll wait outside."

Dominic closes the door quickly and Parker chuckles into my shoulder. "Great, I'm gonna have to walk by Dom with a huge boner now."

He eases himself off me, and I miss his warmth, but he wasn't wrong. There's no mistaking the bulge in his pants and I feel bad about that, but in a good way. "Sorry, but at least it's Dom. He won't give you grief about it. He'll save all that for me."

"I'll leave you two then." He fans his face with a grin. "I'll be in the fridge if you need me."

I snag his wrist before he gets too far and place a kiss on his knuckles. "You never told me what you came back here for. Did you need something?"

"Oh. Not really. I just wanted to tell you I had a great time last night and let you know I'm ahead of schedule today already." He snorts. "Okay, no. I just came back here to see you. That's all. I just wanted to see you."

With a sunny smile, he opens the door where Dominic is leaning in the hallway. "Hey Dom, good to see you." He loud-whispers. "If I knew you were on the way, I would have practiced more restraint. What can you do?" He whistles down the hall, leaving Dom shaking his head with a small smile.

"I assume this was what your text was about?" He looks at his phone. "I've got about ten minutes before I need to scoot. Jade will have my hide if I'm not there with coffee on the busiest day of the year." He pulls out a chair and sits. "I see you took my advice completely and are having fun. Not what I meant, but if it works..."

I run a hand over my face. "I'll give you the abbreviated version. We've been out twice. Last night was like a date. We shared things about ourselves. I've realized there's a lot more to him than what I've seen the past few months. Oh, and I already imagined sex with him, so there's that."

Dom's eyebrows shoot up. "That, I was not expecting so fast, but it's obviously freaked you out."

"What do you mean, not expecting so fast? Did you know he had a crush on me this whole time?"

He has the audacity to laugh at me. "What is this, high school? We talk about crushes? I could tell he was interested, yes. Most of us could. You were the only oblivious one. When I told you to have fun, I meant to enjoy life. If that means taking Parker home, then I suppose you should do it."

"That's my problem. I don't know how to ask him to come home with me and I don't know how I should approach it. Other than a couple of make out sessions and telling him I wanted to get to know him, I don't know how to handle it from here."

"Not what it looked like to me a few minutes ago. Seemed like you had it handled very well." He laughs and I throw a pen. It lands on his chest with a smack.

"Asshole. Shut up for a minute and listen." Dom straightens up, back to being serious because he knows I need him. "Am I being stupid? He's got life goals, he's my employee. What if... what if I make him like me and he gives up on himself?" Because that is a fear. Sure, I was a grumpy bastard and I've found a reason to not be, but things change. I'm all twisted around and the only thing I know for sure is I want him with me and not just at work. I want him in my life. After that, I'm clueless.

Dominic softens. "O, that's not how it works. He's his own person and always will be. You know he's overcome a lot. Just like Micha, he's done well and refuses to wallow. Remember when he dated that biker guy in the summer? You didn't want to admit it then, but I knew. I knew you were already thinking of what's best for him. You liked him then, but didn't want to admit it." He pauses before standing. "Owen, you'll never know if what's best for him is you, unless you try. If we all had crystal balls, life would never have mistakes — or adventures. Everything would be boring."

I meet him at the door and hug him a little harder than usual. "Thanks. Sorry you walked in on us. It's safe to say I won't have a problem with him at your party."

I walk Dom out, and he gets his coffees to go for him and Jade. We confirm the delivery for the staff social and he's off to start his day. I stay out front with Paige, greeting customers and chatting to regulars. Giving free coffee cards to people or cookies to kids. It's a procedure I've had every year since I opened. But this time it feels different, and I know why.

I'm smiling. A real one. And I owe it to Parker.

SEVENTEEN

Parker

I'M WATCHING OWEN MINGLE with the customers, and he's different. But it's a good different. He's always been confident and commanding, but you could never tell if he was happy. His stony expression was always exactly the same. It made him appear intimidating to most. But to those he allowed close to him, you knew that wasn't the case at all. He's kind and generous and he keeps most things to himself. He thinks all he needs is The Screaming Bean and life will be full. But I've watched him enough to know that's not all there is to him.

His smile reaches his eyes today; the skin crinkles at his eyes when he laughs with Mr. Pine, an elderly man who comes in three times a week to sit with his coffee and a crossword at the second table, by the window. He adores Owen and comes here just to say hello and take a few minutes of his time each day. Owen, I'm told, spent an hour one snowy day getting Mr. Pine's car out of a snowbank for him. The man had misjudged the bank and buried one side of his car in the snow. Owen doesn't notice, but Mr. Pine glows under his attention. He's his own personal superman. Owen sits with him every day, but today, he's more animated than usual and Mr. Pine is laughing so hard he's wiping his eyes. When Mr. Pine leaves, he's happy as always, but Owen... he's captivating.

His joyful presence fills the room, and in all the best ways. His laughter is more frequent and his smile hasn't left his face. The people of this town are seeing the real Owen today, and I couldn't be more thrilled to be here for it.

"A penny for your thoughts. Or a rag for your drool?" Paige elbows me, smiling.

"My thoughts cost more than a penny, thank you very much. As for the rag... maybe?" We both laugh. Paige knows how I feel about Owen. I suppose everyone will know more than that if things go well between us.

"How did your dinner go yesterday?"

I told Paige I finally just asked Owen on a sort of friendly date. I'm surprised she took this long to ask me about it.

"It went really well. Things were said. Plans were made." I wiggle my eyebrows, not wanting to voice it out loud just yet. Owen might not want the staff to know if we hook up. Although, I trust Paige to not say anything. She squeezes my arm. "I hope it works out, Parker. He's definitely happy today and not the usual fake happy, you know what I mean?"

I most definitely know what she means. Paige heads out to clean up tables and I meander back to the kitchen, double checking everything is turned off and shut down for the next seven days. I've never worked anywhere that gave me the entire week of Christmas off. When I was hired, it was a bonus in my books. However, I had hoped I'd have my own apartment by now. I had plans of lounging around in jammies and reading while eating my body weight in junk food. It's still possible I could do that, but it's not the same at the shelter. I said I'd help with the cats and the ladies might need help for dinners. It's not a bad thing to be needed, but one of these days it's just going to be me, doing what I want. Right now, it's Owen I want, and I'll take him in any way I can get.

I could be given no better Christmas wish than lying naked with Owen. Biting my lip, I imagine what he must look like naked. I wonder if he is hiding more tattoos — and wouldn't that be fucking hot? A dreamy sigh escapes my lips and I jolt when a pair of large, warm hands rest on my hips.

"What are you thinking about, making that sound, sunshine?" Owen's voice is a purr next to me as he nips my ear.

I turn around into his arms. "If you must know, I was just imagining you naked and searching for more tattoos." I lick my lips as his eyes widen and I laugh at his loss for words. "I may be all sunshine and happy here, Owen, but I'm not afraid to tell you what I want. Or what I want to do, or taste. You get the picture?" He swallows hard and his fingers clench on my waist.

"You sure know how to catch me off guard."

"Nah, you'll get used to it. It's almost closing time. What do you need me to do to get this day wrapped up, boss?"

He tugs me closer and his breath passes over my ear, lighting a spark across my skin that finds its way to my groin. "I need you to say yes to coming home with me tonight."

Santa seems to have got my letter after all.

"There's no way I could ever say no to you."

He places a soft kiss on my lips and backs away. "I hope that never changes."

He leaves me alone in the kitchen floating on a cloud, dreaming of what tonight will bring.

The snacks have been consumed and Owen has given all of us his Christmas gifts. We've all laughed and talked in a social setting, which doesn't normally get to happen. It's comfortable and so much like family, my heart pangs just a smidge thinking of what it would be like to have an actual family. These are my co-workers and a few are friends, but they all mean something to me just the same. We don't all meet up at tables to share food on holidays, but we care about each other. That's clear by the gifts we've all exchanged tonight.

"Merry Christmas Parker. I hope you have an enjoyable week off." Paige wraps me in a hug and I breathe in her peppermint shampoo.

"I'm sure I will. You have fun too, okay? Say hi to your gram for me."

"I'll do that. She still wants you to come one day and teach her how to make that pie dough."

I chuckle. "Just tell her it's practice. She's doing it right. It takes time."

I kiss her on the cheek before she gathers her things and all that remains are me and Owen. I chuckle to myself when I realize I said goodbye to all the staff and saw them out, just as a host would. I took over Owen's job in a way. As the boss, he should have been doing that, but I sort of swooped in and stole his thunder.

He's moving chairs back and cleaning up some of the mess we missed and...he's humming a Christmas carol.

"You've got to be kidding me." I shake my head, a smile forming on my lips as Owen looks up from his task.

"What? Is something wrong?"

"You're humming. And it's a song I know very well."

"I'm not humming." His cheeks turn a shade of pink and I never, ever thought I'd see the day when Owen was embarrassed enough to blush.

I stride over to him. "You're humming Santa Claus is Coming to Town."

He laughs again. "Busted. I guess I'm in the Christmas spirit." His eyes drop to my lips and I know exactly what spirit he's in. The same one I've been in since he came into the kitchen.

"Hmm..." I run a finger down his chest, thrilled I can touch him this way. "I'd rather have you in something else." I rise on my tiptoes and suck his bottom lip gently before backing away. "I need to stop by my place first, if that's okay?"

He rubs the back of his neck. "Ya, that's fine." He croaks.

"Did you change your mind, Owen?" *Please say no.*

"Not at all. Just nervous." He shakes his head and continues tidying up. "Can't believe I just said that." He mumbles and I'm once again struck by how different Owen actually is when he lets you see him.

"Don't be nervous, boss. It's just like riding a bike. Only the bike is me." I laugh as he grumbles again and shakes his head. But he's smiling.

After a quick stop at my room to pack a bag and make sure the ladies watching the shelter for Jacob don't need anything, I'm once again in the front seat of Owen's Bronco. This time I'm heading to his place. I don't know what he has planned. He could want me there to wax the kitchen floor for all I know.

"Hey. You're quiet. Everything okay?" His hand squeezes my knee before returning to the steering wheel.

"Sorry, I'm just up in my head. I'm fine." I reach over to squeeze his thigh in return, but he grabs my hand before I can remove it, lacing our fingers together and holding it there. Such a small thing should not be throwing my heart into a flutter. But it is. Every time he lets me closer, it raises my hope that he sees more than just a fuck with his baker.

"So, what are we going to do tonight? Did you have a plan, or are we just going to wing it?"

"Promise you won't laugh and I'll tell you."

I can't keep the chuckle inside at his serious tone. "Looks like I already failed."

He turns the bronco up a long, winding country lane. There are several street lights lining what has to be his driveway, which ends at the most cozy cabin-like house. It could be in a Hallmark movie. "This is your place?"

He kills the ignition and turns to me. "Yep. Welcome to my little slice of paradise."

I grab my bag and meet him in front of the vehicle, and he points out things as we walk up to the mammoth wrap around deck.

"That's the field where my parents used to have horses. There's a small barn back there. I don't know what to do with it yet. I had renovated it for a studio of sorts, but I don't have any hobbies so I left it all dry walled for now. You can see it in the morning." He steps up to the door and unlocks it, motioning for me to enter before him.

We enter a small mudroom, and there's a bench on each side and wrought iron hooks attached to rustic slabs of wood for hanging your coat on. Under each bench are cubby spaces. Some have wicker baskets and others hold pairs of shoes and boots. It's very rustic, but cozy — something I didn't expect from Owen. I guess I thought his place would be sleek and modern. We each sit on the bench to remove our snowy boots and he tosses me a pair of sock type slippers as he pulls his own pair on.

"It can get chilly on the feet until I start the woodstove. I should have warned you, but that's why I have extra slippers out here."

I pull on the massive pair of sock-like slippers with grippy feet on the bottom and giggle. "As long as I don't need to run in these, we're good." I follow behind him into the rest of the house with my giant duck feet. A short turn to the right and the rest of the home comes into view. "Holy Shit Owen. This place is amazing!"

Owen laughs as he walks over to start the pellet woodstove in the corner of the open concept sitting room. You would never guess from the outside that this was the inside. One giant room makes up most of the ground floor. A sectional sofa is arranged facing an old stone fireplace. A massive flat screen TV hangs above the fireplace. To the left of the woodstove, there's a set of patio doors and three enormous picture windows which must have an incredible view in the daylight.

Behind the sectional is a 6 foot kitchen island that doubles as a work surface and dining space. A smaller table for two is tucked off in the corner.

I shuffle over in my giant slippers, mouth agape at the beauty of his stainless-steel appliances and black counters. It's a dream kitchen for any chef. I spin around, almost stepping on my oversized slippers and crashing to the floor. "Owen, do you cook? This is the perfect kitchen!"

He dips his head. "Um, ya. I like to cook when I'm around. I've always liked it. Nothing fancy, but my mom taught me how to do the basics."

I shouldn't be surprised. He makes soup from scratch for Dominic three times a week. He knows how to cook. I just didn't think he'd know how to cook this much and have a dream kitchen. He opens a cupboard and takes out two wine glasses. "Do you like wine? I have a homemade peach wine from this summer. It's really good."

He makes wine? I would have sworn he was a beer guy. "I like wine. That sounds awesome." He surprises me again by opening a small fridge under the glasses, a wine fridge, and pulls out a bottle. I watch him remove the cork and pour us a generous glass each.

"Let's sit in the living room, it's more comfortable." He carries our glasses and I follow him. He places our glasses on the coffee table and takes his position on the end, throwing his right arm across the back of the couch. I sit beside him, close but not too close yet. I really want to snuggle into his side, but I'm going to let him lead.

I'm curious about this man now that I'm on a personal level and I want to talk. I want to know all about him. "So you mentioned your parents used to have horses? Did they used to live here?" I take a sip of the wine and it's so peachy it's like I took a bite of one. It's smooth and sweet and could spell trouble if I drink too much of it.

"This is where I grew up. I already told you about my dad. Mom kept a horse for a while, but it was never something she wanted to do on her own. This house became mine after mom died. I was raised here, but as you can probably tell, I did a fairly substantial renovation." He sips his wine and his fingers find their way into my hair. He absently massages my head and I'm filled with a longing to be part of this every day. The end of day glass of wine while snuggled on the sofa and just being together. The family feeling I've always wanted. Cheddar would love lying around a woodstove.

"Is there anything original to it? I can't imagine the inside is even remotely close." He stands up and walks to a large bookcase beside the old fireplace and pulls out a photo album.

"These are old photos of me as a kid, as well as how the place looked before I completely gutted it." He turns towards the back to show the pre reno pics. He's smiling with a sledgehammer and so is Dominic. There are lots of pics of them doing some serious manual labor together. "Who's taking all the pics while you do this?"

A small smile ticks up. "Jenny. Dom's wife. She was here most days when Dom came. She wanted to help, but she never got to see the finished work." He blinks back some tears and I'm shocked to feel myself do the same. I never even knew her, but I know she was Dom's wife who died far too soon and obviously a good friend of Owen's too.

"Did you do all this yourself?"

He chuckles. "Oh no. I'm not that talented. Dom and I did most of the demo and I hired contractors to do almost everything else. I knew after mom died, I wanted to stay here but I had to make it something of my own."

I silently flip through the album, marvelled at how much the inside has changed. "What happened to the spiral staircase?" It was in the photos but it's nowhere now.

"Ah, I had to take that out and replace it with something more practical. You can't move furniture up and down a spiral staircase easily."

He takes our wine glasses, almost empty, and refills them in the kitchen. "Come on, I'll show you where the new staircase is and where it leads."

I take my refilled glass, and he leads me to a door off the kitchen. Behind the door is a staircase. I follow him up and it opens up to another large open concept room. Not just any room, but it's Owen's bedroom. My mouth goes dry as I stare at his bed, wondering what he sleeps in and if he's a snuggler. Above the bed is another bank of windows in an arch. There's a door that leads to an ensuite bath, double doors to a giant closet and a set of French doors which I can only assume lead to a deck.

I'm rooted to the spot, close to hyperventilating, because I'm in Owen's bedroom.

EIGHTEEN

Owen

I DIDN'T THINK I'D lead Parker to my bedroom so fast. I don't even know what I want to do with him. My mind is all over the place, bouncing from thought to thought like a hummingbird among the flowers.

I should have just stayed on the couch talking to him. Romance has never been a strong point of mine. I never seem to know the finer points of it. But once he mentioned the staircase, it seemed the next logical thing was to show him. The fact it went to my bedroom wasn't a factor. But now he's standing in my inner sanctuary, very close to my bed. The same bed I jerked off in while thinking about him.

"Do you like hot tubs?"

He breaks out of his trance. "Who doesn't?" His sunshine and mischievous grin sets butterflies loose in my belly.

"One splurge I made on the remodel was to add a deck off my bedroom for a hot tub. I soak out there a lot. Helps calm the mind before bed." I open the French doors and place the bottle of wine on a table out there to keep it cold. I raise an eyebrow in question to Parker. "Would you like to join me?"

He bites his lip. "I would love nothing more, but I didn't pack a suit."

I shrug, trying for nonchalant but not sure if I achieved it. Of course he didn't pack a bathing suit. Why would he? I had my own selfish reason for not telling him. "You can go buff or keep your boxers on. Your choice."

"What are you going to do?"

I tear my shirt off and unzip my pants. "Whatever you're comfortable with, I'll do the same."

The boy doesn't even take a moment to consider before he blurts, "Nude. Let's get naked!" I laugh as he rips off the oversized slipper-socks with so much force he almost falls on this face. "We have all night, Parker. Don't hurt yourself."

I've never been modest about my body, and undressing to sit in the hot tub is such a routine for me that I don't even consider how it may seem to others. When I hear a squeak from the other side of the bed, Parker stands frozen, his eyes popping so far out of his head it's like someone squeezed him too hard.

"What? Are you okay?"

"Do you always just strip and show people..." He waves his hands at me, "...that? Do you always drop trou so fast?"

"Sorry, I'm used to being alone. If it bothers you..."

It's obviously not a problem because Parker has his clothes off faster than a magician pulling a rabbit out of a hat, and I'm stunned at how easy it is for him to stand before me naked. I don't want to take too much time staring, but I like what I see. A lot. So much for taking things slowly. First, I invite him into my bedroom. Now it's naked in my hot tub. I should probably look up the definition of *slow* next time because I'm sure it's not this.

I grab two towels from the rack near the door and my wine glass. Without turning around, I open the door and step out into the cold. I set my glass on the table and drag the cover off the hot tub. Steam billows up into the frosty night air. I take the steps into the tub and settle into my usual spot, reaching across for my wine. Parker is still at the doorway. "Come in and I'll get the jets going."

He tiptoes across the snow, holding his wine high and cupping his balls. "I've never been outside naked. Freezing your balls off is a legit thing I see." He copies my movements and slides into the hot tub with a hiss before standing back up again. "Is it supposed to be this hot?"

"Well, it is a hot tub for a reason. If it's too hot for you, we can go back inside."

"No, No. I'll be okay. I just need to adjust to it."

I press the button to start the coloured lights and the waterfall. Once Parker has gotten more comfortable, I start the jets. Sinking lower, I let my shoulders bear the pulses of the jets and sigh, allowing the inky blackness of the sky with its tiny points of light to calm my mind. I lean back and search the stars like I always do, but with Parker out here with me, my thoughts are even more chaotic than normal.

This is so unlike me. It's been years since I've tried to impress anyone. Are hot tubs even romantic anymore? I have no fucking clue, but we're here now and I've had my first peek at what Parker hides under his clothes and it was a feat of strength to not stand and stare at him. Tall and lean with miles of young skin, it made my mouth water. He laid everything he tried to hide under that spandex suit bare, and I was dying to touch him.

I find my glass and sip my wine while eyeing Parker. He's staring at the sky and gulping his wine like water.

"Are you okay Parker?"

He sighs, letting his shoulders sink under the water. "It's hot, but once you get used to the temperature, it's really nice." The noise of the jets and gurgling water is the only sound we hear as we sit and stare into the stars. The lights from the hot tub splash colour over his face. He looks good in the yellow one.

"Your wine is fantastic. Did you bring the bottle?"

I chuckle and reach for the bottle outside the tub. "It's one of my favourites for sure. Slow down though." I pour a half glass for him and return the bottle to the table. "It sometimes sneaks up on you."

He giggles and slides closer to me, wrapping his legs through mine. "Sneaky is fun sometimes. Especially when it's *hands* that are being sneaky."

"Fuck!" I jump as his hand on my dick gives me a squeeze. "You should warn a guy."

"If I warn you, then it's not being sneaky." He swallows most of his wine and slides closer. "Although, if I wasn't being sneaky, then I could be dirty. Oooh! Dirty would be better, wouldn't it?"

He obviously drank too much too fast. I'm used to him being forward, but this is new. I'm all for alcohol and losing inhibitions, but not if he doesn't know what he's doing. His hand cups my balls and the moan crossing my lips is wanton. It's needy and I'm wanting more. Parker laughs again, sloshing his way up and over to once again sit on my lap. I welcome the lack of clothing between us this time. He drains his glass and I take it from him before he ends up dropping it somewhere.

"Parker, maybe you should slow down and... oomph"

Before I can finish my warning, his mouth is on mine. His hands grip my shoulders as he grinds hard against me, and I gasp into his mouth. He draws back, resting his forehead on mine, still rocking his impressive erection against me. "Sorry Owen. I thought you were going to tell me you wanted me to slow down and not touch you. I don't want that."

I don't want that either — now that I have him naked and slippery on my lap with his tongue down my throat and my hands on his ass.

"I know we're naked in a hot tub together, but don't feel you have to do anything. If all we do is fall asleep together, I'm okay with that." It wouldn't be the end of the world. I do long for someone to wake up to, but now, as he snakes his hand between us and wraps it around my dick, I want it all. Badly. I want to kiss him. I want to come with him. I want to cuddle him after.

His hot breath passes over my ear as he whispers, "I told you I'll do anything you ask me to, Owen." His tongue traces the shell of my ear and my breath hitches. "I want to ride this cock." He squeezes me underwater and even with the hot water surrounding me, I shiver. "I want to ride your face." Parker trails his tongue down my neck.

"Fuck Parker... you... *fuck*."

He chuckles. "That's the idea, yes." His teeth take my earlobe in a firm bite and my hands on his ass pull him closer. How does he know what I like right away? He's barely done anything and I'm so lit up by his words and his touch, I feel like a breeze from a butterfly's wings will set me off.

"I want to paint you with my cum so fucking bad, Owen." His own tiny mewls of desire are sending me to the moon. We need to get out of this tub before I blow and have a mess to deal with. As cool as that may be, it's a lot of work to clean up afterwards. Maybe that's my problem with romance. I'm too practical.

"You have quite the mouth on you." I lean forward and suck a mark on his neck. His head drops back with a guttural moan. Seems I've found a weakness in him as well. "You want me to leave my marks all over your body? You probably want to look at them in the mirror and jerk off to them when I'm not there." I'm rewarded with more moans, and I can't remember the last time I enjoyed being with someone this much. Maybe we drank some wine, but spurring each other on; the filthy talk — the whole thing is exhilarating and I can't think of a better way to spend the Christmas holidays than all wrapped up with this beautiful creature and leaving hickeys everywhere on his body. It's like I'm sixteen all over again and I'm fucking there for it.

"Owen." The alarm in his voice stops me in my tracks.

"Parker? What's wrong?"

He rests his head against my shoulder. "I don't feel good. Everything is spinning."

Shit. I knew he drank the wine too fast. "Can you hold on to me? Do you think you can do that?"

He tightens his arms around my neck, and I stand, guiding his legs around my waist as I carefully step out of the tub and take the two steps inside. "Do you feel sick? Or do you need to lie down?"

"Not sick. Just not good." He mumbles into my neck, and I lay him down on my bed, both of us still dripping wet. Now that he's on my white duvet, I can tell how red his skin is. He must have found the tub too hot, but didn't want to say anything. Coupled with the fast drinking of the wine, it appears my sunshine baker doesn't have the tolerance for drinking in a hot tub.

"I'll be right back." I smooth the hair off his face and walk to the bathroom. I run the cold water and soak a few face cloths and fill a glass of water for him.

I return to find him still very pink, and place a cloth on his forehead and one in each of his armpits. "You've overheated. Drinking in the hot tub isn't something you can do, I'm afraid. It's one or the other, not both."

He manages a small smile. "I overheated because I was with the sexiest man on earth. You darn near killed me."

"Feeling like shit and still with the smart mouth." I support his head so he can sip the water. Now that he's out of the tub and cooling down, the pink in his skin is fading, but it will take a while for the spinning to go away.

"I'm sorry I ruined whatever you had planned, Owen. I was looking forward to it."

"It's okay Parker. Tomorrow is a new day." I grab a dry towel and pat him dry as best I can. When I get to his feet, I look up to see how he is, and he's no longer got his eyes closed, but he's watching me. He reaches out a hand and as I take it, he tugs me gently down.

"Thank you."

"For what?" I knit my brows. Why is he thanking me?

"For taking care of me. Thank you."

He closes his eyes again, and I spend a beat too long staring at his flushed face. My heart is breaking for Parker. This is new to him, having someone care and take care of him when he's not well.

"You don't have to thank me, but you're welcome." I towel myself off and notice my cock has finally realized the party's over; both a blessing and a curse.

"Owen?"

"I'm here." I lie next to him on the bed and slip my hand gently into his.

"My mouth will still be here in the morning. This isn't over."

I chuckle and pull a light sheet over his body. "It's only just begun. Now go to sleep. I'll be right here if you need me."

He says nothing more, but his chest rises and falls with the slow and steady rhythm of someone who has fallen asleep. I ease off the bed and sneak out to cover the hot tub and retrieve the wine and our glasses before returning to my spot and slipping my hand back into his.

If I can at least make him feel safe and cared for while he sleeps, the night is still a good one.

Nineteen

Parker

MY MOUTH FEELS LIKE I ate a bowl of flour. What the hell did I do last night? I blink my eyes and lick my dry lips as I jolt awake. This isn't my bed. I'm at Owen's. The previous night comes flooding back.

I turn my head to find the other side of this mammoth bed empty, but he'd been there. The blankets are pulled back and there's an indent in the pillow. I wasn't drunk. I'd reacted to the booze and the heat of the tub. I remember our entire night, including how Owen had laid me down and taken care of me. He'd cooled me down with cloths, and he'd left water for me and held my damn hand until I'd fallen asleep. He did all that after I'd crawled over him and rubbed on him like some animal marking its territory. Talk about being a cock tease.

I throw my arm over my eyes with a groan. "The guy probably has blue balls as bad as me." I may have passed out after working us both up, but my body remembers every single bit of what had happened before my world had started spinning like a souped-up merry-go-round and I'd needed to lie down. It was going so well, too. A smile tilts my lips at the memory. Owen was so into it. He was dishing it back to me and I was there for it. I knew what I was doing, and right now I want to keep doing it. I give my erection a squeeze and hope like hell he's still up for continuing this today, because I don't want to leave here until we've made us both orgasm so hard that fireworks go off.

Rolling over, I find a glass of water on the nightstand next to me and chug it down. I shuffle over to the ensuite and use the mouthwash on the counter. A glance at the clock by the bed tells me it's only 6 A.M, which is a late sleep-in for me. When you're used to being in a bakery by 4 A.M, anything later than that is a treat. I wonder how long Owen's been up for... and where he is.

I fumble through my clothes, looking for my boxers, but change my mind. They'll just get in the way of what I want. Bare-assed, I head to the stairs and hesitate. What if it's too much to show up naked? Maybe he has guests over? It's unlikely, but maybe I shouldn't be so over the top, just in case he changed his mind. Doubling back, I find my boxers and pull them on before searching out Owen.

As I reach the bottom of the stairs and the door that I know is off the kitchen, I hear music. Christmas music. I creak the door open, and I'm met with the amazing smell of coffee and pancakes. Stepping into the kitchen, I have to bite my lip to contain the mix of laughter and disbelief threatening to bubble out of me. Owen is swaying along to Christmas carols played by an orchestra as he cooks. He's standing in front of his stove, a Santa hat perched on his head and — as luck would have it — a pair of boxers and nothing else. Owen hasn't heard me yet. The music and his humming has covered the small amount of noise I'd made. He flips a pancake and reaches for his coffee cup on the counter. I stand rooted in place, admiring this picture of domestic happiness: Owen in his kitchen being himself with no care in the world. I know even before he turns around, that he's going to be smiling, and I can't wait.

As he flips another pancake onto a pan and places it in the oven, he sees me, and the most adorable pink tinge reaches his cheeks. "How long have you been watching me?"

I walk over to him and reach up on my tiptoes to plant a kiss on his cheek. "Long enough to wonder if I woke up in another dimension." I flip the pom pom on his hat with a chuckle. "Where's Owen, and what have you done to him?"

He takes my wrist, tugging me closer. "You tell me." His lips dust over mine. "What have *you* done to him?"

His blue eyes sparkle with mischief as he releases his hold and turns back to the pan. "There's coffee ready if you want it and there's hazelnut creamer in the fridge."

"Did you get that just for me?" I pour myself a mug and find the creamer unopened as my heart leaps into my throat. He got it specially for me. He doesn't use flavours.

"I did. I was hopeful you'd still be here in the morning."

What did I expect? He invited me here. He's my boss and knows I don't need to work for the next ten days. But beyond that, I didn't think he'd have prepared to have me here for breakfast. Nor did I expect to see him in his kitchen in a Santa hat, not even close. I add my creamer and inhale the sweetness of hazelnut and dark roast coffee. My fave combo, enjoyed with my favourite person — that's a great way to start the day.

"Well, I'm still here." I place my mug on the table and walk back over to him. Wrapping my arms around him from behind, I drop a kiss between his shoulder blades. He stills for a moment before I feel his hands on mine and he pulls one to his mouth, feathering a kiss on my wrist. "A guy could get used to waking up to this every morning."

"A guy certainly could." Owen turns off the element and slides the pan away before he turns in my arms and engulfs me in a hug.

"I'm sorry I passed out last night. Unless you spiked my drink, that never happens."

His chest rumbles with a laugh. "You can't drink *and* hot tub, that's all. It happens to some people. I'm just sorry we had to find that out last night."

He pulls me closer, allowing his hands to coast down my back and grab my ass to bring me impossibly closer. At least he's not upset with me. "I hope we can continue where we left off... if you still want to, I mean."

He pushes me away so he can look down into my face. His blue eyes allow me to see right into his soul. "Why would I change my mind?"

I sigh and push out of his arms. "Because I let you down last night. Because you came to your senses and know you can do better than me?" I shrug a shoulder, convinced none of it and all of it is true. That he's only putting on a fancy breakfast charade to ease the let down. Maybe I imagined the whole thing.

He turns and takes the platter of pancakes from the oven. "Sit down." He nods to where I've placed my coffee cup, and his authoritative tone has me dropping into the chair with no argument. He places the pancakes on the table and from the fridge, retrieves a gorgeous fruit tray. All the strawberries and melon pieces are cut in fancy shapes and assembled in a gorgeous presentation. As I'm gaping at the detail on the fruit, Owen clanks a can of whipped cream next to the fruit, drawing a laugh from me.

"I thought you needed that for a pie?"

He laughs as he takes the seat opposite me. "I didn't need it all, but once I had it, I brought it home because I didn't want to sneak it back where you could see me."

We place food on our plates in silence, and I'm not sure what I should say now. My confidence from only a few minutes ago has flown out the window. I've made a mistake, I know it. This is the type of situation I never find myself in. It's too good to be true.

"Parker, don't do that."

"Do what?"

"You've stopped being you. I want you to be yourself. It's one thing I admire about you. Your perpetual smile and annoying singing. It gives me hope we can all be happy no matter what comes our way."

He chews and waits for me to reply, but I wasn't expecting that from him. "Not that I thought you were using me for sex, because I know you're a decent guy and we've been having fun, but since we work together, I wanted to be sure you were still okay with... uh... sleeping with me." God I couldn't sound more lame if I tried. I never cared that he was my boss before. Now I'm convinced it's an issue.

Owen's eyes widen, then he swallows his food before bursting into gut-busting laughter. I've never heard a better sound than his laughter. He wipes a tear from his eye and catches his breath. I didn't think I said anything that funny. "Parker, if I wasn't okay with you being here, I would never have asked you here. I most certainly wouldn't be cooking you breakfast in my underwear." He sips his coffee before he continues. "We were supposed to have this conversation last night, but I jumped the gun and had you naked in my hot tub before we got that far." His sly grin reappears. "Can't say I didn't enjoy the bit we had, though."

"Okay, let's have the conversation now, then. Can we do that?" Because dammit, I need to know what he's going to talk to me about.

"I don't know where we will go with this. But you've shown me how to enjoy life again...and to be perfectly frank, you've also shown me how much I miss having someone in my life to share things with... one of them being my bed." His blue eyes stare me down, pinning me in my seat with a heat that brings goosebumps to my skin. It's really hard to think about eating anything other than the man across from me right now. "I will never mistreat you. If this only lasts for a few days and we go our separate ways, so be it. But I do know I want to spend time with you naked and see if you're just as much fun in bed as you are out of it. If I'm wrong about you wanting that too... well I'm sorry, but I think you feel the same way."

He pops a strawberry in his mouth with a grin and I'm stunned. I've wanted nothing more for months, than to be where I am right now. Now that I'm here, I'm questioning everything for no reason. Nobody is in love, both of us have had sex with other people that went nowhere. Why am I suddenly hung up on what will happen after? When I've already slithered naked all over him and... oh my god, heat flushes my cheeks as I remember having him in my hand. I need to get a grip and grab hold of this opportunity while it's in front of me. Seize the day and all that crap. Whatever happens will happen.

With that final thought, I push my chair back, breakfast abandoned as another stronger appetite returns. I want this man. I always have, and I want to finish what we started last night.

I take the two brief steps to meet him at his chair and pluck a large, juicy strawberry from the platter. Taking a bite, I let the juice squirt out of the corner of my mouth and run down my chin. I take another bite as I step closer, and Owen is exactly where I want him. His chest is rising quickly, and his hands reach for my hips, but I back up a step.

"I want nothing more than to have you wring me dry and fuck me until I can't remember my name, Owen. You're all I've thought about for months." I stuff my hand in my boxers and stroke my dick that's rapidly coming to life.

His chair crashes to the floor as he launches himself into me, smashing his mouth over mine and lapping the strawberry juice with a moan. "You're the sexiest thing I've ever had in my kitchen." He backs me up into the kitchen island, caging me in and devouring my mouth like there's never going to be a next time. I'm gasping for air, clawing at his back and wanting to be impossibly closer to him. When he finally allows me to breathe, his teeth nip along my neck and collarbone, drawing a moan from my lips. I know he's leaving marks, and I want them everywhere.

"Owen..." My breathless plea for him to keep going isn't ignored. His large hands grip me tightly and hoist me onto the island.

"This is the perfect breakfast." He lifts my leg and peppers kisses and bites to the inside of my thigh as I grip the edge of the counter for dear life. "Lie down Parker."

His hand gently pushes me back and I lower myself onto the island, spread out like a buffet for him, completely at his mercy. Fingers slide into the elastic of my boxers, and I raise my ass slightly so he can take them off. My cock springs out, smacking me in the stomach, and I want him on me — everywhere at once.

When he steps away, I lift my head to find him staring at me. Somewhere along the line, he lost his own boxers and he gives himself a squeeze. "Do you know how hot you are right now? Laid out in my kitchen like the perfect midnight snack. I want to eat until I can't eat anymore." His voice is raspy and trembling and I'm lost in it.

Propping myself up on an elbow, I spread my legs as wide as I can and stroke my length. "You want to eat me here in your kitchen?" I prop one foot up, brazenly spreading myself for him. "I think I told you I want to ride your face. So if you want to eat, let's start with that." His chest heaves as he steps back to me. "Come and eat me, Owen."

"Jesus, you and your filthy talk." He passes his tongue down my thigh and I hiss with pleasure.

"You love it." I pant as he repeats the process on my other thigh, coming close to my balls but stopping just short. I whimper and drop my head back.

"I do. So much." His tongue flicks across the head of my leaking cock. Just a taste. I need his mouth on me everywhere. I lift my head to find his gaze locked on my face and the whipped cream in his hand. He cocks an eyebrow in question and I groan, dropping my head back again. Of course he'd want to torture me.

The whipped cream is chilly on my heated cock, but it feels amazing and his mouth hasn't even touched me yet. It seems to take forever for him to place all his whipped cream and when I lift my head to see what he's doing, a chuckle escapes my lips. There's so much whipped cream on me I don't know how he's going to find my dick under it all. "Is a cock sundae on your menu by chance?"

"I could never say no to a creamy dick." He winks before leaning down and sucking my balls into his mouth.

My hips shoot off the counter and he uses the opportunity to place his hands under my ass and lift me higher. I can't even find the words to egg him on with. Whipped cream is melting and running down my crack and he chases it with his tongue. "Fuucckk." I moan and grab at the edges of the counter again to steady myself as Owen buries his face between my cheeks and eats me out, driving me higher and higher, only to pull back just as I want him to go further.

I'm panting from the effort of steadying myself — almost in a shoulder stand — and from the relentless rimming. My arms are trembling and Owen senses my fatigue. He gently lets me down until I'm flat on the island again. He's kissing and licking anywhere but my dick, and I want to scream in frustration.

"Are you ever going to suck my dick?"

He laughs next to my belly button, warm breath sliding across my skin, leaving more goose bumps in its wake.

Fuck, even his breath turns me on.

"I could..." He flicks his tongue across the tip, and I bite back a groan. "Or I could let you come on me like you promised."

My eyes fly to his and his mischievous cream covered grin taunts me. "Can't I have both?"

He holds out his hand for me. "You must be getting uncomfortable on the island." I take his hand and he easily pulls me up. Before I let him lift me down, I grasp his face, chasing all the whipped cream from his lips and smashing my mouth to his.

"You're driving me crazy, Owen. I want to come so bad I can't stand it." It's a miracle I've lasted this long. His tongue is magical, and I'm quite fortunate to have it at my beck and call. But patience is not my strong point, and this proves it. Instead of drawing out the sweetest and stickiest oral sex session of my life, I want it to end.

He helps me hop down and as soon as my feet hit the floor, I walk him back into the door leading upstairs. His back hits the door with a muffled thump, and I drop to my knees and swallow him down. Fuck, he tastes so good. I don't need to cover him in anything. He's addictive on his own.

He's just as close to coming as I am as the pull on my hair comes far too soon.

"Parker, stand up."

I scramble to my feet, squishing myself against him as his hand takes both of us together in a slippery, sticky stroke. I rock into his fist, clutching at his shoulders and panting like I ran a marathon. If I'm this out of shape for sex, I should consider more exercise.

"Look at me when you come. Do it."

His words are the final straw, and I do as he asks. Staring into his ocean deep eyes as rope after rope of cum fills his hand and paints his abs. I shudder and look between us as Owen moans and bucks against me with his own orgasm.

He slumps against the door and pulls me against him. We're covered in cum, sweat and whipped cream residue, but there's no place I'd rather be. Why I doubted myself this morning, I don't know. If this is what being with Owen is like, I'll sign up indefinitely.

"You're really amazing, you know?" He kisses the top of my head and I tilt back to look at him.

"So are you. A guy could get used to being eaten for breakfast if it's done like that every time."

He chuckles. "Don't get used to whipped cream. I don't normally do food and sex. It was a spur-of-the-moment decision."

"I can live without it but kudos for the creativity."

He tugs my hand to lead me upstairs. "Let's get showered and do it all again, but without whipped cream this time."

I laugh as he pulls me up the stairs in his haste to shower. As I pass by the mirror to step into the shower with him, my breath catches at the sight of so many marks on my pale skin.

My fingers dance over them on my chest. Marked by Owen. My breath leaves in a whoosh as I step into the shower with him, my cock already waking for round two.

TWENTY

Owen

I PRESS START ON the dishwasher and turn around to find Parker humming and dancing while he Lysols my kitchen island. The kitchen is almost back to normal, but I'm never going to be able to sit here again without imagining Parker spread out for me. Meals will never be the same.

Leaning back on the counter, I keep watching Parker. I've never had such uninhibited sex before. Or such an amount. It's barely 1 P.M and we've been at each other all morning. When he stretches over and his t-shirt rides up, I glimpse a hickey on his ribs. Another first for me. I've never been with anyone that loved to be marked as much as he does. I had no idea this is what would happen when I asked him back here. I thought we'd have sex and perhaps have dinner and enjoy each other's company. I'm not complaining about coming so much I feel like I'm getting a dehydration headache, though. One thing that I hadn't prepared for is how well we get along and how easy it is to be with him. Annoying singing and dancing aside, he's... easy to be with. The work I've had to put into other people isn't there. Parker feels like an old friend and your favourite sweater — comfortable and something you reach for over and over.

He turns around finally and finds me watching him with crossed arms and a small smile on my face.

"You creeping on me, boss man? Staring at my ass while I'm slaving away over here cleaning up your mess?"

"I'm fairly certain you were part of that mess, and I didn't hear you complaining."

He laughs and snaps the lid back onto the container of wipes. "No, you sure didn't." He leans back, mimicking my position. "I'd even go so far as to say you can have me for breakfast any day of the week."

I laugh and walk over to him. "Insatiable is what you are." I drop a kiss to his lips and take the container of wipes back to clean off my stove top.

"What do you normally do on Christmas break, anyway?" Parker plops himself onto the couch and speaks over the cushions. He's taken the seat closest to the woodstove as well. He likes to be warm. When I finish my job and I'm satisfied we've cleaned the kitchen to health code standards, I sit beside him and throw my arm over his shoulder. He snuggles into me and fits perfectly, resting his head on my chest.

"Nothing much. I usually go to Dom's for some kind of lunch or dinner, then I hang out and watch movies. Sometimes I read, sometimes I do crosswords. I sit in the hot tub a lot. Whatever low stress stuff I can do to just unwind."

"You know what reduces stress? Cats." He peers up at me with his deep brown eyes, the lashes so long they kiss his cheeks. "Did you know that? Petting animals reduces stress."

"Good to know. Cheddar helps with that, does he?"

"Can you come stay with me tonight?"

I sit up straight and peer at his now pink cheeks. "Come again?"

"I thought you said you couldn't anymore today?" He chuckles and I return it. One track mind this one.

"What do you mean, stay with you? It's Christmas Eve. I'm sure you have other people to be with tonight."

"Well... not exactly. I mean I do, but I'd rather be with you... and I have a favour to ask." He sits up and climbs onto my lap. Even though I said I couldn't come again, there's something about him that makes me wonder if I was lying.

"You can ask me." I smooth my hands up his back and wait as he licks his lips.

"You wanted to have fun, and I think we've got that figured out." He slides his hand up my neck and into my hair. It feels good. "I have to take care of the cats at the shelter for the next few days and I was wondering if you'd like to help me?" He rushes on. "Don't feel you have to say yes. If you don't want to, I get it. I mentioned it to you after the market, but I wasn't sure if you meant it. I thought it might be fun, and a way to get to know you better." His lips touch mine in a light kiss. "I also want you to stay because I like waking up with you."

His request catches me off guard. I wasn't expecting him to invite me to his place. I said I'd help him when he'd asked. We were having fun and we should roll with it, but in my mind, it was only going to happen in my space, not Parker's.

My hands have a mind of their own and soothe his back. "Parker... I would love nothing more than to spend more time with you, but.."

He pushes away from me, but I hold him closer. "I get it. It's fine. It's too much too soon." He squirms, turning his face away, but I notice the way his smile falters.

"That's not it." I grab his chin, forcing him to look at me. "I like you and everything about you. I don't want to send the wrong message. Christmas is always a time for families and couples. We're just figuring things out with us. If it won't be awkward with the residents, I can go." Because nothing would be worse than trying to explain over Christmas dinner you're not a couple, just fucking. Not exactly smooth dinner conversation.

"Oh. I wouldn't show you off as a boyfriend or anything. I just wanted to continue our time together and keep having fun. In and out of bed if you wanted." He sits back on my thighs and lets his hand trail over my chest. "There are no strings. I didn't mean to make you think there are."

"I think we can safely say we're friends. And we have sex."

"Amazing sex."

He wiggles his eyebrows and the carefree Parker returns, causing me to slap a smile on and lean up to plant a kiss on his lips. His kisses bring me to life. As my heartbeat quickens with his hand in my hair, I most definitely want to keep having the sex.

"Sure, I'll come stay with you. It'll be fun." A genuine smile graces my face when Parker smiles back at me.

"We should go soon, then. The volunteers were in this morning, but now it's all me for the next three days."

He climbs off my lap and the urge to pull him back to me and make out like teenagers while the parents are away is so strong, I ball my fists to keep from reaching for him.

He heads for the stairs. "Let's pack our things. The sooner we get it done, the sooner I can reward you."

Since I like rewards, I do as I'm told.

"You sure you're okay staying? I only have a double bed. It could get squishy."

Parker drops his bag in the corner of the room and gestures to his bed. It probably will get squishy as he says, but I can sleep anywhere. I'm also not worried about the sleeping arrangements. Mainly because I'm hoping we'll do little sleeping.

"I wouldn't have said yes if I didn't want to, Parker. Don't even worry about it."

He checks his phone and fires a text message off before sliding it back into his pocket. "Let's get over to the shelter and deal with these kitties, and we'll be back by suppertime." He rubs his hands together, motioning for me to follow him.

I follow him out of his room and down the short flight of stairs to the sunken main living area of the shelter. The giant Christmas tree is lit up and there are stockings hung across the fireplace. The coffee table is covered with dishes of chocolates and candies. A plate of cookies sits covered on a side table and Cheddar, Parker's giant cat, is curled up on the sofa. It's a Norman Rockwell scene suitable for a postcard and enviable for anyone wanting to feel like they belong. It's been years since I've been in a setting like this. I've been to Dom's since his wife passed and I, of course, have The Bean decorated, but this is different. The lengths Jacob has taken to make the kids here feel at home, are visible even to me. Even the scent of freshly cut evergreens drifts across the air.

"It's nice, isn't it?"

Parker's voice brings me away from my daydream. "It's beautiful. Very warm. I can tell Jacob worked hard at this."

He peels back the saran on the cookies and holds the plate out to me. I take a sugar cookie sleigh while Parker takes a gingerbread man. "Jacob and Austin never had a home life like this." He waves his hand towards the picture perfect Christmas scene. "He tries to make everyone feel like they're family. Whether he's known you for a day or a year, he wants you to feel at home." He crunches into his cookie and leads me to the kitchen as I eat my own. "He knows you're here, by the way."

"Jacob knows I'm here? Am I not supposed to be?"

"Do you want milk? Water?" He pokes his head into the fridge as he finishes his cookie, leaving crumbs behind on his shirt.

"Water is good, thanks." He passes me a bottle of water and I pause before brushing off the crumbs on his chest. "Did you make these cookies? They taste like something you'd make."

"Oh? How would you mean that exactly?"

"They're beautiful and sweet. Makes me want to have more."

Why the hell did I just say that when I already told him I didn't know what would happen with us? I promised I'd never hurt him, and that comment can definitely mean something.

He snorts. "You think I'm beautiful?"

My brow furrows at his tone, but I'm also glad that's what he took out of my statement. "Of course I do. Why do you say it like you don't believe me?" My voice is more growly than I intend, because again, he's lacking the confidence in himself I always thought he had. I brush a thumb across his cheek and rest my palm there. "You're a beautiful person, inside and out. Don't let anyone make you doubt that."

"Okay." He whispers.

I forget for a moment we're no longer in my kitchen and crowd into him, wedging my thigh between his legs and pinning him to the counter. Leaning closer, my lips ghost over his ear. "I can't wait to have more of you naked later." Rocking my hips into him, he gasps and grabs my biceps.

"Okay."

I chuckle against his neck. "Have I reduced you to one-word answers?"

He giggles. "No, it's because Brandie is watching from the doorway, and I don't want her to hear my dirty talk right now." His voice squeaks as I push off him quickly and indeed find an audience.

"I'm in no rush. You guys take your time. I have all night to watch."

"Sorry. I thought we were alone."

"It's a shelter. You're never alone. Unless you're in your room with the door locked. Even then, if we want to get in there, we will."

I guess that makes sense. They're here to help the residents and need to be watchful, but does she have to watch Parker so closely? He's only here because he can't find an apartment. His time of being here as a lost youth is over. Although now I know him better, perhaps I'm wrong. I watch as he helps Brandie find things for the supper that's being made tonight, and I lean against the opposite doorway leading to the entrance.

He tosses a playful grin my way over his shoulder. "Let me get Brandie squared away here and we'll get on with our cat visit."

I nod and observe him in his element, a kitchen. While he's a baker by trade, he sure knows a lot about whatever they plan to make tonight. Sounds like a special Christmas eve dinner of prime rib and Yorkshire pudding with all the fixings is on tap, and I'm suddenly quite happy to be invited.

"Oh, did you make that yule log thing you wanted to? And did you hear about your application yet?"

My ears perk up at Brandie's questions. Parker has said nothing to me about his application except that he applied. It's not a secret, so why do I feel sad at the thought of him leaving and not want to hear what he says? I should leave and let them talk.

I clear my throat. "I'm going to use the restroom before we go." I leave the kitchen before I can hear anything on his updates and close the bathroom door behind me. I don't need to use the restroom, but I need to get myself together. Staring at my reflection in the mirror, I see a man in his mid-30s who's missed out on a lot of life. Those little lines by my eyes aren't from laughter. They're from constantly working and scowling into screens, turning down invites to go anywhere because I needed to do just one more thing, or I was simply too tired to be social. There's no grey hairs yet, thank god for good genetics, but there's a change in me. Even I can see it.

I turn on the water and splash some on my face, wondering if it will wash away the change I notice. It doesn't. How does a guy like me turn into a... well... a guy like me, when he lets his guard down and allows someone in? In the short time I've been with Parker, I've come to enjoy his company and remember what it was like to have someone to care for. Hearing it mentioned about his application, reminding me the threat of him leaving is very real, threw me for a bit. I'm obviously not ready for him to leave.

With a heavy sigh, I pat my face dry and resign myself to the fact I'm going to have to deal with the day when he's no longer in my life, and it's not something I want to think about now. Realizing I'm attached to a sweet man isn't what I thought would happen today. Maybe it's just being here with all the family-like atmosphere and Christmas stuff that's making me sentimental. Whatever it is, I'm not ready to hear whether he's leaving or not.

I exit the bathroom to find Parker in the entrance's alcove, waiting for me. His adorable face and his adorable grin aimed my way, and that warmth spreads through my chest again.

"All set?" He hands me my coat and shrugs into his.

"Sure thing. Let's do this, and by the sounds of things, there's an amazing feast happening tonight. You should have led with that when you asked me to come."

He pouts. "I thought I was enough to get you here." He winks before turning away, but I snag his coat to spin him back around. He's still playful and flirty Parker, but I see things so differently after only being here a short time.

"You are enough."

I kiss him. Hard.

"Now let's stop making these poor animals wait."

TWENTY-ONE

Parker

I LEAD OWEN ACROSS the parking lot to the shelter next door. It's not enough time for me to get control of my feelings. They're bubbling all over like an unwatched pot. He's got me so twisted around I'm not sure which way is up anymore. I don't know why he left the conversation with Brandie, but it wasn't to use the restroom. I'm almost positive he wasn't embarrassed about getting caught making out, either. It's not the first time someone has walked in on us. So what happened?

I unlock the door and type my code into the alarm system before locking the door behind us again. "Have you been here before?"

He ducks his head, and I smile. "No. I never had a need to. I donate though when there's... ah, fundraisers and stuff."

Owen walks over to the plaque on the wall and takes it in, scanning all the adoption photos. "Hey Micha is in these!" A smile crosses his face as he looks closer to find our mutual friend in more of the photos.

"He is. He insists. Pet adoption is a big thing for him. You probably already knew that, though."

He chuckles. "I guess I did." He points to the plaque. "This is Jacob's brother, right? The one he's gone to visit?"

I step closer to him because he feels too far away. "Yes, and Logan. His husband. Have you not met them?"

"Only briefly at one of the town events. I think at the ground-breaking for this too. I brought coffee." He laughs and I do too. God, I love the way his eyes sparkle when he laughs, and that little dimple pops up on the right cheek. It's so small you have to look for it. But I know it's there.

I give him a tour of the place so he knows where to find everything we need for the cats. "I'm going to assume you know how to operate a washer and dryer." We've paused in the laundry room to gather some clean blankets.

"I can manage. Give me some credit." He bumps my shoulder with a grin, and my heart flutters.

We enter the cat kennels and dump all the clean blankets in a pile. I immediately go check on the litter with the runt that will need some bottle feeding. Momma cat and all seven kittens are snuggled and asleep for now. I gesture for Owen to come closer.

"We'll leave these until it looks like they are more awake. We'll need to bottle feed the little brownish one. He's the runt and Dr. Kody doesn't think he's getting enough to eat with such a big litter."

"Is that normal?" He looks at the sleeping puddle of kittens and I can almost see the hearts jumping from his eyes. He wants to help them all. I know that look because I get it myself all the time. Every single time I come here, I want to save them all. But my budget wouldn't allow it and there's the slight problem of being homeless still.

"It happens sometimes. He's gonna be okay, though. As long as we keep helping out, he'll be fine, just smaller than the others."

Owen steps back with a nod. "I trust you. Where do we start?"

I freeze to the spot for a moment, tumbling those words over in my mind. He trusts me. For what exactly? Is he trusting me with his life? Trusting he won't get peed on? Whatever it is, those three words have me looking at him differently.

I lead him over to the opposite side of the kennels and show him how to move the cats, where to put them and how to clean their cages and refill everything. I know some of their personalities and try to introduce him as we go.

"This is Mabel. Total sweetheart, she's going to want to cling to you like a baby. If you want to hold her, I can take care of her kennel while you do that."

Owen's eyes widen. "Um, like, just hold her? I've never really just held a cat before, to be honest."

"Oh, well, consider this your first!" I pop open Mabel's kennel and scoop her up, immediately passing her to Owen. Mabel chirps and wraps her paws around his neck, snuggling into him.

"This isn't normal, is it?" His giant paw of a hand strokes her fur as he tries to look at her face.

"No, it's not. She's super snuggly and she'll start purring shortly. She loves everyone."

I tend to her kennel, watching Owen out of the corner of my eye as he pets the cat and walks around the room with her like she's a baby clinging to him. My heart flip-flops in my chest and I squeeze my eyes closed.

He notices I'm finished and brings her back over. "How come she's not been adopted? She's so adorable."

"She's older. Not everyone wants an older cat. They want the kittens; the babies they can mold into whatever they want." I pause. I'm no longer talking about kittens, and Owen's eyes are trained on me. He doesn't miss a thing.

He places Mabel back in her kennel, and she snuggles with the teddy bear she has. "We don't have too many more and then we'll feed the kitten." I close the latch on Mable's cage and run straight into a wall of Owen.

"Want to talk about it?"

I sigh as his muscular arms wrap around me. Words I wasn't expecting come pouring out. "I was an eight-year-old in foster care. I was too old for any of the families to want to adopt me. Everyone wanted newborns or toddlers, not a kid who was set in his ways and scared of his own shadow."

"I'm sorry you had to go through that. It's their loss for not seeing how awesome you are. I bet you were a great kid. Happy and helpful."

He looks down at me, and I know he means it. They're not empty words.

"Thank you. I know you mean that, but it will take me a while, if ever, to believe it."

He doesn't placate me. Instead, he holds me, stroking my back and kissing the top of my head as I struggle to rein in my emotions. I feel like the jets in his hot tub, whirling and swirling with no real purpose, and I need to get through this. I can usually keep all this stuff shoved down and never let it out. Being with Owen is cracking all the walls I have to keep that shit hidden. When I've finally had enough time to feel settled, I pull away from him. "Let's feed the little dude and give momma a break."

I show Owen what to do with the kittens and we set up an area for momma cat to stretch out and have space. She has the biggest kennel in the place, but when you have seven kittens and a litter box and food dishes to share it with, it's very tiny. The kittens are three weeks old and exploring and on the move, so we set up some gates to make sure there are no escapees or injuries. Momma cleans herself while the kittens tumble and explore and Owen sits to join them. I set up the kennel for them to return to when we're done and take our little guy to be bottle fed.

Like some bizarre twist of domestic life, I sit in the chair bottle feeding the little runt I call Squirt and watch Owen play with the kittens on the floor. He dangles feathers on a string and bounces balls for them. He even tosses a few toy mice at them. I imagine what my life would be like if I ever had a husband and family and wonder if this is what it would be like. When Owen sets those blue eyes on me and I see the worry in them, I feel like I'm dangling over the edge of a cliff, and I don't know if I want to fall or scramble back up to the top. I don't want to purge my issues on him, but if he keeps being so damn comforting, my dam is going to shatter.

"Have you ever thought about getting a pet?" Watching him with all the cats tells me he'd be a good owner. He's sensitive to their needs, and that speaks volumes about the person he doesn't let anyone see.

"I've always wanted one, but I'm not home enough. Just doesn't seem fair." He dangles another feather for the kittens. "How did you pick Cheddar?"

He wrangles a few kittens, returning them to their kennel two at a time while I decide how I want to answer. It's not a simple answer to give.

I swallow hard. "More like he picked me." A hollow laugh passes my lips as I snuggle the kitten closer with its bottle. "I was at a shelter in the city. I'd been there for a month, and it wasn't the safest place for me. I was just a boy, and the place was teeming with adults, both male and female. I thought I might find an ally, but they were no better than the people I left behind."

Owen finishes putting the kittens and momma cat in their clean kennel and lowers himself onto the floor next to me, running his hand along my calf. It's a gesture of warmth and comfort, something I've been searching for my entire life. "I used to spend as much time outside of the place as I could because it felt like a toxic abyss, one that I might not get out of the longer I stayed. I went in at the last possible moment every night to claim a bed."

I hated my life then. I hated everything at that point. I didn't want to die, but I sure as hell didn't want to live either.

"So, while I was outside one night, I was walking along a path near the park, and I saw a box. Just a box. Nothing special about it, really, but something pulled me over to look inside." The kitten has stopped nursing and I ease the bottle from his mouth. He seems stronger today. I snuggle him closer, running a finger between his eyes and massaging his tiny paws.

Owen rustles next to me. His hand is on my face, one giant thumb wiping away a tear I didn't know had fallen. "Sorry. This is always an emotional story for me." Water is already bursting through the dam I built. It's going to pour out now because I can't stop it.

"You don't have to share it with me if it makes you uncomfortable."

"No, I want to." I focus on the little guy I'm holding. "I opened the box, and this little fluffy orange body was lying there. At first I was sad that maybe a kid had lost his pet, and this was where they left him. Then I was mad. But then it twitched. This little thing was alive." God, humanity is a disappointment some days. "Someone had just thrown him away. Left him in a shoebox to die."

The dam has burst. Owen is going to hear it all and I hope I survive the aftermath.

I shudder a breath, and somehow Owen is even closer to me than before. He takes the kitten away from me and gently places him with his family, and I watch as Squirt snuggles into the kitten pile of siblings. Owen returns and pulls me to my feet, once again wrapping his arms around me. The strong arms I've already come to feel safe in. I release the torrent of tears and a sadness I've been holding back. Sobbing into his chest, I remember finding Cheddar and how I knew he was a fighter, just like me. "I smuggled him into the shelter that night and warmed him up. I hid him in my duffel bag with everything I owned and kept him next to me. So badly, I hoped I was doing the right thing to help him. It must have helped because I woke up the next morning to a tiny meow from my bag." I sneak a peek at Owen, and his eyes are shiny. My big guy doesn't want to cry. "He was so loud they told me I had to get rid of him or leave. I grabbed a piece of toast and never went back. It was pure luck I arrived here that night. I walked most of the way."

"Parker, that's almost 200 km. You walked?"

He pulls me even closer, and I hear a muffled curse as I cry harder.

"I walked until a nice man stopped and asked if I wanted a ride. He dropped me at the... here... that's how Jake found me on his doorstep. Exhausted with a newly revived kitten in my pocket."

"And you kept him and named him Cheddar." He smooths a hand up and down my back.

"I did. That cat saved my life just as much as I did his." I gulp in air, frantically trying to calm down, but it's all out now, and it's up to Owen to decide if he wants to stay. Finding and rescuing Cheddar was both a high and a low of my life. Not everyone knows about it and how I got here. Something told me I needed to tell Owen, and it came pouring out, and like a faulty tap, I couldn't stop once I started.

I can feel the fuzziness slipping in, and I can't stop the tears. My legs are shaking as I sag. I can't punch any of this back down now that it's out. My cat. My past. My fucking inability to have anyone love me.

I collapse into Owen.

TWENTY-TWO

Owen

PARKER HAS SLUMPED INTO me, and I'm holding most of his weight. I ease him back into the chair he was in and kneel in front of him. He's so pale and his tears are still flowing as he squeezes his eyes shut. My heart is pounding as I try to figure out what to do or say. I've never dealt with anyone in such an emotional state, but I know enough to know what I do next is going to make a difference. I just don't want it to be bad.

Squeezing his hands, I run my thumbs over his knuckles. "Parker, sunshine, I need you to tell me if there's anything else we need to do for the kittens. Can you do that?"

He sits silently for so long that I'm about to try again, but he speaks up, his voice barely above a whisper. "We're done."

"Perfect. We need to get you back to your room now. Can you walk with me, babe?"

Jesus, what happened in the last hour to this funny, bubbly man? He's an empty shell. I reach over to the pile of towels we brought over and do my best to wipe the tears and snot from his face. It's like the light in the lighthouse went out and he doesn't know where to go anymore.

"Come on sunshine, let's get you home." I grab his elbow to guide him from the chair and he stands, wobbling, until I wrap an arm around his waist to hold him up. He leans into me, pulling his feet along like bricks of concrete.

I struggle with him through the doors of the shelter, fishing the key out of his pocket to lock the door behind us. I half drag, half steer Parker across the lot to Auslo's Loft and climb the steps to the entrance. I bite down a curse, forgetting the residents have codes for the entrance and not keys.

"Parker, can you enter your code so we can get inside, please?"

He stares blankly at the keypad for so long I fear I'll have to call someone inside for help. Finally, he lifts his hand and punches a code with the speed of a sloth on sleeping pills and the door opens. I help him take off his shoes and coat and lead him through the kitchen to his room. It smells heavenly and my stomach growls with the amazing aroma of beef and gravy. The ladies are setting a table and when they see me supporting Parker, Janice rushes forward.

"Do you need our help, Owen? What happened?"

Parker mumbles, "Just Owen." So I continue leading him that way. "We're okay. I'll find you later, but don't hold dinner for us."

"Of course, we'll save you each a plate, love. Give us a shout if you need anything." In a lower voice, she whispers. "If you call Jake, he can help."

I nod in acknowledgement and hoist Parker up the stairs. Once inside, I close the door and lower him to his bed. His eyes are bloodshot and puffy, skin still pale and my heart breaks at the pure sadness etched on his face.

"What can I do for you? I'd love to run you a bath, but I know you don't have a tub."

"I'm tired." He whispers.

I search around his room and find some discarded sleep pants. He still hasn't moved, and I know this is going to take some effort on my part. Like a wet noodle, Parker allows me to undress him. The only sound he makes is the occasional sniffle, but his eyes follow my every move. I change into my own sleep pants and wonder where it all went wrong today. I asked him about Cheddar, and this happened.

I pull the blankets back. "Come on sunshine. Snuggle in." He slides over to take the wall side and I slide behind him, big spoon to his little spoon. He holds my hand with a strength I wouldn't think he had after today. Kissing the back of his neck, I make a promise to myself to let nothing like this happen to him again if I can help it. It's killing me to see him like this.

"Please don't leave." His voice is barely a whisper, but I hear it loud and clear.

"I'm not going anywhere. Get some rest."

I wait until his breathing evens out, and he's sound asleep before I ease myself away to find his phone and sneak into the bathroom.

It doesn't take me long to find Jacob's number since he's his most frequent contact, and I enter his number into my phone and hit call.

I peek through a crack in the door to find Parker still sound asleep before Jacob's voice comes over the line.

"Hello?" There's lots of laughter and noise in the background and I feel horrible for coming to him on his vacation and when it sounds like a party is going on.

"Hey Jake, it's Owen. Can we talk?"

"Owen! Ah... ya... give me a sec."

I hear muffled conversations and noise, then it's quiet and it's just Jacob.

"Is everything okay, Owen? I wasn't expecting to hear from you."

I sigh. "I'm sorry to bother you, and I don't know if everything is okay. Parker had some kind of meltdown today. I was hoping you'd be able to help me."

"Oh. Shit. He was probably due for one soon. I should have been there."

"What? No. You deserve to be away, and I'm here for him. I just don't know what to do. Or what happened, really." I peek out the door and Parker is still out cold. "He's been asleep for almost an hour now. I helped him take care of the cats and we talked about getting pets and the next thing I knew he was crying and snotting and couldn't stop. I almost had to carry him back here."

Jacob clears his throat. "Did you talk about Cheddar by chance?"

"We did. That's what started this whole thing."

"He doesn't tell many people that story. First, you should know that if he did, he trusts you completely."

"Oh. Wow. Okay... what do I do? Tell me everything I need to do here, Jake. It's Christmas, and he's going to be angry he missed it. I'm not leaving him alone."

That's not even up for negotiation. I promised I wasn't going anywhere and to be honest, I don't want to.

"Short answer is just be there and take care of him. He's usually able to function after a day, but he won't be back to normal for a few days. He'll be quieter and he might be clingy, but Owen... he needs someone to accept it all. If you can't be there to do it, I can try to reach Micha..."

"No. Nobody else. We already had plans, Jacob. I'll be here."

There's some noise in the background and Jacob's muffled voice speaks to someone else before he comes back on the line. "It's a lot to handle Owen, you sure about this?"

"Completely. Does he need a doctor? I can get him to a doctor."

"It wouldn't hurt for him to go back to therapy, but he doesn't want to. You have to understand, Parker feels like he has something to prove. He wants to do it his way. Just be there. Get him into a shower, force him to eat, listen to him if he talks." More laughter and shouting come across the line. "Listen, I need to go. I'll text you anything else, okay? Thank you for being there for him."

"Thanks Jake, have a good Christmas. I'll be in touch."

Ending the call, I let myself out of the bathroom and sit down in the chair in the corner of his room — the one that he uses to hold laundry and not actually sit in. I park myself there and watch the sleeping lump across from me while I turn Jacob's words over in my mind.

Parker trusts me.

He opened his heart to me and needs someone. As I watch his purple duvet rise and fall with his deep breaths, I replay the whole day. The sex, the hesitant way he asked me here, the fun we've had the past few weeks. We've had a lot of fun together, in and out of work. We've learned about each other and I knew he had a rough childhood, but I never suspected it went so deep that asking an innocent question about how he got his cat would cause him to go over the edge.

A scratch comes at the door, followed by a tiny paw poking through the crack, and I chuckle. I quietly cross the room and open the door for Cheddar. "Hey big guy, sorry I wasn't thinking about you. I had to make sure your dad was okay first." He rubs against my legs, and I pick him up before placing him next to Parker and the big orange puff ball snuggles into Parker. Even in his sleep, Parker's hand finds the cat and strokes him before falling still again.

I return to my chair and watch both of them this time. Jake's words spin around and around until I suck in a breath.

There's only one thing this means, Parker has feelings for me.

The next morning, Christmas morning, I drag Parker into the shower and force him to wake up, even a little. But he's not into it. He doesn't want to join the rest of the residents for Christmas morning, and it breaks my heart.

"Can I bring your breakfast up here for you, sunshine? I need you to eat something."

"Just cereal."

I got words! This is good. "I can do that. Any kind you like?"

"Fruit Loops or Honeycomb, something sugary."

I smooth his hair back as he lies down on the bed again, watching me. "I'll be right back with breakfast for you."

I fly down the stairs, almost slamming into Brandie at the bottom.

"I'm so sorry. I need cereal for Parker."

She shows me the pantry and pulls a bowl and spoon out before leaning against the counter. "He's not joining us today, is he?"

I shake my head. "I don't think so." I pause before adding milk to the bowl and take a banana from the fruit basket. He needs to have good food too. Christmas be damned. "Was there anything he was supposed to do today? Something I could help with instead?"

She pats my arm. "I think you're helping where it's needed most right now. We'll be okay. Won't be the same without him, but it's a small group."

I tuck the banana in my pocket and take the bowl of cereal with milk up to Parker's room.

"Fruit loops and milk for you." I hand him the bowl and a tiny smile crosses his lips as he takes it from me. "I also have something in my pants for you." I wiggle my eyebrows and roll my hips in the worst possible imitation of being sexy, making sure the shape of the banana is obvious in my pants.

He snorts and milk dribbles down his chin. I silently congratulate myself for getting him to smile, even if it was just a quick one. "It's a banana. You and your filthy brain." I smile and place the banana on the bed while he eats his cereal, eyes aimed at the floor.

"Thank you."

"Don't thank me for bad jokes or I'll keep making them. You don't want that."

He hands me the bowl and I place it on the dresser for later as he crawls back to his place on the bed. Sad brown eyes find mine, and my heart skips. "Can you just snuggle with me for a while?"

"Of course I can, whatever you need."

I slide in next to him and he drapes himself over me, tangling his legs in mine. I soothe my hand up and down his back, and then it hits me. Like an arrow making the bullseye on a dartboard, this feels right. Parker may not be himself right now and we've got a long way to go to really know each other, but right now? Holding him, bringing him fruit loops and a banana and forcing him into the shower? It makes me feel complete. Caring for someone on such an intimate level is something I never thought I needed.

I drop a kiss to his head and hold him tighter. "I'm not going anywhere. Rest if you need it. I'll be here."

His arms wrap tighter around me as he rests against me, once again falling asleep.

TWENTY-THREE

Parker

THE ROOM IS DARK, my snowflake night light isn't spinning its patterns and Cheddar is draped across my feet like a fuzzy log. When I turn my head to see the time, it's almost 9 P.M... and Owen isn't here. I flick on my bedside lamp and sit up. His bag is still in the corner so he hasn't left completely and my heart slows back down.

I settle back and stare at my ceiling. I'm a fucking mess. I broke down for the first time in years, and it was in front of Owen. Just when I think I can't embarrass myself any more, I come up with a killer of a show — and on Christmas Eve. I've even missed Christmas Day. I wiggle my legs to draw Cheddar's attention and he crawls up to me, flopping beside me with a chirp and a purr.

"Who knew you'd cause some of my finest moments, Cheesy? Good thing I love you."

He's not the only thing I have feelings for. Owen, by all rights, should have dropped me in my room and fled as fast as he could. Nobody wants to be responsible for a screw up. Yet he's still here, bringing me cereal, forcing me to shower and holding me until I fall asleep. Only a few people have ever seen me like this, and none of them have cuddled me as I slept. Until now.

Does this mean he's just being nice, or does this mean he really cares about me? I shouldn't get my hopes up if he does care, though. Things can change too soon. It's best I don't allow myself to get attached. I need to pursue one goal at a time, and it's got to be a career first. As much as I want the love and belonging that always lies just out of reach, I need to not let this distract me.

My door clicks open, and I turn to see Owen slide in quietly.

"Hi."

"Hey, you're awake. How are you?"

He sets a plate on the dresser, and I get a whiff of turkey and gravy and my stomach growls. We both laugh at the volume of it.

"I'm hungry, apparently."

I sit up against the wall, crossing my legs as he hands me the plate of food.

"I got you a little of everything. I didn't know what you liked or if you'd even eat, but I wanted to be prepared." He rubs the back of his neck. "I already ate. It's delicious."

I pick up the fork and jam some stuffing and turkey in my mouth as Owen gets undressed. I watch him as he folds his pants and shirt before placing them neatly on the back of my chair before settling next to me. This is what it must feel like to have a family or someone who loves you enough to be there through everything. My heart aches at what I've been missing all these years. If I had this to come home to, would I even have these meltdowns anymore? It's a tempting thought.

"I went over and took care of the cats for you today. I even fed the little guy his bottle." He smiles proudly and I have to return it.

"Thank you Owen. You didn't have to do that."

"I did it to help you and you said the volunteers were all busy. I couldn't let them be hungry on Christmas day."

He squeezes my knee and I occupy my mouth with food in case it blurts out something it shouldn't. "Did the kids at least have a good day? Brandie and Janice handled the meals for them, no issue?"

He laughs. "Oh yes. Meals were devoured and presents were shared. I ducked in and out when I could."

"You could have joined them all day, though. I slept for most of it." I push around the food on my plate, saddened that he didn't even enjoy Christmas dinner with me, like I'd wanted when I asked him to come back here.

He nods and forces me to look into his ocean eyes, and I want to cry all over again. "I could have. But you needed me. I said I would be here, and I meant it."

I have a hard time swallowing. I'm not used to people being there for me. Yes, I have great friends who will come running, but they love me differently. This is different. It makes me hope for things I've never had before, and I'm scared shitless about having my heart broken.

"How did the bottle feeding go? Everyone doing okay?" A change of subject seems to be best to get my mind and heart off the path it's heading.

"Everyone is great. I gave Mabel extra hugs and sat with her. In fact, I think I might know a lady who would love to adopt her. Next time I see her, I'll ask." He takes my plate and sets it on the dresser again, before settling and continuing his story. "The little one drank well and was playing with his siblings. They were so cute. I probably played with them far too long, but the mom seemed grateful. Ever see a cat look at you like that?" He chuckles. "I swear whatever the cat equivalent to having a bath by herself is, that's what she had."

I smile, noticing how he's grown animated as he talks and he's truly into it. "Squirt really held his own, playing with his littermates. Is that what parenting feels like? I was so proud of him fighting back." He laughs again and squeezes my hand.

I laugh back. "It's very satisfying to see them flourish and beat the odds. Thanks for helping. Really."

A comfortable silence rests until I realize I missed the ugly sweater party. I groan. "Owen, I've ruined your whole holiday. You missed the ugly Christmas sweater party at Dom's."

"You ruined nothing. Shit happens. I spoke to Micha, it's fine." Another gentle squeeze to my knee. "He offered to have us over one day this week if you're up to it."

"What did Micha tell you?" I pick at the edge of the duvet. Micha and Jacob are the only ones that ever had to deal with me like this. They know what it's like. I hope they at least encouraged Owen to put up with me.

"Nothing I didn't already know, Parker." He cups my cheek, turning me to face him. "Only that you're special, amazing and a good person. I can agree with that." He brushes his lips over mine. "You're also kind, a ray of sunshine on any bleak day and someone I hope to get to spend more time with."

I blink back threatening tears. "Even after what happened? I'm a bent paper clip in your very ordered life."

"I liked you just fine before this happened. We all need help in our lives. This is yours." Another gentle kiss has me sigh against his lips. "I'll take the wonky paper clip if it means you'll still sing with a wooden spoon in my kitchen to annoy me."

I laugh and melt into him, relishing the gentle touches and kisses, the whispers across my ear. Of all the people I ever thought would be the one to help me through one of my breakdowns, I never thought it would be Owen.

"I don't do it to annoy you." I straighten up and look at his handsome face. "I do it to make you smile. You have the most amazing smile."

"Do I?"

I trace my fingertip across the lines near his eyes. "You have these adorable lines here that crinkle when you smile, and when you laugh... they're super sexy." I trace the spot on his cheek where his dimple shows up. "Right here, when you smile really wide, you have the cutest dimple that pops up. It's not huge, but it's there. When I sing and get extra silly, it's because I'm trying to see your dimple."

He clears his throat, and I lay my head on his chest. His voice is scratchy. "Nobody ever told me that before. I've never noticed."

"That's unfortunate, because those two things can really make my day."

"I'll try to remember that."

Cheddar chirps and crawls up between us, wedging his way in, so we have to separate and let him get comfortable. We both laugh and adjust ourselves for comfort, Cheddar in the middle with two hands petting him, and Owen and I spend the most beautiful night sharing stories about anything and everything. I feel the most normal I have felt in the past few days, and I don't want this little cocoon away from adulting and real life to ever end.

"I'm coming!"

I bounce down the steps to the kitchen, leaving my room finally after being holed up in it for almost four days.

Four days of being tended to by Owen and feeling like I was at the center of his life. Four days of the heady feeling of being the subject of his sole attention. Today though, it ends. I need to get back the feeling of normality. We're meeting Dominic and Micha for lunch at the diner and spending the evening at Owen's. Dominic and Owen want to go snowshoeing on Owen's property, Micha and I... well, we'd rather stay warm.

I find Owen leaning against the wall in the kitchen, waiting for me.

"Sorry, I had to pack, and I wasn't sure what I needed."

"You need yourself and an appetite. After that, we'll figure it out. Let's go."

"Let me just say a quick bye to Jacob." I dash down the hall to the office and Jacob is typing furiously at his laptop. His head whips up at my arrival.

"You're off then?" He takes his glasses off and rubs at his eyes. He's always so stressed and tired. I really need to spend time with him to find out what's going on.

"Yes, I'm heading out. I'll be back tomorrow to check on Cheddar. Don't expect me back tonight, though."

He nods before turning back to his laptop. "Jake... let's catch up soon, okay?"

He smiles, it barely reaches his eyes. "Find me when you get back, and we will. Have fun."

I scurry back down the hall and shrug into my coat, joining Owen for the short drive to the diner.

"Everything okay with Jacob?"

We exit his vehicle, and he holds the door open for me to go inside. "He seems exhausted and stressed. I'm going to catch up with him when I go back home next."

I see Dom and Micha at a table and wave. Owen's hand on my back, even through my winter jacket, thrills me. It's a quiet gesture to most, but to me, it's an indication that he cares. That he's with me.

"Parker!" Micha leaps up and hugs me, like he hasn't seen me in forever. Well, I suppose it's been at least a month since we've caught up. In Micha's world, that *is* forever.

"Hey Micha! How are things?"

As we all get comfortable and order, it doesn't escape me that Owen has taken my jacket and hung it on the post for me. He now sits with his arm over the back of my chair, and I'm close to hyperventilating with him sitting so close to me in front of friends. Sure Dominic caught us in the office, but this is different. It's in public.

Dominic is deep in conversation with Owen about paths on his property and some kind of outdoor stuff. Micha leans in close.

"Are you guys a thing or what? I feel like I'm missing most of the story." He sucks on the straw in his root beer, glancing at Owen to make sure he's not paying attention. "Like, he's sort of claiming you right now and you're blushing."

I lean across the table, meeting Micha in the middle, and our noses almost touch. "We can't talk about this here." I hiss. "Nobody is making claims."

"Dom says Owen is smiling more. That has nothing to do with you?"

"I'm not talking about it here."

He sighs and leans back in his chair. He pokes Dominic to get his attention. "I'm gonna go pee. We'll be back." He kisses Dominic on the cheek, stands and tugs on my hand. "I don't go alone. Come on."

Owen bites back his smile, and that puts me more at ease. Seeing him comfortable, knowing I'm going off with Micha to talk about him. He's not stupid and I know he heard us. "Excuse me."

Micha tugs me down the hall to the restrooms and pulls me inside. "I do really have to go. But we need to talk."

He steps into a stall and locks it behind him, continuing to talk over the door. "From what I know, Dom told Owen to have more fun. Before you know it, he's dressing up as Santa and Dom catches you two making out in the office." The toilet flushes and he exits, still talking while he washes his hands. "Then you disappear for a few days after Owen has you spend the night. I know you had one of your episodes and I'm sorry, P." He dries his hands and places his hands on his hips. "So... what's your story? You two hooking up or what?"

"Jeez, way to get to the point."

"Well, as much as I would love to spend all day talking to you, we're in a public bathroom and our lunch will arrive soon. Don't make me miss my chicken fingers."

I laugh. "I wouldn't dream of it." I lean against the wall, stuffing my hands in my pockets. "I don't know what we are. That's the truth."

"But there might be something? You must be banging, at least. He's got that look."

I snort. "Micah, when did you become so invasive on everyone's personal business?" I look him in the eye. "And what look are you referring to?"

He laughs. "Now you want to talk, I get it. The look on his face when you sat down, when we left the table, hell, when you entered the diner. The look that says he can't wait to get you naked. I'm going to assume it's already happened once."

"It has." He wiggles his eyebrows, waiting for details, but I can't do that. He knows this. "I'd like it to keep happening. There! Are you satisfied?"

"I'll have to be because we have to get back to the table. I've at least confirmed one thing." We exit the restroom and walk back to the table. "That Owen has finally let himself enjoy life, and he's smitten with you."

I pull on his arm to stop him. "What? He can't be smitten. Who even uses that word? Are you seventy? How do you know this?" Talk about a rapid fire of questions and why am I holding my breath while I wait for his answer?

"Parker, he spent three days with you at the worst time of your life. I offered to take his place, and he said no. That means something."

He prances back to our table just as the food arrives, leaving me gaping after him. Owen stayed because he's nice. That's all this is.

At least that's what I'm going to keep telling myself.

TWENTY-FOUR

Owen

"I'M SORRY DOM AND Micha changed their minds about snowshoeing. It would've been fun."

We're on our way back to my place, and I'm not overly disappointed with the sudden change of plans. I've been thinking about getting Parker naked since the last time I had him here. I'm also no fool. Micha dragging Parker off to the restroom was his way to get info from Parker and left me with Dom to field many of the same questions.

Other than knowing I enjoyed being with Parker for both the good and the bad, I really didn't know what, if any, label to put on this thing with us. It started out as fun and I'd like to keep it that way, even though he could be leaving. That's months away, at least. Might as well seize the day. Turn over a new leaf, or whatever new age crap they spout these days.

"Somehow, I'm sure Micha is fine staying inside and snuggling. He's not what you would call a fan of winter."

"I know that." I squeeze his knee. "So, what would you like to do instead? No cats to worry about it, no rushing anywhere. Just us."

He looks out the window as I drive. Nothing but trees and snow passing by. I wonder what he's thinking? We've been through a lot together the past week. I know he didn't like me seeing him have a breakdown, but it gave me a greater perspective on what lies underneath the surface of my sunshine baker. I have a whole new respect for him, if I'm honest with myself. I was privileged to grow up with a family and wonderful memories, something so many take for granted.

I've seen so much more of Parker than I ever thought I would, and while I only meant to have fun, I feel like we could have more if we wanted it. I'm not sure he does, though. This is a means to pass the time until he puts his life on course. If I try to ask how he sees this going, it may just spook him off and I'm shocked to say, I'm not ready for that.

He turns his adorable face towards me. "Surprise me. Just leave out the hot tub this time." He laughs and I follow along.

"It's a shame that didn't work out for you. You could always try it without wine and see how it works."

"I prefer bubble baths, I think."

"That can be arranged." I run through what I hope is a romantic — or at least seductive — idea in my head. "I have an idea then."

We drive up my long and winding driveway and the motion lights switch on when we get closer to the house. "It's so cool how it knows you're home. It's like all these little lights whisper, "He's *here*" and turn on to greet you." Parker chuckles and my breath catches as he looks relaxed and happy for the first time in days.

"Did I just make it weird? I made it weird, didn't I? Sorry, too many books as a kid. I have an active imagination."

Clearing my throat, my voice comes out raspy and sore. "No, it's not weird. It's cute and you look beautiful right now." He does. I had to blurt it out because my mouth was working faster than my brain and I didn't want to keep it inside.

Parker stops laughing. His flushed face and parted lips set my heart pounding. "I guess I one-upped you on making things weird. Sorry."

"It's okay."

We exit the bronco and for the entire walk up to the front door, my heart is in my throat. My hands itch with a need to grab him and kiss him. Like an addict needing a fix, I must touch my lips to his or I'm going to lose my mind.

"You know, I didn't have time to ask you last time. Does your w..."

Whatever Parker was saying, I don't let him finish. I kick the door shut with my foot and grab his arm to spin him and pin him against it before smashing my mouth to his. It's all teeth and battling tongues as we both claw at each other in a frantic effort to get closer.

My arm gets stuck in my coat and Parker's gets caught on the door handle as we lurch through the mudroom, laughing and kissing.

"Owen, stop... my boots."

I laugh as I let him go long enough to loosen the laces on his boots while I rip mine off, throwing them into the mudroom and hoping they land somewhere safe-ish.

As soon as Parker is upright again, boots removed and the rest of our winter gear leaving a trail from the mudroom to the living room, I reel him into me again, kissing along his collarbone and nipping lightly. Not enough to leave the marks he likes — not yet anyway.

"Why is it... ah... whenever we're here... oh god... "

I smile against his skin as I find his sensitive spot right at the hollow of his throat and nip at it. "Do you have something to say, Sunshine?"

"I could if you'd stop doing... gah... that."

I reluctantly take my lips off him and step away, pushing my stiffening cock to a less uncomfortable position. "What is it? Is this not okay?" *God, I hope it's okay.*

"Uh... I don't actually remember what I was going to say." He breathes, his flushed skin glows, and he's so damn beautiful. His puffy pink lips and the scratches on his neck from my stubble, are perfect.

"Did you want me to stop?" *Please say no.*

"Not at all. I just didn't think this was your plan tonight. I thought you had something special planned."

Oh. That.

"You're right. You wanted me to surprise you, and I had a plan." I pass a hand over my face. I don't want to keep that plan though, because I'm an impatient bastard. "Would you believe me if I said this was part of my plan?"

His deep laugh is full and a delight to my ears. "I wouldn't believe you one bit." He steps into me, circling his arms around my waist. "But I'm also not complaining if you want to go off plan."

"Good, because I'm so far off plan I'm going off-roading." I kiss him again. He's addictive. "The good thing is, we'll end up dirty either way."

We kiss and stumble towards the couch, falling on it in a heap of tangled limbs. He rips his lips from mine, and I freeze. "I remembered what I wanted to ask."

"What?"

"When we came home, I was going to ask you a question, but you got all up in my face and I didn't get to."

"Okay, ask away." For the love of god, I hope it's a good question.

"I was going to ask you how your pellet stove worked. How is it always so warm in here when you come home and it's a wood stove? Doesn't it need to be fed or something?"

"Are you seriously asking me this right now? You've stopped the prelude to sex with that question?"

He slides a hand over my straining cock, drawing a gasp from my lips. "I didn't stop it. I just remembered what it was."

"It's on a timer. Is that a good enough answer for you?"

He laughs and takes his shirt off, pitching it behind him somewhere before he's back on top of me. "You could have said magic for all I cared. I just wanted to ask before I forgot again."

We somehow work the rest of our clothes off and he's right, it's very warm in here and I'm not talking about the wood stove heat. I'm so hot for Parker I could combust. After the last four days of him not being himself, I've missed him. Everything about him and I'm so damn happy to have him back. When was the last time I ever felt like I missed someone? Too damn long.

"I've always wanted to have sex by a fireplace. A big romantic scene, you know?" Parker is losing his clothes faster than a kid loses their mittens and I'm racing to keep up with him.

"Is that what you want?" I trail more kisses down his neck. "I can make that happen, you know."

He pulls away and looks into my eyes. That silly smile is back, and it makes my heart flop like a fish out of water. I struggle to get my socks off with one hand while the other slides up this thigh. "But the floor is hard, and I don't know if I'll like that."

"I can solve that problem." I hop over to my ottoman, still struggling to remove a sock and whip out a soft blanket, brandishing it with pride. "See?" I spread it on the floor in front of my fireplace, which is really not a fireplace, but if it's what he wants, I'll make it happen. I also can't hold out to move this some place else either. "Spontaneous fireside sex, as requested."

I'm down to my boxers, finally, ready to send them flying, but Parker is only watching me. "Parker, get your half naked ass over here."

He crosses the few steps toward me, shucking his pants along the way. "That's not a very thick blanket. What about my back?" He grins again, egging me on and, of course, I take the bait.

"I'll be on the bottom." I pull him against me, greedy hands grasping his firm ass. He wraps his arms around my neck, pressing into me with a contented hum.

"How generous of you."

"I'm a giver. What can I say? Let me be your cushion."

"You already are." He whispers against my lips, and the rush of hurrying to get naked and get each other off grinds to a halt with the truth of his words.

I swallow hard. The playfulness dissipates with every second I gaze into his soulful brown eyes. My hands caress his face, and my heart beats an erratic rhythm. "Then let me do it again."

With a reverence that wasn't there earlier, I kneel at his feet, peeling his boxers down with a kiss to his abdomen. I run my nose along his thigh, ending with a kiss on his hip and tugging him to follow me down to the floor. I lose the rest of my clothes and settle him on top of me.

"Do what you want." I rasp. My hands still grip his hips, holding him against me like I'm afraid he's going to float away like a child's untethered balloon.

"What are the odds you have lube down here?"

I snort. "Very good." I reach my hand over, grabbing the foot of the ottoman and dragging it towards us. Leaning up, I dig around inside and find the bottle I was hoping was still there. "Ta da!"

He raises an eyebrow in question. "If you must know, sometimes I'm too lazy to go upstairs and if I feel like jerking off, it's right here."

A smile flirts with his lips as he takes the bottle from me. "You're full of surprises, aren't you?"

"Not at all. I'm just practical."

He squirts some of the liquid into his hand and slides it down my cock. "How is it practical to keep lube in your living room?"

I groan as he slides his slicked-up hand in a torturous drag along my throbbing dick. "Because this TV is better for porn."

His hand stops its ministrations and his breath hitches. Ah, the dirty talker likes that idea. "Sunshine, you like that? Thinking of me rubbing one out while I watch someone else?"

He licks his lips, turning his burning gaze to mine. "Yes." His voice is barely a puff of air, a squeak in the giant room.

"Come here." I pull him towards me and make him sit on my thighs. His glorious cock twitches, and this could be over quick. I sit up and nestle us together, pulling him closer until I can have my lips on him. Guiding our hands, I wrap us together around both our lengths, my hand covering his, and roll my hips. "Show me how you'd do it if you were here watching."

"Jesus Owen." His hand moves at a rapid pace, hips matching as he slides us together.

I let him take over, using me in his own fantasy. He's beautiful. Fucking beautiful. His skin shines with a thin layer of sweat and his chest and neck are pink with arousal. I lean back on my hands and watch him let himself go, using me like his own personal pleasure device, and I'm loving it. I'm loving all of it.

"Parker..." I gasp as my orgasm comes out of nowhere, far too soon, and I paint myself with hot ropes of cum. Parker never stops, and I watch him rush to his finish, eyes blazing and never leaving mine as he comes all over me with a groan.

Something else comes out of nowhere and it hits me like a tonne of bricks.

"That was so fucking hot. Next time you should play your favourite movie." Parker falls onto my chest, and I wrap my arms around him.

I roll his words around: *next time.*

He wants a next time and that couldn't make me happier. He wants a next time, but I just realized I want more than that.

I want him all the time. Forever, if he'll stay.

Twenty-Five

Parker

I HUM ALONG TO the song on the radio, deep in concentration as I pipe an icing decoration on a special birthday cake for a woman turning eighty. It's not a wedding cake, but it's keeping my eye on the prize. I need to have my cake skills in top form if I want to work with the best. Besides, I know Hazel is going to love the extra flower decorations I added.

The days back at work have all blurred together, and it's already mid January. Working with Owen every day and spending almost every night with him has been amazing. Our new dynamic is easy. I get to wake up with him most mornings and it's a refreshing change to have someone who understands the ridiculously early mornings. The bonus is seeing that gorgeous smile on his face all day. He's been a different person since we started whatever it is we're doing.

We haven't labeled ourselves and I honestly don't know what he thinks of this arrangement, but I know one thing, I love whatever it is. He accepts my quirks and quarks, sometimes joins me singing in the kitchen now, and the sex we have is out of this world. It doesn't matter if it's a quick and dirty morning wake-up or a longer, intimate session. Every time he touches me, I see stars and wonder if it's something else, or just the newness of us.

"Hey Sunshine." Speak of the devil. Owen enters the kitchen, plants a kiss on my cheek, and continues to the fridge.

The fact he's given me a nickname hasn't escaped my notice. I love it. It makes me feel beyond special to have captured his attention to the point he gives me a nickname. Every time he says it, my heart bounces around like a ping-pong ball.

"Hey yourself, handsome. What are you up to?"

He exits the fridge with a refill box for the milk machine. "Paige is low on milk, just hefting this out to her."

He stops next to my table, admiring my cake. "Hazel will love that. How did you know she likes orchids?"

The flowers I sculpted are delicate lady slipper orchids, and I know she loves them because she told me. Hazel ended up being the one Owen thought would be perfect for adopting Mabel, and he was right. Mabel took to her new home and owner like a duck to water, and I was thrilled. She talked my ear off about the orchids that grew in the bushes near her house. I even remembered it was the pink one she loves the most. When her daughter ordered the cake and invited us to the party, I knew I'd make them for her.

"She told me the day we brought Mabel over. I thought she'd like them."

"She'll love them. They're gorgeous." He sets the milk down and gets closer, leaning his head down for an eye-to-eye view. "You're so talented, Parker, truly."

I feel the heat rise in my cheeks with his praise. "Thank you. I'm proud of them."

He bites on his lip and nods his head. "You should be. You're good at what you do and could teach people yourself, you know."

Owen picks up the milk and leaves me alone with my cake and his words. A heavy sigh leaves me. I can't teach people. A few pretty orchids aren't enough to prove myself. If I want any kind of status to back up my work, I need the experience I'll get from the apprenticeship at Cake Holes. I should hear from them soon. The next intake start date is February first, and that's only a few weeks away.

I cover the cake and set it in the fridge for pick up tomorrow. My stomach churns now that I realize the window of acceptance is closing in. I haven't even planned on how I'd get there yet. The packing and the driving. What will the accommodations be like, even?

I snort a laugh. I'm not accepted yet but I'm planning like I will be. Perhaps my positivity will help the offer magically appear.

"Hey Parker, you want to come over for dinner tonight?"

Owen's smiling face — the smile that never leaves now — appears at the kitchen door. "Of course. Can we drop by my place first?"

He nods his acknowledgement and disappears again, leaving me surprised for an entirely different reason. One that wasn't part of my plan.

How do I deal with Owen if I leave?

An alarm is going off. I think. It's also really warm. Blinking my eyes open, I finally register it's Owen's alarm sounding, and he's spread half his body on top of me like a hunky man duvet. If I didn't need to reach the alarm, I'd be loving it. But he's freaking heavy in his sleep.

Heaving his arm off me and struggling to reach over him, I flail at the alarm until I mercilessly hit the right button and it silences. "Owen." I'm still tangled in his limbs and he's barely coherent. "We need to get up or we'll be late."

"A few more minutes." He mumbles into my chest, and I chuckle.

"We might be late if we lie here too long." I run my fingers through his hair. I'd love to spend the morning in bed like this today, and every day, if I could.

"It's okay. I know the boss." He squeezes me tighter as I laugh louder.

"Okay boss-man, take what you need. Just remember, it's not my fault you're tired this morning."

He snorts, still with his eyes closed, but a smile dances on his lips. "It's totally your fault. If you weren't so damn delicious, I wouldn't have stayed up so late tasting you."

I smack his shoulder. "Don't blame this on me. I'm awake and I was just as involved as you were."

He cracks open an eye. "You were." His hand finds an ass cheek with a firm squeeze. "You were an MVP in the cock riding event. Gold medal for enthusiasm. No half-assed involvement from you." He laughs at his own joke and my cheeks heat as I remember last night's... events.

"I think that's a compliment on my level of participation."

With a quickness I wasn't prepared for, he wraps me up and flips me on top of him. His sleepy eyes find mine as he pulls me down for a kiss. It's not a quick good morning peck. It's lazy and heated, consuming and passionate and it's so overwhelming I break away and push off him with a laugh.

I roll out of his arms and off the bed. "We need to get up! No distracting me."

I grab my phone and my overnight bag and head to the bathroom. I look over my shoulder and catch my breath when I notice Owen watching me with those baby blue eyes. That's not a casual glance and I need to get a grip before I jump to conclusions and embarrass myself.

I start the shower, expecting Owen to follow me, but he's still lying on the bed. Oh well, he'll get here when he's ready. We all have sluggish mornings. My phone chimes and a quick glance shows Jacob's name on the screen. I read the message and almost drop the phone.

Jacob: There's a letter from Cake Holes here for you!

I lock the screen with a shaking hand and swallow back the lump in my throat.

Looks like the day I've been waiting for is finally here.

TWENTY-SIX

Owen

I ALMOST TOLD PARKER I was in love with him this morning.

At the last moment, I reeled it back in and swallowed the words down. This is only fun for him. He has his whole life in front of him still and doesn't want to get serious with an established older man. Not that I'm that much older, but my life is already on its path. I'm not striving to find myself in a world of cake creating and struggling to find my professional path. I've already done that, and he needs to as well.

Even though he's had a shitty route in his life and needs someone who loves him just as he is, it can't be me.

"You're really quiet this morning. Is everything okay?"

Parker's voice brings me out of my gloomy thoughts. His hand on my thigh causes me to look over at him as I drive us to work. I snap my eyes back to the road before I get lost in his warm, brown eyes and remember how he bit his lip as he rode me like a champ most of last night.

Or how he fell asleep on my chest, and I stared at him so long I didn't fall asleep until two hours before the alarm went off. The real reason it was hard for me to get up today wasn't the marathon sex, but me lost in my head and accepting this was turning into something — for me, at least.

"I'm just still tired, I guess. I'm okay."

I squeeze his hand to reassure him, and he returns to gazing out the window. There's nothing to see there in the dark of an early winter morning, but I suppose it's better than staring at me and wondering why I'm so quiet.

"It's not me, is it?"

His question catches me off guard. "Of course not. If there was something you did that was bothering me, I'd tell you."

He nods, but as we pull into the parking lot, I can tell something is off with him, too. His bubbling morning attitude is flat and dull, and the smile doesn't reach his eyes. Before he can exit the vehicle, I grab his hand.

"Is everything okay with you?"

"Right as rain, boss." I'm still sure he's hiding something. It's all over his beautiful face. The little lines between his eyebrows are back and the ones around his eyes are missing. He's struggling with something he doesn't want to share with me. While I can understand he may think I can't help, I feel hurt that he won't tell me.

"Never bullshit a bullshitter, Parker. I know something's wrong."

He sighs, looking outside again and avoiding my eyes. "I don't want to talk about it right now, *please*?" The begging in his voice gives me pause. I won't be another person in his life to strong-arm him into doing what he doesn't want to do.

"Let's get the day started, then."

I open the door before he can answer and wait for him to follow me. Once I know he's crunching in the snow behind me, I walk to the front and let us into The Bean. We do what we do every morning and follow the routine we quickly came to find comfort in, but today there's something missing, and I don't know what it is.

Twenty-Seven

Parker

I MAKE MY WAY to Owen's office late afternoon, before my shift is over. He hasn't come to the kitchen all day, except to silently bring me a fresh coffee and then, he avoided looking at me. I haven't seen him smile all day, and that makes me... well, sad. I hate not seeing the big guy smile.

I knock lightly and push open the door to find Owen staring at his computer screen.

"Hey, Sunshine." He looks at his phone. "Whoa, it's home time already, is it?"

"Ya, I just wanted to come and tell you I'll spend tonight at home. It's been a few days and I should really visit with Cheddar."

The first genuine smile I've seen since this morning shows itself and a weight lifts from my shoulders.

"I think that's a good idea. He probably misses you."

He stands to stretch and once again, I'm caught up with wondering where his mind went today. I wanted so badly to tell him I loved him last night, but I didn't. I couldn't.

Now I'm torn again. I walk into his arms and relish the feel of the safety he provides.

"Not as much as I'll miss you. I sleep great at your place."

His arms squeeze me tighter as he plants a kiss on the top of my head. "I sleep great when you're there, too."

"I'll see you tomorrow then?"

"Of course. Give Cheddar a hug for me."

I leave him be and gather my things to walk the short distance to Auslo's Loft.

I need to open that letter.

I've been staring at a piece of paper for thirty minutes now. Not just any paper. It's an envelope that has the power to change my life. This ordinary white envelope, sealed by a stranger's slobbery tongue, can turn my world upside down.

I run my finger over the return address again, Cake Holes Bakery. Why am I hesitating to open this? I've been waiting for months for this to arrive, but now that it's here... I don't want to know. But I do... and that's my problem.

Cheddar hops up beside me on the bed as I flip the smooth white envelope over and over through my fingers.

"Are you going to open it or just handle it all day?"

I whip my head to the open doorway where Jake is leaning, arms crossed and watching me. "Give me time. I will."

"Pfft. Parker, you've been sitting there for fifteen minutes already."

And standing for the other fifteen minutes, until I decided I needed to sit down for whatever I found inside. Good or bad news, I knew I couldn't take it standing up.

Jake enters and takes the space next to me, unoccupied by a lump of orange cat.

"What's your issue? I thought you'd be excited?"

"I am.. but it might be a decision I have to make, and I don't know what I want to do if there's a decision." Fuck, I'm not prepared for this. This was supposed to be a simple moment. Open letter, I'm in and celebrate. Open letter and I'm out, eat lots of ice cream and wallow, then go back to work. I wasn't expecting the situation with Owen to come into play. Not even a little. He was something I never thought would happen to me, much like the letter in my hand. Of course, the stars charting my life had to have them both happen at the same damn time.

"Is this about Owen by chance?" Jacob runs a hand down by back and I drop my head to his shoulder.

"Yes, it's about Owen. He's unexpected, and I don't know how to proceed now. This was supposed to be a simple thing. Now, I don't know, because..." I trail off because how do I describe what it is with Owen? We weren't supposed to be this close. But he's made himself a part of my life in unforgettable ways. The thought of no longer having him wrap his arms around me and taste all my creations while he beams at me with pride — something I've always wanted — makes me want me to hide under the covers. How do I walk away from that? How do I give up the man that makes me feel so comfortable in my own skin and appreciates me just as I am?

"Does he know? Like, does he know you might leave?"

I run a hand through my hair and huff a sigh. "He knows I applied and that I want to make wedding cakes. We've never talked after that, because..." My voice breaks. Because we haven't made it into anything serious. We're having fun. While Owen has been nothing but amazing and showing me everything I've never experienced, there is no air of seriousness. We haven't talked about staying together. I don't even know if he sees us staying together. He's never said. He knows I may leave the bakery if I get this offer, but does that translate to him understanding I might leave him too? Fuck, it's a mess.

"I get it. You don't have to talk if you don't want to." Jacob pauses and gives me a squeeze. "But I want to know if you got in, Parker. I've been waiting along with you."

"You're right. You deserve to know, and Austin too. If it wasn't for you guys, I wouldn't even be doing this."

My heart is slamming so hard, I fear it's going to break a rib. I swallow the bile building in my throat and slide a thumb under the flap, slowly ripping the envelope open. I wipe a sweaty palm on my thigh before removing the folded papers inside.

I finally open them and my eyes blur as the sheets flutter from my fingers to the floor.

"Parker?" Jacob's voice is so far away, but he's beside me. I gulp in air and turn to him.

"I got in." My voice is a whisper. "I got in!" I shout, throwing my arms around Jake. "I can't believe they picked me... holy shit."

Jacob is pulling out his cell phone. "Can I tell Austin?"

"Of course. He deserves to know." I pick up the papers I dropped and start flipping through all the details, none of the information sinking in, except one sentence. In bright red ink right after the acceptance, the deadline looms.

I have ten days to plan and report for my first day.

Ten days left to choose between the man I'm in love with and the career I've always wanted.

TWENTY-EIGHT

Owen

I'M RUNNING LATE AGAIN this morning and this time I can't actually blame Parker, since he didn't stay over, but I'm going to blame him. He's all I've been able to think about since I woke up. I missed him more than I thought I would last night and the only thing I want to do right now is find him singing in the kitchen of The Bean and taste his lips on mine.

I shake my head as my feet crunch through the snow and carry me across the parking lot, closer to the one person who occupies my mind, both awake and asleep. I still can't believe the young man I hired such a short time ago, the one I swore I'd have nothing to do with, has worked himself seamlessly into my life. As I enter The Bean with a renewed purpose, a slower music beat than usual drifts from the kitchen through the empty dining space, causing my smile to fall slightly.

My heart leads my feet to the kitchen door, and I pause outside. The melancholy music is not what Parker usually chooses. If I know anything about him, it's music that always betrays his mood. The normal uplifting tunes I'm greeted with are absent and I don't want to interrupt. Instead of entering the kitchen as I've always done on the mornings when we haven't spent the night together, I head straight to my office.

I busy myself with settling in and try to shake the sour twisting in my gut, but I'm not alone. Parker stands at my door, pale and sad. A cloud hanging over the sunshine he carries everywhere. Fuck, I want to take him away and erase all of whatever is bothering him; be the one to erase whatever has caused such a shift in his effervescence.

I walk over to him and let him fall into my arms and I inhale the scent of his banana scented shampoo, the fresh baked goodness that seems to never leave his body, and I press him against me, imprinting it all on my soul.

"How come you didn't come to the kitchen first?" He rests his cheek against my chest.

My hands slide up and down his back. Whether to comfort him or myself, I'm unsure. "It sounded like you needed alone time. You had sad music. I wasn't sure if I should interrupt."

He laughs softly against me, the feel of it vibrating through my entire being. But it's not a contented laugh. The joy is missing. "You picked up on that, did you?"

"Are you okay?" I squeeze him tighter, not wanting to let him go.

"I... I don't know. Can we talk later?" Parker pushes away from me, his warm brown eyes roaming my face, searching for an answer to a question only he knows.

I drop a kiss to his forehead while my heart pounds at the seriousness of his tone. "Of course we can. What do you need me to do for you?" *Let me help.*

He answers by pressing his lips to mine and I'm drowning. I chase after his tongue like it's the one thing to pull me from the water and I'm craving him more than ever before. When he pulls away, his lips shine and his cheeks are rosy. I'm struggling to breathe. "Just that for now. I needed that." He runs his hand down my chest, each fingertip burns a trail under my shirt. "I'll find you after lunch."

With a final peck to my lips, he leaves the room.

I release a stuttered sigh and sit at my desk before the weight on my chest brings me to my knees.

I can't concentrate. All I can think of is how sad Parker was and the sinking feeling in my gut. He's about to tell me something I don't want to hear.

I grab my coat and tell Paige I'm stepping out for a bit, and I wander down to Dogwood Pond to clear my head. It's a clear winter day in January, meaning it's cold and sunny. As I walk down the snow packed trail to the pond, I remember how Parker and I walked here after the Christmas Market just a short time ago.

That was an amazing night. I smile to myself, remembering all the flirting and how I realized there was more to him than just a cute, smiling face. I loved how he had friends wherever we went and how he had a zest for everything, no matter how small. No one has drawn me out of my grouchy self like him. That night I smiled so much my face hurt. My belly hurt from laughter and the realization Parker was someone I enjoyed being with. He kissed me that night and filled a hole in my life I never knew was there.

My feet come to a stop at a snow-covered bench. I brush it off, taking a seat to look out on the space on the pond that's been cleared for public skating. A young woman is on the ice with a toddler now, as he shuffle-skates his way towards her. I watch in silence, a smile playing on my lips as I remember when I was small and started learning to skate too.

"Is this seat taken?"

I'm startled by my best friend's voice. "Only for someone wanting to freeze their balls on a bench in January."

He dusts off a spot and settles next to me, watching the same little boy skating.

"How did you find me?"

Dom chuckles. "Are you kidding right now? I've known you for almost thirty years and whenever you need to think, you like to go where it's quiet." I glance his way, but he continues to speak while facing forward and watching the tiny skater. "When you miss our standing lunch date and you've left The Bean, it's a safe bet I might find you here."

I say nothing, because I don't know what to tell him yet. I don't have to apologize either. Dom knows I'd never stand him up without a good reason.

"Do you want to talk about it yet?"

Another young skater is now on the ice, marginally more stable than the other one because of the hockey stick he clutches.

"I'm not even sure what it is, to be honest."

"You sure about that?"

I'm not sure about anything right now. But I know something will change soon and I don't know how to process it.

I run a gloved hand over my face, choosing my words carefully. "I think Parker is going to leave soon."

Dom nods. "Right, Micha said he applied to some fancy cake place in the city. Supposed to be a tremendous opportunity if he gets accepted."

The little hockey player shoots the puck into a net and his dad lets it go in. We clap for the goal and whistle a cheer, and we're rewarded with a stick wave from the little guy.

"I fell in love with him, Dom. I fucking fell in love with the damn guy." I swallow the lump in my throat. "Some fun, huh?"

"I figured. You gonna tell him?"

"I can't tell him. He needs to make the life he wants without me influencing his decision."

"What if he wants your input?"

I stare out at the skaters, not actually seeing them anymore. What if he asks for my opinion? I'd have to lie.

"If he asks, I can't tell him. Dom, he has his whole life ahead of him. It's a huge opportunity and he can't stay here because of me."

"What if he wants to, though? Ever think of that?"

Too often. "I'll see if that's what's on his mind tonight, but I won't come between him and his dreams. It's not right." As much as I want to be part of his dream, it's not my place to insert myself like that.

I stand and dust off my butt. "Still want lunch? I'll buy at the diner since I stood you up."

"No, I'm okay. I'll pop by to see Micha before heading back, since I'm here. I'll grab a snack later."

We walk up the path together and before Dom takes the turn for Micha's grooming shop, he pauses. "You know, O, he's an adult too. He's capable of making choices. He won't be able to make one if you don't tell him how you feel." He claps my shoulder. "In fact, you saying nothing is making the choice for him. Neither one is right."

I know Parker is capable of choices, but I don't want to be responsible for him making one he regrets.

I kill the next hour in my office doing mindless book work. Parker was in the middle of negotiating a special order with a woman when I returned. I gave him a wave, and he acknowledged, so I just had to wait. Waiting was not a strong point for me. I hated waiting for anything, especially when it had me in knots like this.

When he finally appears at my door, the relief I was hoping for doesn't come. He closes the door behind him and stands in front of me, scuffing his feet on the floor and looking anywhere but directly at me. His voice is a broken whisper.

"I got a letter yesterday."

"You heard from the bakery then?" My heart is thudding so hard and fast I feel like I might need an ambulance. I asked, and I need to know the answer, but I don't want to hear it.

"I got accepted." His words are barely audible, leaving his lips with great reluctance, like he already knows they will break me.

"That's great news Sunshine. It's everything you wanted." I step forward and fold him into my arms. Both so he can't see the shine of my unshed tears but also because I need to hold him close. "I'm so happy for you."

"I only have ten days left." He swallows hard and hugs me tight. "Ten days is all I have left here."

"We'll make it the best ten days ever, I promise."

He moves away, swiping at his eyes. "Right, the best days."

"What do you need me to do for you?" I swipe at his wet cheeks, barely holding mine back. "Um... accept my notice today, with my apologies, of course. I didn't think... I thought I'd have more time..."

As he trails off, I know what he's thinking because I'm thinking it too.

Ten days is not enough to say goodbye.

TWENTY-NINE

Parker

TIME MOVES AT WARP speed when you have a deadline. Logan's dad, Mr. Larkman, will lend me a car until I have time to find a used one for myself. With no rent to pay for the last eight months, I've saved up quite the tidy sum and Jacob had insisted I contribute nothing financially, since that's not what the shelter is about, even if I'm no longer a lost teenager.

With my transportation at least temporarily settled for the six-hour drive I have to face, the next hurdle is my accommodation. The bakery has a group house I am more than welcome to use. It's close to where I'd need to report every day and as I scour other listings for rooms to rent or affordable apartments, I'm dismayed to find the group home is my only choice. My reason for being unhappy with it, is because they don't allow pets.

"I'll take care of Cheddar while you're gone, Parker, you know that. He's happy here." I know Jacob is right and Cheddar will be fine, but he's been my buddy for eight years. I've never been without him. I'm already leaving

Owen behind. Leaving Cheddar is another gut punch I wasn't prepared for. I'm doubting if this whole thing is a good idea anymore.

The sigh leaving my lips carries the weight of a thousand worlds. "I know you won't let anything happen to him. I'm just gonna miss him. It's a long time to be away."

It's a six-month apprenticeship, and it's going to feel like six years without my cat. Longer, if I'm offered a position after that.

"Parker, you've made it through things worse than this. You can do this. You've got an entire legion of people to support you with this. This is your dream." He squeezes my shoulder. "It still is, isn't it? It's still your dream?"

"Yes?" I rub my eyes, the scratch of exhaustion taking hold of me. "I should be happy about this. I mean, I was, but... why do I feel like I have to give up everything else I have for one opportunity? Why can't I still keep what makes me happy and do this?"

Jacob only has a shoulder squeeze for an answer, because there is no answer. Better yet, the answer is simple. Nothing comes easy for me. From the drug addict mom, the abusive foster homes and the less than spectacular boyfriends, all of whom never wanted me for me. To the first shelter I escaped to, only to find they were no better than anywhere else I had temporarily called home. The hope of finding a place to belong is still a mirage glimmering in the distance, out of reach. Just once, I wanted the easy button.

I wanted to have the dream job and my apartment and a boyfriend who loved me for me. I wanted to keep my cat close and see him every night when I needed a purring, unconditional friend after a long day. These aren't big things to wish for.

"Thanks Jake. I know I have you. I'm just overwhelmed."

He stands up, and I follow him to my door. "Get some rest."

Closing my door, I return to my bed. Cheddar immediately snuggles next to me and I stroke his fur, wondering if my sacrifices now will pay off in the end, and how bumpy this road is going to get.

Each day that brings me closer to the coveted apprenticeship at Cake Holes Bakery makes me more reluctant to leave. I should be happy, but I'm not.

Each night I spend with Owen makes me feel even worse, because now we have an end date. I don't want to fall asleep every night because it's less time I can memorize his smile, see his dimple show up when he's happy and get lost in his ocean blue eyes. It's less time I can feel the safety of his arms. It's just less time with him.

I am painfully aware my crush turned into something more. After he spent the days during my meltdown with me, it's been clear that every single thing he's done for me since, has been out of kindness and a care I've never been on the receiving end of. I hoped it meant this was love. But he hasn't said those words to me and my heart aches to hear them cross his lips. To whisper those three words to me and give me the one gift I've never had.

My mind locks away every detail of our last few days together. At work Owen arrived before me and greeted me with a coffee, made just how I like it. He hung out in the kitchen more than usual under the premise of inventory, but I know he wanted to be with me. He even canceled his lunch dates with Dominic all week, instead, taking me someplace special every day.

One day he packed a picnic and drove us up to the lookout outside of town with a view of Dogwood Pond. It's January and rather cold to have a picnic, but he had the back of his Bronco piled with warm, snuggly blankets and a thermos of hot chocolate. I still remember how the warm chocolate tasted on his lips when he kissed me with a tenderness I felt to my bones. How could I ever forget?

Yesterday it was a lunchtime visit to his place, because he insisted I needed to snowshoe before I left. The weather was perfect, he said, to see the beauty of winter. I didn't want to argue about winter not being beautiful. We followed a path on his property that led us to a small, frozen pond. We sat on a bench, which he had obviously come out earlier to clear off for us, and he told me how he used to spend hours at this pond as a child, catching frogs and minnows and the occasional fish to brag about. Again, he had a lunch for us in a backpack and we ate and talked about anything and everything. I learned he's afraid of wasps and snakes which made me laugh so hard I thought I'd die from the pain. But I didn't. He showed me the icicle formations along the trees from the recent thaw and freeze cycle and I had to agree, winter could be beautiful. Especially when you shared it with someone you cared about. Everything could be beautiful then.

That night, I stayed over at Owen's. We didn't even go back to work. He surprised me by turning the hot tub's temperature down so I could handle it, because he wanted me to see how it is for him at night, to experience it without feeling ill. We avoided the wine altogether and it was the most relaxing evening I'd ever had. We soaked in the now really warm, not extra hot tub, and it was something I could get used to. We made pizza together after, goofing off and laughing before settling down and ignoring the TV show to make out like shameless teenagers on the couch. Making out that led to us being naked in front of the fireplace — the real one, not the pellet stove — in yet another choreographed scene by Owen that had my heart aching for this to mean something more.

It's getting harder to leave. All Owen needs to do is tell me how he feels, and I'd stay. I'd drop it all and stay, if only he'd ask me.

My room is now packed, boxes piled in a corner. Only a few personal items sit on the dresser, along with my bedding that I'll strip tomorrow and pack. Owen will be here tonight for the last time and while I look forward to him spending it with me, I dread the morning.

THIRTY

Owen

IT'S BEEN DIFFICULT TO keep a smile on my face as Parker's last day arrives. Like a storm cloud covering the sun, there's no brightness. The last thing I wanted to do was smile, but I did. For Parker. There's a saying that never made sense to me when I was younger: if you love something, let it go. I could never wrap my brain around why you'd want to do that... until now.

Now I understand and I wish I didn't. Every night we spent wrapped up in each other, I could see the unasked question hanging there just out of reach. Suspended like a soap bubble from a child's wand before it flies away with a breeze on an amazing adventure. Strong enough to survive the journey in the gentle breeze, but not the sharp poke of grass beneath your feet. I can't tell him how I feel and have him throw away an amazing opportunity just for me. Like the soap bubble, I need to let him find his own adventure.

I have to let the best thing I've had in my life for the last ten years leave me behind and hope that maybe, just maybe, he comes back someday. If he doesn't, well, the rest of the saying is, it wasn't meant to be.

As I walk the steps up to the shelter entrance for the last time, I almost change my mind. But I selfishly want this night with him.

Once I'm buzzed in, Parker meets me in the mudroom, the same place he kissed me for the first time. I wonder if he remembers it like I do. My heart squeezes as my eyes blink away the memory.

"Hey."

"Hey."

I chuckle, but it's flat. "When did we start being awkward with each other?"

He tries to smile. "About ten days ago, I think."

He steps into my arms, and I squeeze him hard before releasing him.

"Can we take a walk?"

"Sure, we can do that."

He grabs his coat and his oversized pom pom hat that always makes me smile, and once he's dressed, we go outside. I take his hand and guide him to the path leading to the parking lot down near the pond. The one where the Christmas market had been set up only a month ago — *how has it only been a month?* — where I realized there was more to Parker than just another smiling face. He was kind and generous and beautiful inside and out. He hid his broken pieces from everyone, never showing his cards until he trusted you, in true gambler style. When he shared parts of himself that night, I was honoured to be included.

Our feet crunch in the snow and our breath hangs frozen in the air, moisture suspended just like I want this night to be. Frozen in time and not moving forward to the morning when Parker is gone. I want the arms on the clock to stop right now and strand us here forever.

"I want to take you along the boardwalk by the pond if that's okay?"

His mittened hand squeezes mine and I feel it grip my heart. "Of course, I love walking there."

As we cross the parking lot to the entrance of the path, he stumbles and I pull him closer to me, my breath catching at his nearness.

"Sorry. I didn't see that snow chunk." His lips play at a smile but he's hiding something too.

A chuckle slips out as we cross the area where the food trucks were. "I still can't believe you ordered a hard taco in December."

"Me neither." His sunshine smile returns as I hoped, and I commit it to memory. I'm going to need it on replay when he's gone.

We walk along the boardwalk, our heavy steps echoing across the cold winter air. The feeling of finality is settling over me, making it harder to breathe.

"I'm really glad you brought me to the market that night. I don't know if I ever thanked you."

"Well, you kissed me and decided to spend more time with me, so that's thank you enough for me."

Passing under the light post I sneak a glance at his face to find him blinking away tears and swiping at his face with the back of his mitten. Maybe this was a bad idea, coming here if we're both going to be teary-eyed. I haven't even given him his gift.

"You're going to be amazing. This bakery isn't going to know what hit them. You've got this, you know. You have an army of supporters cheering you on."

"That means a lot, Owen. Thank you for the confidence, truly." He turns his face away from me as we come to the end of the boardwalk and meet the path to loop us back up to the shelter and I know he's trying to hide his sadness, pushing it down so I don't see it. But it's impossible to not see it when I'm reflecting the same thing.

I have us stop next to my Bronco and I pick up the small gift bag from the back seat. It's nothing big and fancy, but I thought it would be something he'd appreciate. Something to remember me by even if it's only for a little while.

"You got me a gift?"

"I did. I... I wanted to give you something to remember us." Because once he's gone and living his life I'll be as faded as an old photograph left on the corkboard.

He removes the tissue paper and t-shirt I had made for him and laughs. A sound that sends my heart tripping to know I caused it.

"A t-shirt that says *Bakers rise to the occasion*. I love it, Owen. Thank you."

He stretches on his tiptoes to kiss me on the cheek, but I turn my head to kiss his lips. "You're welcome Sunshine."

He takes my hand, like he always does, and we make the short walk up to his room. When I step inside, my heart shatters. I've been here every night since I knew he was leaving, but seeing the boxes piled in the corner and all the touches that made this his home missing, it's real. It's happening. There's no more time. There's no more countdown and how many more nights. This is it. He'll be gone.

"Wow, it's really empty, isn't it?"

"It is. I can't believe I have enough stuff to fill all those boxes. It's definitely more than I came with."

I settle next to him on the bed. "Well, at least two boxes have to be filled with all your crazy costumes for Halloween, Thanksgiving and Christmas. Maybe even three."

I'm rewarded with a smile. "How are you ever going to handle not having a costume-crazed baker around?"

"I don't know. It's going to take some getting used to. It's going to be quiet."

The walls are crushing me, and I don't want to make small talk with this beautiful creature. I don't want to be a simple memory, one he picks up here and there when he remembers his time at a coffee shop at the beginning of his career. I want to be a real part of his life. I want to scream for him to choose me, choose us, but I can't.

Instead, I smooth my hand over his cheek and bring my lips to his and hope he knows I see he's worth it, worth everything.

My lips trace a path along his neck, hitting the hollow in his throat that drives him crazy.

"Owen..." My name, a breathy whisper from his lips is a sound I'll store forever. We work to remove each other's clothes. My skin is too tight and my heart races as my fingers fumble with every zipper and button.

My lips and tongue follow the map of his body, covering every inch I can. Sucking and nipping my way down his smooth skin, I leave the marks he loves behind.

Don't forget me.

His body writhes, begging for more and less at the same time. My tongue, for the last time, works in tandem with my fingers to make his body sing. This body I'm not ready to leave behind.

"Owen..." My name in his breathy voice crossing his kiss swollen lips is torture to my soul, but I want to hear it again. I swallow his throbbing cock, burying my nose against his soft abs as he thrusts his hands into my hair with a strangled gasp. I choke on his length and the tears that come to my eyes mask the real ones threatening to spill. Tears, because I love him and he'll never know.

Working him open with my mouth and fingers, I drive him higher. I worship him and commit every moan and gasp to memory. Every squirm. Every touch and every kiss.

"Please Owen." My beautiful boy pants, reaching for me with clutching hands. "I need you."

I pepper kisses over his freckled nose and reach for the condom, but his hand wraps around my wrist.

"No. I want all of you and we're safe. Please?" His voice cracks with his plea and it's more than I can handle.

"Are you sure, Sunshine?"

He nods and grips my shoulders tighter.

When I finally slide home and fill him slowly until I bottom out, I bite my lip in a bid to hold back the words I want to tumble freely from my lips. Parker's hands grip my biceps as those soulful brown eyes, the ones I'll see every time I close my own from now to eternity, lock onto mine as I make love to him.

This is no longer about sex. Not a quick get off to satisfy a need. It's more than a physical act. This is us joining body and soul and it's ripping me to pieces. There are not enough bandaids in the world to hold me together.

"Owen..."

Parker comes apart underneath me, moaning as his gorgeous body shudders, spurting streams of cum on his chest. Pulling out, I finish myself over him with a strained groan as I coat him with my load. Panting more from the emotions swirling in the room than the physical act, I mix our mess on him together, hoping in a bizarre way it makes me a part of him and keeps me close to him for longer.

When I finally meet his eyes, the tears sliding down his cheeks are my undoing, and I finally let my own flow. His voice cracks with his plea, and I have to look away.

"Tell me to stay, Owen. Please."

I really want to. Oh, how I want to.

"I can't do that, Sunshine."

A sob escapes as I press a hard kiss to his lips and seal my fate. I had meant to spend the night wrapped up in him, but I can't do this. I find my clothes and dress in the low light of his nightlight and leave the room. The door clicks closed behind me before I hear his sobs grow louder and I race away as fast as I can.

If you love something, let it go.

I did, but I don't know how to move on. And nobody told me it would hurt this much.

THIRTY-ONE

Parker

T HE HATCHBACK CLOSES ON my borrowed Ford Edge with a hollow thud. I loaded the last of my boxes in the car, moving in a fog of sadness I just can't shake. All of my possessions, every single thing I own, fit in one car's trunk. Even my bedding.

The bedding I didn't wash this morning like I wanted to because it carries the woodsy cologne and musk of Owen and washing it away felt too final. Too much like I was throwing away the key and never looking back. It's pathetic, but so am I. After he rushed out last night, leaving me covered in cum and a crying mess, I couldn't move. I felt like a load of concrete had been dumped over me and I had no desire to fight my way out. I had hoped so damn badly he would tell me he loved me and beg me not to go. The fairy tale I wanted, the one I pictured for years, would finally become a reality. But he didn't say what I wanted. When the words he said left his mouth; the ones promising me nothing, they slammed an industrial sized door on my chance of a happily ever with them.

Stuffing my messenger bag onto the passenger seat, I lock the loaded car and go back inside for the final round of goodbyes. I don't want to hear them, but it's a necessary social activity. Even though I no longer feel social, I have to paint the smile on my face and get back up. I always get back up when life knocks me down. If I didn't, I'd be a part of the pavement now, smashed so far in, you wouldn't even be able to find me. This time though, it might take longer than usual to get on my feet.

I force the smile on my face and find Jacob waiting in the kitchen for me.

"You're all packed up, then?" He dusts his hands off on his pants with a crooked smile. If I didn't know better, I'd think he was sad to see me go.

"Just a final round of hugs, then I'll hit the road."

"I'm gonna miss you around here." Jacob pulls me into a tight hug, smacking me on my back, and I feel my tears well up again. If I cry anymore, I'm going to be dehydrated. I can't possibly have any more tears left.

"I'll be back to visit as much as I can. We get a break in a month." I pause. "That sounded shorter when I read it. A month until I see you and Cheddar again. Ugh."

I wander to the common room and find my giant orange cat curled up on the sofa. "Hey Cheesy, I gotta go. Can I have a last snuggle, big man?" He cracks an eye open and chirps when I pick him up, hugging him close. I bury my face in his fur. "Jake is gonna take care of you and I'll be back before you know it, buddy." He purrs against me and my heart cracks. Fuck, I'm going to miss this cat.

Placing him back on his spot, I find Jake standing in the doorway, waiting. "Take care of him. Send me a pic every day, please. Don't let him forget me." I swipe at the lone tear that trickles down. I can do this. I'll be back in a month. Four weeks. Thirty days. They all sound like forever right now.

"You sure you'll be okay to drive?"

I nod. "I'm sure. Once I get out of here, I'll be better."

Jacob smiles softly. "You made a choice, Parker, it's what you wanted. We'll get you through it." He hands me a small bag. "I got you road snacks. All your favourites."

"Aww, thanks Jake. I'll call when I get there."

"Please do. Austin and Mr. Larkman have already asked for updates. That means they hound me until they get them."

I pull him in for a last hug, lingering too long before I let go.

"It's not an end, Parker, it's a new beginning. Go show them how awesome you are and be the best baker they've ever seen."

With a last nod, I speed walk to the car before I do anything stupid. I enter the coordinates for the rooming house and cue up my driving music. It's back to the 90's grunge bands for today's trip. With a honk and a wave to Jake, I start my journey towards my goal of an acclaimed baker.

This is what I've always wanted.

I'm ripped from my sleep the next morning by a thundering knock on my bedroom door. I'm so tired and disoriented I take a hot second to remember where I am. I arrived at my rooming house by 6 P.M and lugged all my boxes up to the tiny shoebox of a room I was assigned. It has a single bed, which I wasn't aware of or used to. Instead of finding a store to buy new sheets, I collapsed on the bed and rolled myself into a burrito with my duvet.

"Parker!"

I finally free myself from the duvet and swing open the door to find... someone I haven't met yet.

"Uh, I'm Parker."

The man rakes his eyes over me; displeasure oozes from every inch of him. "Did nobody tell you there's an orientation meeting today?" He glances at his very large and expensive watch. "It's in twenty minutes."

"What!? I thought it was tomorrow?" My brain is racing to remember the last time I checked my email — or any kind of correspondence. This last week I spent consumed with Owen, I shut out the rest of the world, unwilling to accept our bubble was ending.

"You should have had an email Wednesday with the last minute change. If you can be downstairs in fifteen, I'll take you there. If not, you're on your own."

The man leaves me there in my doorway without another word. After I close the door, I stumble and frantically root through my suitcase to locate some clean clothes while I load my email on my phone. I'm half dressed before all the emails come flooding in and sure enough, there's the change in the meeting date with URGENT at the top. Only it's not dated Wednesday like he said, it was yesterday while I was driving.

I skim it quickly while I gather my toiletries over to the shared bathroom. A quick brush of my teeth and a splash of water to my messy hair is all I can do before I'm flying downstairs to meet the mystery man from this morning. I find him leaning on the front door, swinging a set of keys in his hands with a sneer on his face.

"Thanks for waiting. I haven't checked my email for a few days." I chuckle, but his face remains the same. "You already know I'm Parker, but you didn't tell me your name."

I stick a hand out to him in the customary greeting of a handshake, but he grabs his coat from a hook and ignores it. His people skills are amazing. "Follow me."

I snag my coat and shove my feet into my boots, jogging to catch up with him. He walks to a gleaming, metallic blue BMW parked at the curb. It's so sparkling clean I'm inclined to think it never leaves the garage in the winter. I settle into the passenger seat and try to focus on where we're going so I can get there myself next time.

Since my companion is obviously not one to carry idle chit chat, I pull out my phone to read the email in full, in case there are other surprises I've missed. I curse silently. There's a *lot* I missed. I scroll through the email only to find out I don't have a break in a month as originally planned. In fact, because the bakery has taken on a high-profile event in the neighbouring city, it needs the help of all the students in order to deliver on the contract. It doesn't specifically say that, but I'm not stupid. I see what they're saying. They want to use the free student labour. That changes my plans, but I'll have to consider all of that later. We've arrived at the meeting location; the building I will spend a lot of time in for the next six months.

My still nameless companion parks in the space marked No Parking. I roll my eyes at his thoughtlessness and hope I don't have to deal with this guy after today. I follow him into the building and notice the signs pointing the way to classrooms and test kitchens. It's a facility away from the bakery itself. A separate entity where all the magic happens in giant ovens and mixers. A bolt of excitement runs through me now that I'm finally through the doors.

Rude guy leads me to a classroom, and we must be the last to arrive. I know there were only six of us chosen for this program and five people were already seated at the table across the front. I move to sit with the people in the front, since that's where students usually sit, and my silent chauffeur takes a seat at the very back of the classroom and slouches in a chair with his arms crossed.

"You must be Parker."

A lovely woman in her mid 40s, with a pierced eyebrow and rainbow-streaked hair, smiles and holds her hand out. I shake it, relieved that someone here knows how to be polite. "I'm Sarah. Lovely to have you. I trust Anthony didn't give you grief today?"

I glance back at the man and find him glaring my way. "Nope, all good." I shake her hand and smile, a full smile for the first time in days, and it feels good. Anthony can shove his attitude.

I get comfortable and smile at the woman next to me, but she greets me with an icy stare. What is with the people here? Common friendliness has been wiped away much like fingerprints left on the stainless-steel countertops.

Sarah speaks and introduces the instructors. She tells us about herself, and I'm drawn in by her open friendliness and warmth. The rest of the people here feel so cold I feel like I should have brought a sweater. Nobody is returning smiles or trying to be friendly. It's unnerving.

"Are there any questions about tomorrow?" Sarah's voice brings me back to the present and I realize I zoned out, missing most of what she said. I'm saved from embarrassing myself when she asks me to stay as everyone else leaves and there's no sign of Anthony.

"Sorry to single you out, Parker."

"That's okay. I missed half of what you said, anyway." I wince. "Sorry. I didn't get the email about the changes, and I wasn't ready this morning. I'm probably not making a great impression, am I?"

Sarah pats my arm. "We made an error, and you were the only one with the short notice. We didn't have your email until you returned your offer, and it was overlooked. I wanted to apologize and make sure you didn't have any questions. As you probably noticed in the email, you missed a meet and greet session last night."

I noticed that. I was disappointed, but I'd hoped to be able to at least have coffee or something with one of my new classmates today and maybe make a friend. The empty room tells me that won't be happening, though. It's Sarah or nothing and I need cheerful company.

"Grab your coat. You and I are going to have a brief tour, and I'll catch you up. Then we'll have a coffee."

"Aren't you one of the teachers? Isn't this against the rules or something?"

She snorts. "Parker, there's no rule saying I can't be a nice person to a student. I was once in your shoes. I'd like to make it easier if I can."

Her friendly smile sets me at ease. I'll take the offer of a friend. It's been a rough twenty-four hours.

"So who is Anthony, anyway? He's not a real ray of sunshine, is he?" I zip my coat and follow Sarah outside.

She laughs, and it's a full laugh, one that instantly makes me like her. Nothing fake about Sarah except the pink colour of her hair. "He's not sunshine, no." We stop at a bright red Chevy Suburban and she opens the door for me. "It's best to just ignore him. He's angry because his dad won't sell the teaching school. Anthony does the accounting and is also a glorified gopher to his dad."

She rounds the truck and hops in on the driver's side. "He was sent to pick you up when we realized last night that you hadn't got the info in time and may have missed it." She pulls away from the curb and narrowly misses a parked car. I check my seat belt and clutch the door handle as she continues down the street.

"So he's mad because he works for his dad?"

"Pretty much. He wants the money, that's all. He's a schmuck." She signals to turn right and completely cuts off a car at the intersection, leaving much honking in her wake. I think I just felt gray hairs spontaneously appear and I clutch the door harder.

She peels into a parking lot, bumping and bouncing us as she slams on the brakes in a parking spot, whipping my head forward.

"We're here!"

Thank God. I scramble to unbuckle and get out of the death trap before Sarah notices my hands shaking.

"This is the bakery in all its glory." She waves her hand towards the building with a smile. "You'll decorate here mostly and bake at the building we just left. There wasn't enough room here to renovate and add more ovens. That's why they're offsite."

She leads me inside and gives me a tour of the place. I'm salivating over the awesome setup for decorating. Every tool or gadget I could ever want for decorating is here. This is where great bakers start. I never thought I'd get here. They picked me out of all the applicants. I made the top six. This is what I always wanted, to be learning with other great bakers. To be noticed for my talent and respected in my field. I'm so damn close to it. I should be far more excited than I am right now. Something is missing.

"Parker, you okay?"

I snap my head around to find Sarah watching me closely. "Uh, ya just thinking. Thinking about stuff."

She takes my hand and leads me from the decorating area out front to the bustling Cake Holes bakery cafe and we squeeze into a tiny pink and black pleather lined booth. We both order regular coffees and I take a moment to ground myself again. After they deliver our coffees in record time, Sarah puts it all out there, shocking me with her observations.

"Tell me who you left behind to come here."

I sputter over my coffee cup, sloshing some onto the table. Wiping up my mess with a nearby napkin, I inhale several deep breaths. "What makes you think that?"

She smiles again, and it makes me want to hug her, because I could really use a hug right now. "I can tell these things. You've got a broken heart oozing from every pore on your body." She squeezes my hand in a gesture of support. "Tell me all about it. Get it off your chest now, because for the next few months, you're going to be run off your feet and stressed more than you could ever imagine. If I know what makes you tick, I can help you if you struggle later."

Something about Sarah exudes a trust I can't explain. Few people know my story. I keep those details close to my chest. But with arriving late, cold shouldered by the other students, not to mention the unfriendliness of

Anthony earlier, I know I need someone to talk to and lean on. I could call Jacob when I need to, but he'll be working a lot. The only other person I want to call walked away from me.

Summoning the image of the door closing behind Owen right after I asked him to tell me to stay, is enough to bring fresh pricks of tears to my eyes.

So I talk. And I talk some more. I spew out my entire story with Owen, my crappy childhood and even leaving Cheddar. A second coffee has me telling her my hopes and goals for after this apprenticeship, and my shoulders sag after having talked to someone. She listens the entire time, and when I finally let her get a word in, her words are what I needed to hear in the greatest of ways.

"We all make choices in life, Parker. Sometimes they're good and sometimes they suck eggs. But every single choice we make brings us to where we are today. Every choice moves our chess piece along, sometimes forward and sometimes back." She stacks sugar packets on the table, moving them to illustrate her point. "Sometimes we get so close to that elusive checkmate, only to have it snatched away." She sends a sugar packet sailing my way. "But we regroup and make a new plan, then keep going after it." She tucks all the sugar packets back in the container on the table and I'm stunned at how accurate her analogy of my life is. But then she drops her bomb of wisdom. "You made a choice to come here. Don't forget that. That choice is a move towards your goal... but goals change."

She drains her cup and stands, pulling me into a hug. "Yes, I'm a teacher here, but I'm a friend first. Nobody ever accused me of playing by the rules."

I can't stop myself from smiling. Sarah is like a breath of fresh air and it's easier to breathe. Until I realize she's going to drive me home.

THIRTY-TWO

Owen

I STARE AT MY blank laptop screen as I sit on my couch in a stained t-shirt and sweatpants. The days and nights have all blurred together since Parker left. Well, since I made him leave by not asking him to stay. I tried going to work and following my routine, but I couldn't. I ended up snapping at everyone like a grumpy old dog, even Paige. I couldn't make the soup for Dom because it kept me in the kitchen too long and everywhere reminded me of Parker. Everywhere I looked, he was there. The apron he used was still hanging in its spot, looking as empty as I felt. Even the silence was a reminder that he was gone. I missed his damn annoying singing.

I didn't even interview the new bakers that applied. I canceled their interviews, telling them I changed my mind, and the position wasn't being filled. That part's true. I can't hire someone to replace Parker. Something about it makes my stomach turn. It feels too final. I can't accept that. Instead, I made sure the other kids knew how to make cookies from frozen batter and make cupcakes from a mix. It filled the pastry cases with items from a box and not filled with the joy and love Parker brought to his work. It gave the patrons something to shove in their gob with their coffee and it would have to suffice.

I've been working from home and sleeping so poorly, I don't even know what day it is anymore. One thing I know, though, is what it feels like to be heartbroken. The worst thing about it... I did it to myself.

Tires crunch up the driveway, but I couldn't be bothered to look and see who was stopping by to drag me out of my house. I just want to be left alone. A vehicle door closes and for a long time, I hear no other sounds. I should be concerned, but at this point I don't even care if it's a kid destroying my house or stealing my car.

A knock, so faint I barely hear it, comes from the door. The second knock is more confident, so I drag myself off the couch to answer. Throwing the door open, I find Jacob on my doorstep and that's not at all who I expected to see here. He has dark circles under his eyes and his hair is an unkempt mess, which is not like Jacob.

"I wasn't sure if you'd answer." He wrings his hands together before shoving them into his pockets.

"Well, I live here and I'm awake, so... what are you here for, Jake?" If this is some lame-ass attempt to check up on me, I might lose my temper. People need to stop checking up on me. I'm fine.

"I need your help. Well, I hope you can help. You're my only hope at this point."

With my arms crossed, I lean on the door frame. "I find it hard to believe I'm your only hope. Obi Wan I am not." God, I sound like such an asshole. Since when am I rude to people asking me for help? I'm more fucked up than I thought I was.

"It'll be easier if I show you." Jacob takes the steps off the porch and returns to his car. He spends a few minutes retrieving something from the back seat and returns with a bag and a small animal carrier. His eyes are glistening, and for the first time, I notice how truly upset he is. "Can we come in?"

I step out of the way, holding the door so he can enter. After toeing off his shoes, he continues to the couch uninvited and opens the pet carrier door. "When Parker left and couldn't take Cheddar, he asked if he could be the shelter cat until he was able to come back." He inhales a shaky breath. "Putting him up for adoption wasn't a choice for Parker. He wants to take him back when he can, so I agreed to take care of him. I thought he'd be okay since he was comfortable there and knew us." He swipes at his eyes and my heart lurches. "He's been lying outside the door of Parker's old room for days. He won't eat or drink. I've had him to the vet, and they can't find anything wrong. They think he's grieving and…" A giant sob escapes, and now Jacob has me rushing over to comfort him.

"Did you bring Cheddar here, Jake?"

Sniffling, he nods and reaches into the carrier. "Since he knows you and you were with Parker so much, I was hoping maybe being with you would bring him around or something. It might be a long shot, but I can't stand seeing him so sad. You both mean a lot to Parker..." He trails off, knowing how it sounds. We both meant so much to Parker, but he left us both behind. Being reminded of that only crumbles my heart more. Except, I forced him to leave me. Cheddar was an innocent bystander.

Cheddar allows himself to be slid out of the carrier with little fuss. I've never been one to attach to animals, but this cat and I did bond, I can't deny that. His sad eyes are a mirror of mine and fuck if it doesn't make me want to make him feel better. He's not his normal attitude-filled ball of pumpkin fluff. There's no chirping and purring and I don't know if it's possible, but he looks like he's lost weight.

"Oh Cheesy, my man. What are you doing to yourself?" At the sound of my voice, he perks up to look at me. Jake hands him over and once he's in my arms, it's like the hug I didn't know I needed. He plasters himself to my chest, hoisting himself to snuggle into the crook of my neck. I know how this cat feels; missing the person who was the center of his life.

"He misses you too." Jacob says softly, stroking Cheddar's fur. "Do you think you could keep him and see if he comes around for you? Maybe he'd eat for you?"

I'm not a monster to turn down a cat that is obviously grieving and a friend who is trying to do what's best for another friend. I'd also be lying if I say it doesn't feel good to have him with me. He's like an extension of Parker, and that makes my heart hurt a bit less — to have his cat with me.

"What do you think, Cheese man? Want to stay with me for a while?" I stroke his fur and he snuggles even closer. "He can stay Jake. Just tell me what I need to do."

Jacob runs back out to his car and returns with a litter box, litter, and a cat bed. "I wasn't sure if you'd take him, but I came prepared. His food is in the bag on the kitchen counter with his dishes." He sits back down next to me on the couch, and I know what he's going to ask before it's out of his mouth.

"I'll be okay. We both will. We just need time. Broken hearts are hard to mend, but we'll figure it out." I kiss the top of Cheddar's head. "Won't we buddy?"

"If it helps at all, it broke his heart too." Jake says in a whisper. "It wasn't easy for him."

I try to reassure him with a smile, but it feels as fake as the eyelashes on Tammy Faye Bakker. "It was a choice, Jacob. We have to accept it and move on, and one day light will shine again. It could be next week, it could be in six months. I don't know, but I have to believe it will." If I don't believe life will return to normal and I can find another way to be happy, then I'm just as hopeless as I was before I met Parker.

Jacob walks to the door, and I trail behind him, not letting Cheddar go. "I'll keep you updated on how he is. I still have your number."

With a final pet to Cheddar, Jake leaves us alone and I settle back on the couch with the grieving cat. I peel him off my chest and lower him to my lap. With a feeble meow, he peers up at me and my heart breaks for him. Even his whiskers are drooping. But I can't let him wallow like I have. We have to go on with things. As much as I want to hide in my house forever and not face The Bean void of my favourite baker, I have to face it soon. Maybe this is just another reason to remain single in the future. Maybe it's one of those life lessons that are supposed to make you learn something about yourself and have a magical epiphany. Whatever the reason is for putting me on this path, I don't like it and neither does Cheddar. And it's my fault we're both here.

Cheddar doesn't want to move off me. I try to place him on the couch, but he clings to me like an octopus. It's impossible. He's far too big to carry around and also try to have a free hand to do anything, but I have an idea. I carry him with me upstairs and with one hand I dig in my linen closet for a loose sheet. Sitting on the bed with him in my lap, I manage to first invent new swear words, but I also fashion a kind of sling I can wear to hold him against me. I saw a young woman in the coffee shop once with her baby in a sling and I thought it was genius.

Once I wrangle the contraption around me and adjust it on my shoulder, I scoop Cheddar up and place him into the pouch. He initially objects, but his feeble meows tell me he'll take what he can get if it means he's attached to me. I stand up and snug up the sheet straps, carefully tucking in the ends so I don't dive headfirst down the stairs.

Feeling rather proud of myself for creating my cat sling, I head back downstairs and set up his litter box and food dishes. I've never had a pet before. Jacob's information, along with the experience over Christmas at the shelter, is all I know about cats. Now I'm thrown into this whole cat-dad thing. It's also infinitely harder doing anything with a cat strapped to my chest with a sheet. It's like a toga party gone horribly wrong.

I set his litter in the mudroom, making sure he has a bit of privacy and ease myself back to my place on the couch. My hand absently strokes his fur, and I feel a bubble of anger. I shouldn't feel angry. I shouldn't be the one to control his choices, but I did nothing to convince him to stay, either. He asked me. He wanted me to ask him to stay because he would have if he knew I saw him as worth it. If he knew I loved him, he would have stayed and thrown his dream away. I chose the coward's way out. I couldn't tell him to stay for my own selfish reasons; he had to go chase the dream himself. I wouldn't stand in his way.

"I'm sorry you got dragged into this, Mr. Cheese. I didn't think you'd take it this hard." I've turned a loveable cat into a droopy, clinging mess and I've sent off the center of my world, the person I love most, because I really am an ass.

The day fades into night and I drag myself to bed with Cheddar still attached to me. I show him his litter box and his food, but he's not interested in either. We cuddle under my blankets and go to sleep, finding a little comfort with each other and hoping tomorrow brings a better day.

Dominic doesn't bother knocking and enters the house with his key like he usually does.

"Owen, buddy, this has to stop."

He finds me in the same place I've spent most of my days. On the couch in the same clothes.

"Is that a *cat* strapped to your chest? When did you get a cat?"

Cheddar is getting better and eating out of my hand now, but he still likes to snuggle up with me when he takes his mid afternoon pre supper nap. "It's Cheddar, Parker's cat."

Dominic's eyebrows hit the ceiling. "Want to tell me what's going on?" He settles next to me and peeks into my pouch to see Cheddar. I wake him up and bring him over to his bowl while Dominic watches me. "Let me see if he'll eat and I'll explain."

I slap some fresh, canned food into his dish, and he sniffs at it before turning his sad eyes to me. "I'm not spoon-feeding you forever, Cheddar. If you want to stay here, you're gonna have to eat by yourself."

MEOW

"I know, but I'm going to go back to work soon. I need you to eat."

He looks back at the bowl and takes a small bite, then licks his lips before diving back in for more until he's finished his whole bowl. I pump my fist in the air. "Yes!"

"Why are you so excited to watch a cat eat?" Oh right, forgot about Dom. I wash my hands and remove the cat sling before flopping down next to Dominic.

"Jacob brought him over because he wasn't eating. I think he was grieving Parker. He hoped I could help. Did you know pets do that? Grieve I mean?"

He nods slowly. "I guess it makes sense. So he's here, and he's doing better?"

"That's the first time he's eaten from his bowl since he's been here. Definitely better. He still wants to sleep on me all the time, though. That's why I strap him to me so I can at least do stuff."

"What exactly have you been doing? Other than not showering or shaving?" Dominic scrunches his nose.

I pass a hand over my face, feeling the building stubble there — closing in on beard territory. Jesus, how long have I been here?

"Uh, not much I guess."

Dom sighs. "Owen, I love you, but Jesus Christ, you're stubborn."

"He has to figure out what he wants with his life, Dom." I throw my hands in the air. How many times do I need to have this conversation? "I told you I wouldn't make him choose." I'll drag myself into a shower soon and I'll walk out the door just like I used to. Soon. Soon-ish.

"Maybe he figured it out, and it was you he chose! But you wouldn't give him the one thing he was hoping to hear. Ever think of that? Maybe he found a different dream he wanted to chase, and it included you."

The silence hangs heavy as I consider his words. Is it possible? Could he keep me and follow his baking dreams? My mind spun as I tried to picture how it could work. My heart lifted when it all clicked. I can make it happen if he'll let me. If he'll forgive me.

"I've made a huge mistake."

He chuckles. "I know. I've been trying to tell you that."

"I need your help to make this right." My heart pounds at the idea unfolding in my head. Parker once told me, the only thing you can do is ask for what you want. The first time he did, I said yes. The second time, I said no... in the most heart-crushing of ways.

I need to make it right and ask for what I want. What I hope is what he wants too.

"I'm going to need a cat sitter for a day or two. I have a road trip to take."

THIRTY-THREE

Parker

I 'M DISTRACTED TODAY. I messed up the easy cupcake icing job and got yelled at. I made the wrong size cake this morning and got yelled at. Now, I've made the wrong colour of gum paste flowers and again, I got yelled at.

I want to go home and snuggle with my cat that I miss with a fierceness I didn't know was possible. I want to fall into the comforting arms of Owen, just like I was doing every morning until I came here. The reminders of our last night together that covered my body are mostly faded. Some, just pale marks in the background, others gone completely. Every day one disappears, it feels like another day bringing me closer to having him out of my life for good. I don't want that.

I never felt more like myself than when I was with Owen. He made me feel so alive. I was invincible. A superhero who could do anything. Owen made me feel like I achieved the greatest thing in life: to be loved for me. No conditions to lose weight or get a different diploma. No turned-up nose to find out my mom was an addict and my foster homes never kept me. He didn't even care that I lived in not one, but two youth centers.

I love Owen, more than I need the air I breathe. I love him. I don't think I'm supposed to be here in a stuffy bakery that prides itself on the elite clientele it attracts. The bakery that doesn't foster kindness to its students.

Except Sarah. She's the only friend I've made since I've been here. While I didn't think it would bother me being the odd one out in the group, it's starting to chafe. I've been through enough in my young life against my wishes. Why am I making myself do this when everything I wanted was what I left behind?

"Parker, you know you can talk to me. You've got that look."

I glance around and notice the other students have left; completed their projects while I'm still here because of my morning's mistakes.

"What look is that? The look that says I feel like a failure here and I'm wondering why I ever came?"

"Listen, you've got a friend in me. You know this." Sarah glances around the empty decorating studio. "Look at what your classmates are creating, Parker. Look."

I take the time to observe the skills the others have on display. There are some beautiful creations, but they're good. That's it.

Not amazing. Not different. Just Good.

I return to my cake adorned with a cherry blossom tree. The edible translucent glitter worked into the paste to give the flowers more sparkle, making them pop off the cake. I created an entire tree growing up the side of the cake, not just a few flowers in a bouquet. The blossoms are various sizes and shapes and clusters, and I've even crafted tiny stamens by hand with hardened sugar straws I made myself, dipping the ends into a sugar creation to sit on the end of the stamens. It blows the other students' work out of the water and that's not me being arrogant. It's true.

"What are you saying, Sarah? Is this why I can't seem to fit in here? I'm too good and they don't want me in their group?" I snort. Never have I ever been the envy of others. Unless you count when I had the bed with the cleanest sheets at the shelter one night, but that's not high on my list of enviable moments.

"Parker, you aren't made to fit in here... you're made to blaze your own path, not to follow in the footsteps of traditional stuffy bakers." She shifts to stand in front of me. Her pink hair makes me smile. "You've had a weight on your shoulders since you arrived. You thought this was what you wanted, but it's clearly not, so why are you here?" She takes the shaping tool out of my hand and makes me focus on her. "You remember our talk on your first day, right? Sometimes plans change, and that's okay."

My life plans skip along in my mind. All I've ever wanted was to make cakes and have wait lists for brides years out. I wanted to make a name for myself. I thought I needed a seal of approval from an established professional to achieve it. But now that I look, really look at what I can do compared to the others, I already have the skill to make it on my own. I don't need a stamp from this place on my resume, or to brag about A-list customers and make other customers feel insignificant. I want to be me and take clients of all kinds and be the one everyone loves, not just for what I create with my hands, but for who I am.

The kid with the shitty past, and the sunniest outlook because at some point, life has to give you a break. I've already got what it takes to make it. I don't need this at all. I had it already and I left it.

"I've made a huge mistake." My gut clenches as I think of Owen moving on without me. A new baker and possibly a new boyfriend. Was I ever his boyfriend to begin with?

"No, sweetie. It's not a mistake. It's a learning experience. Mistakes can be fixed." She waves her hand around in the air. "And you learn from them. Just like adding too much dye to a paste you want to alter, the first time you don't wear gloves and stain your hands, you learn for the next time, right?"

I gulp, remembering how Owen left me for the last time. He didn't tell me to stay like I asked. What if I reframe the question?

"I didn't tell him I'd stay. I asked for *him* to tell me to stay. I put the choice to him, and he didn't take it." I shove away from my station and pace. "This changes everything. He didn't tell me because he wanted me to choose for myself. God dammit, I'm an idiot. I thought he was pushing me away because he didn't care, but he wanted me to make my own choice." I sit back in my chair, reeling at my breakthrough. "He wanted me to follow my dreams, and I didn't see that as an admission of wanting what's best for me. I thought he didn't want me. Sarah, what if he loves me like I love him? You think I can fix it?" I've been thinking this entire time apart that he crushed my heart because he didn't care, and I couldn't be more wrong. He cared too much.

She takes my hands again. "It's worth a try, isn't it?"

"How much trouble will I be in if I quit right now?"

She laughs again, that hearty laugh that feels like she's giving the haters a big FU. "They won't be happy about it and you'll be giving up a portion of the fees, but other than that, there's nothing tying you here."

I untie my apron and lay it over my chair.

"I quit. Effective immediately."

Sarah pulls me into a hard hug. "Go get him, Parker. Be sure to keep in touch." She holds me at arm's length. "I'm going to miss you, but you're going places, my boy. I can feel it. Go be who you're meant to be and be with the one you love."

Sarah offers to drive me home, but I politely decline that carnival ride and walk. I need the time to hatch the idea I have anyway, and I need to make some calls.

THIRTY-FOUR

Owen

I PACKED A BAG as soon as Micha agreed to come take care of Cheddar while I was away. I was going to take him with me, but at the last minute, I changed my mind. I wanted the day to be about Parker and me, with no distractions. I took a video of Cheddar to show Parker what we had been up to and how good he'd been instead.

I left as soon as I could this morning and I hope to catch Parker before he leaves for the day. Jacob was more than happy to provide me with Parker's info, but it included a stern warning. The warning was to guarantee I would make his friend happy and be serious about what I have planned. That's an easy warning to live by because I never want to see him sob and hurt like the night I left ever again. It's all I see every time I close my eyes.

I only hope he can forgive me, that we can get back to how we were. Surely he has to know I'd never be that mean? Grumpy asshole or not, I would never intentionally hurt someone I love.

My GPS pings to alert me that I'm almost at my destination. As I creep along the street looking for a parking space, a toque with an oversized pom-pom I'd recognize anywhere catches my eye. My heart speeds up, thinking I have the timing wrong and I'm going to miss him. I can't miss him. I need to see him, hold him, kiss him. Today. Soon.

He's placing a box in the back of a car and I pull to a stop next to it and set my hazard lights flashing. I can't risk him leaving while I find a proper parking spot. I round the front of my Bronco and call his name, my voice cracking.

"Parker?"

He closes the hatchback and steps in between our vehicles. Fuck, he's just as beautiful as ever. My heart pounds, wanting to go to him and bridge all the distance I've put between us. To plead for forgiveness and show him how wrong I was. I have so much to say.

"Owen? What... what are you doing here?"

Hearing my name on his lips, even with his confusion, spurs me into action. I take the few steps closer to him. His cheeks are rosy from the morning chill, his adorable button nose just as pink.

"I came to see you. I... I need to talk to you. If you'll still talk to me, that is."

His eyes widen. "Of course I'll still talk to you. I was hoping to talk to you tomorrow, actually."

My eyebrows shoot up. "You were?"

He waves to the packed car. "I quit yesterday. I'm coming back to Bloomburg."

"Really?" My breath leaves me in a whoosh.

A driver honks as he goes by, not happy for me to be blocking a lane of traffic as people begin their morning commutes.

"Is there somewhere we can go to talk? Where we can be off the street by chance?"

Parker looks over his shoulder at the home behind him. "I still have my key. We could go back inside? If you want to."

"I want to."

Parker shows me where I can leave my vehicle safely and waits for me on the sidewalk, hands stuffed in the pockets of his puffy coat.

"I rented a room here. The other students that did as well have left for the day. It's just us."

He takes my coat and hangs it with his before leading me to the living area. I rub my hands on my jeans before balling them into fists. I'm so tied up I could puke right now.

"Um... Parker... I made a mistake." He opens his mouth to speak, but I shake my head. "Please let me say it all first."

He presses his lips together and nods for me to continue. "I didn't want you to go, but I didn't want to get in your way either. I wanted you to make a choice for your life without me being a factor." My hands are shaking, so I squeeze them together harder. "I should never have left you the way I did. That was a real dick move, and it's something that will haunt me for the rest of my life." Swallowing hard, I force myself to look at him and my breath catches. Please let me not be wrong with what I see in his eyes. "You wanted me to tell you to stay, but I couldn't do that."

"You would have been fine if I'd stayed on my own." He whispers. "Without me asking."

I nod. "Because I love you. I knew I loved you then and I love you now. I only wanted to do what was right."

Silence hangs in the air, along with the words we both said. I pull out my phone to bring up the video of Cheddar, hand it to Parker and hit play. "I've been helping Cheddar through it. Through you being gone. He missed you." Parker's hand goes to his mouth as he stifles a cry.

"You carried him around all the time because he missed me?" Tears flow down his cheeks, and I lean over to brush them away with my thumbs.

"We both missed you. He needed someone, and Jake thought I could help. He was right."

The video stops and Parker stares at my phone, tears still there and I hate seeing tears in his eyes. I hate that I've caused them again. "Please don't cry, Sunshine. I hate seeing you cry."

With a heaving breath, he wipes at his face. "Owen, I was coming home to see you and forgive you. I put you in an impossible position. I can see that now." He moves closer to me. "I didn't want to choose to stay in case you didn't feel the same and then I'd have nothing again. You didn't tell me you loved me, so I left. I was too afraid to ask."

"I should've told you weeks before you got that letter. I didn't realize until you said you were leaving just how much I love you. But I want you to have everything you wanted for your career too, Parker. I know I said I can't make your decisions, but I may have come up with a solution, so you can have both."

He drops his head, and his shoulders shake with gentle sobs. I can't take it.

"Sunshine, come here." I pull him over to me, and he climbs on my lap, wrapping his arms around my neck. I hold him close to me, soothing his back and praying this turns out how I pictured it.

When he calms down, he sits back and wipes his tears again. Then he says what I so desperately hoped for.

"I want both, Owen. So much."

His lips touch mine in the sweetest kiss, and the sweetest words he could ever say wash over me. "I love you too."

THIRTY-FIVE

Parker

I CLUTCH ONTO OWEN after kissing him for the first time in what feels like forever.

He loves me!

My whole body shakes with relief. I had the whole thing planned out, but none of it included Owen showing up here this morning and catching me off guard. My confident mask crumbled as soon as he told me he was sorry. I knew I'd forgive him, because I loved him with everything I had. I always would. We're both to blame in this mess.

When I feel like I can finally speak, I sit back, still stunned he actually showed up here.

I pass my fingertips over his cheek. "I still can't believe you came here for me."

He presses my hand into his cheek before placing a soft kiss on my wrist. "I couldn't stay away anymore."

Finally. Finally, after the shit show called my life, I'm one step away from everything I've ever wanted. "I was coming home because yesterday someone made me see that I didn't need to be here to get what I want."

With reluctance, I peel myself off Owen and find my phone to show him the pictures I took of my cake yesterday. His reaction is exactly what I was hoping for.

"You made this, Sunshine?" He flips through the photos multiple times. "This is fucking amazing."

I laugh, and it feels so good to laugh. "That's what Sarah said."

"I like Sarah already."

"I haven't had the best of times since I got here. It's been shit right from the first day. I've been struggling to be happy to do something I love. Yesterday I made that while the rest of the class did boring roses. Nothing made their cakes stand out. They were all perfectly executed without an ounce of originality. Everyone stayed in their box. I didn't have to think about what I wanted to create. I just made it."

Owen has a lopsided grin on his face as he listens. As I tell him everything that's happened the last few weeks, I get lost in his ocean blue eyes all over again. God, how I've missed him. No amount of time being at a fancy bakery could erase those eyes from memory.

"So, what was your plan once you came back?"

"The first thing was to find you and hope you felt the same as I did." He squeezes my hand and I flash a smile. I hold his hand because it feels like I might float away on a big fluffy cloud. "I made a business plan when I was in college, for my own cake business. I reviewed it last night and made a few tweaks. There's still a few things to figure out like financing, that's a big one, but I have appointments lined up next week." I suck in a breath. "Sorry, I'm rambling. My plan is to open my own space now. No waiting. I can do this on my own without the name of that school. I just never believed I had the talent."

Owen smiles, the best thing I've seen in a long time, and my heart bursts. "Can I help?"

"You already are."

"I said I had a solution, remember?" I nod. "I realized before you left that you had the talent. I thought you knew that, too. We need to learn to communicate better." He chuckles. "I found a commercial space for you. It's still being built, and you don't have to take it if you don't like it."

My jaw hangs open. "You found me a space?" I thought it would take me forever to find what I needed, and he's done it in a few days? "Where? How?"

"It's a long story, but the short version is I met a guy in town who's building a new brewery at the old fairgrounds. You know that one barn that's still decent out there? He's already started renovating the inside, but he mentioned looking at a space in town to sell out of since it's a bit of a drive to the brewery." He smiles again and his dimple pops up, making my heart melt into a pile of goo on the floor. "Anyway, we got to talking, and he thought it would be great to share with a baker and he even had some ideas to cross promote if you can believe that."

Owen mistakes my silence as a negative thing, and his smile fades. "I didn't mean to overstep. You can say no and it changes nothing. I only wanted to show you I was ready to help you achieve your dream."

A laugh bubbles out of me as I throw myself on him again, covering his face with kisses as I half laugh and half cry.

"You didn't Owen. I'm overwhelmed, is all. I'm sure I'll love it. I just thought... I thought I might have to do this without you and you're already starting with all the hard work. I don't know what to say."

I don't think there's a word to describe how I feel right now. I've spent so long looking after myself with nobody thinking of me first, it's a foreign feeling. All of it. Even being loved by someone I want with all my heart is a novel experience. I've been searching for this unnamed feeling forever. It's finally here. I want to squish it tight with both hands and never, ever let it go.

"It took me a while, but I realized I'd do anything to keep that smile on your face, Parker. I never want to be the cause for it leaving again. I'll help you with anything you need, and I'll be your biggest cheerleader. Because when you love someone, you do everything you can, every day, to show them."

He presses a tender kiss to my lips. "I love you, but we have one problem."

I lean into him, running a hand up his thigh. "Is it too many clothes on and no place to get naked?"

He grins again. "Okay, two problems. First one is how to get two vehicles home, but I've got the first problem solved already."

Owen stands and pulls me up with him. "I have a hotel room booked for tonight. Leave your key, say goodbye to this place and come spend the night with me while we solve the other problem."

I place my key on the kitchen counter, as agreed this morning with my housemates. After a last sweep of my room and the shared bathroom, I put my coat on and close the door.

I don't look behind me. My future is in front of me, and when he looks back at me with those deep ocean eyes, I know it's going to be bright.

Epilogue

OWEN

THE SMELL OF FRESH paint still lingers as Parker finishes setting up the display cases and decor in his bakery. His very own bakery is a reality, and I couldn't be prouder of all his efforts. My Sunshine is killing it.

When we drove back to Bloomburg together six months ago, I moved him into my place. I couldn't bear being away from him for another minute. Cheddar had already adapted and loved lying in all the sun patches the windows in my house gave him. He could watch birds at the feeder, and I was building him an outside kitty condo if he wanted to hang in the fresh air with us. So far, he seems content just sniffing at the screen doors, but he's back to his old self since Parker arrived with his stuff and never left.

It was really the only thing I forced on him. I wanted him in my bed every night and to see his beautiful face every morning. Never had I felt such a visceral pull to keep someone close to me before. Thankfully, he felt the same. I've had every day and night of the last six months to confirm to myself I've found the one for me. He's it for me and hopefully, before this afternoon is over, he's going to agree.

"Hey Owen, are there any more boxes out front with baking pans?"

I glance around and see nothing, so I follow his voice back to the amazing kitchen which he designed himself. I'm proud of him, but I'll miss sneaking into The Bean's kitchen every afternoon for a kiss. He's been using The Bean since he came back; getting his name out there to the community. Taking on any order he could while we waited for the space to be renovated. The men who own the brewery split the storefront in half with a single wall and a door to cross over when they're ready. I'm interested to hear their ideas for partnering with Parker. Parker can't wait to get started. I can see him soaring even higher with these new ideas.

Dominic waves to me from the street, and I let him in. "Did you get it?" I whisper.

He presses a small box into my hand. "You owe me for this one. Who forgets the ring on the day they want to propose?"

"I was nervous! I forget things sometimes."

"You also forgot what else you keep in that drawer. My eyes are scarred for life now. Thanks for that."

I squint my eyebrows until I realize what Dominic is referring to, and I snort. "Sorry, I forgot. Not like it's anything you haven't seen before."

"True. But it's different when you see a giant green dildo in your best friend's sock drawer and not hanging on a store shelf." He makes a gagging noise and I punch him in the arm.

He'll get over it.

"Oh hey, Dom. I didn't know you were dropping by."

"Hey, Owen wanted me to drop something off. I was just leaving. Love the place Parker. You've done great. See you both tomorrow?"

He leaves and I flick the door lock behind him. "What's happening tomorrow?"

"Your new bakery, for starters. That deserves a celebration, and Dom offered to host a BBQ."

"Oh, that's nice. That'll be fun."

I lead him over to his counter space.

"How do you organize your custom orders? Are you using a computer or a book?" I know the answer already, but I need him to show me, or my plan is going to fall faster than a lead balloon.

"Both. I need to have the book in case the computer crashes. I just can't trust the computer completely."

"Someone wanted to know if you had room for a custom cake order for New Year's Day."

He frowns and flips open his book. "What kind of cake? Did they say?"

"Yep, a wedding cake."

"Oh, that's cool." With his eyes focused on his book, I suck in a deep breath before pulling out the box from my pocket. "Did you get their name and contact info?"

"I sure did. His name is Owen."

Parker laughs and turns to face me. "Very funny Owen... what?"

Once I have his attention, I drop to a knee as he gasps when he puts the pieces together.

"Sunshine, I love you with everything I have. You make my life full in so many ways, I can't imagine it without you. I want to keep having fun with you forever. Would you put a grumpy bastard out of his misery and agree to marry me?"

He says nothing for the longest time, and I think I screwed it up. Until he sinks to the floor with me and takes my face in his hands for a kiss, leaving me breathless and panting.

"I hope that's a yes." I croak.

"It's a yes. So much fucking yes." He kisses me again and we fall over onto the floor.

With a shaking hand, I slide the ring on his finger. I have a matching one at home already and I can't wait to shout it out to everyone. This beautiful, amazing, ambitious young man is going to be my husband.

I asked for what I wanted, and he said yes.

I hope you enjoyed Parker and Owen's story! If you haven't read book one, you can read about Dominic and Micha here in Twice in a Lifetime.

Jacob's story is up next! That boy is all kinds of twisted up over... his brother's team mate.
If you don't want to miss out, be sure to join my newsletter to be in the loop!

Acknowledgments

I never know where to start, there's always so many who help me with a book. But here's an attempt to cover you all.

Thank you, to you dear reader, for enjoying the stories I create and coming back for more. Your messages and emails truly lift me from dark days and I'm so thrilled you gave my book a chance. Because of you, I keep writing more.

To my city mouse (you know who you are), thank you for being there when the path got rough. Thank you from the bottom of my heart for not letting me fall. Your friendship and support means the world to me.

For all the wonderful members of Neill's Naughty List! You're the best group of readers I could ever hope for! Thank you for laughing at my dad jokes and providing some of your own.

Thank you Jean, you're a gem! We had a rocky start, but we got there eventually.

Thank you Hayden once again for listening to my rambles and keeping me on track. As always, I appreciate you so very much.

For my reader team, a giant thank you! You're all rock stars and I can't love you enough! I am seriously so lucky to have you all on this journey with me.

Finally, thank you to my husband, Superman. Your belief in me never wanes and I love you.

Also By

Nickel City Bandits Series

Off Side

The Perfect Pass (Austin and Logan)

Wounded Winger

Sheltered Connections

Twice in A Lifetime (Dominic and Micha)

Coming soon... book three, Jacob's story!

Lightning Source UK Ltd.
Milton Keynes UK
UKHW021404080722
405575UK00009B/1890